BEYOND
PERFECTION

BEYOND PERFECTION

a novel

JULI CALDWELL

ERIN MCBRIDE

Covenant Communications, Inc.

Cover image by Brian Haigiwara © Brand X Pictures

Cover design copyrighted 2005 by Covenant Communications, Inc.

Published by Covenant Communications, Inc.
American Fork, Utah

Printed in Canada
First Printing: April 2005

11 10 09 08 07 06 05   10 9 8 7 6 5 4 3 2 1

ISBN 1-59156-781-5

For Jane

Acknowledgments

WE would like to thank our friends, our families, and the copious amounts of chocolate that gave us the creative energy to write this book. In no particular order thanks to our parents, for encouraging our overactive imaginations; our sisters (Shantal, Erin, Keli, Natalie, and Stephanie), for giving us something to write about; Jane Austen, whose brilliant social satire *Pride and Prejudice* inspired us to shame-lessly steal her work and apply it to the unique Latter-day Saint culture; Foster and the Lake Mary store, for the chocolate; Joe and Miranda, because Erin Ann said she would; our brothers (Bryan, Jarrod, Kevin, and Scott), because you rock; our myriad collection of ex-boyfriends, for the endless anecdotes (and fodder) they have provided for us; and Cali and Andi, for sharing some of their mommy time with the computer. And Bry . . . just because.

"It is a truth universally acknowledged,
that a single man in possession of a good fortune,
must be in want of a wife."

—JANE AUSTEN, *PRIDE AND PREJUDICE*

A Most Opportune Moment

IT was his shirt that first caught her attention. Elizabeth Benson, Lizzie to those who knew and loved her, had seen him in the school newspaper and at institute activities on the University of Utah campus more than once. He had a spiritual glow that fit the office of institute president. She imagined that he was being trained for the bishopric, most likely from the womb, and that he would prefer to wear a suit—or at least a tie—everywhere he went. Yet there sat William Pemberley, spiritual leader of the Latter-day Saint student population at the largest public school in Utah, wearing a white T-shirt emblazoned with a block blue Y that had a giant screw through its center. She shook her head in mild amusement and disgust, but couldn't seem to remove her eyes from him.

Will stood up from the bench where he sat talking to a very tall, rather slim blond guy. He breathed the fresh spring air deeply into his lungs, and his wiry rib cage expanded, filling out the irreverent T-shirt. The tall blond looked like he could play center for the Utah Jazz. He laughed raucously in response to something Will said, gave him a high five, and started to walk off. Will turned to pick up his full backpack as Lizzie approached him.

"That shirt seems a little unrighteous, even for the U," Lizzie said as he turned around to face her. "You could be disfellowshipped for something like that, Brother Pemberley. Have you no respect?" she said teasingly but meaning what she said.

He grinned sheepishly as he looked down at his clothes. "They're giving them out in the bookstore in honor of the BYU game tomorrow.

Our boys are going to win, no doubt. We could go get you one too." He stepped back to appraise her long, dark hair and blue eyes. He seemed to like what he saw. "I think it's your color."

Lizzie smiled. "Being disfellowshipped is one thing, but my family would disown me if I wore something like that. My dad played baseball for the Y, so he'll be at the game in his Cougar blues."

Will nodded. "You might clash."

Lizzie laughed. "And not just because of our clothes!"

He looked at her again, this time stepping back and holding out his hand. "Will Pemberley."

Lizzie accepted the outstretched hand, noticing his firm grip. The missionary handshake. "Liz Benson," she said. "I've seen you at a few activities. It's great to actually meet you, despite the fact that you have terrible taste in clothes."

He looked aside briefly with a wry grin, taking her comments in stride and brushing them off. "So I take it you're the black sheep of the family, going to the U?"

Lizzie shifted her weight to the other leg, her long brunette locks casually falling over her shoulder, and looked up into his chocolate eyes. "Yeah, I'm the rebel. But I couldn't turn down the scholarship, so here I am."

"Impressive." He smiled, watching the sun glisten on her hair. "You spurned the Y *and* have a scholarship. I respect that." He paused, then glanced quickly at his watch. "Liz, it was great talking with you, but I have a class. I guess I'll see you at the institute dance tonight?"

Lizzie thought a moment and wrinkled her nose. "I hadn't planned on it. I don't usually go. The refreshments are never any good."

"Oh, that's harsh! What if I told you I choose them myself?"

"I'd say you need to broaden your horizons beyond fruit punch and Doritos."

He laughed. "If I promise to get some good food, just for you, will you come and save me a dance?"

"That might just be enough to get me to go," she said after a moment of thought, "if the refreshments were really good."

"Double-Stuf Oreos?"

Liz shook her head. "Sorry, I'm not the kind of girl who can be bought off with a bag of Oreos. I need something better than the dregs of your cupboards. We're talking mint Milano cookies and smoothies."

Will's eyes glowed as he considered her words. "It's a deal. But you better save me a dance for this."

Liz bit her lip and looked down. She knew when a very cute boy was flirting with her, and she loved it. "Okay, deal." She shook his hand again, noticing that he held on for a moment longer this time. He looked away and slung his backpack nonchalantly over one shoulder.

"Deal, Liz. I better see you tonight." He spun and strode away, glancing back one more time before heading into the building across the street. She stood rooted to the spot, watching him, and waved as he disappeared. She smiled a wider smile than she had in a long time as she grabbed her backpack and headed toward her next class.

* * *

To: jbenson47@email.byu.edu
From: Elizabeth.benson@uu.edu
Subject: Encounter with a very cute boy!

Jana,

Oh wow! I just ran into the institute president on campus. He was wearing this awful anti-BYU shirt, and for some reason I felt compelled to walk up to this total stranger and make a sarcastic comment about it. You know me! Why I did this, I have no idea. I think these sorts of things all the time, but I never act on them. Have I said anything about how outrageously cute he is? His name is Will—tall, curly dark hair, chocolate-milk brown eyes . . . yummy! Anyway, he asked if I was going to the dance tonight, and I said no because the food stinks (as it always does). He said he would bring some special refreshments if I would come and save him a dance! Isn't that cute? I doubt I'll show up, though. There's too much studying to be done this close to finals. Besides, I'm sure he won't even remember my name by tonight. But it was fun to flirt with a boy so shamelessly. How many days till Austen gets home?

Love, Lizzie

* * *

To: Elizabeth.benson@uu.edu
From: jbenson47@email.byu.edu
Subject: RE: Encounter with a very cute boy!

Lizzie,

Fifteen days and counting! (But sixteen till I see him! How unfair is it to have an exam at the same time his flight arrives?! It's all I can think about right now.) Do you really not go to dances because of the food? Mom would be very disappointed. How else can she get us married off if we aren't at every dance? Go have fun with the cute boy. One little night on the town won't hurt you. You know you're prepared for your finals. I think you spend too much time with your nose in the books, and going to a dance won't ruin your perfect GPA. Get out and have some fun! And you should still go support institute even if you don't like the food!

Love, Jana

P.S. When you go to the dance (because you will go!) make sure you wear that blue twin set with your khaki capris. And wear makeup! I know you like to go au naturel, and you're fortunate you have the complexion for it, but a little mascara never killed anyone.

✳ ✳ ✳

LIZZIE felt butterflies in her stomach as she stared at the outfits in her closet. There, dangling from the hanger, calling her name, was the silky blue matching sweater set that her best friend and fraternal twin sister, Jana, said looked fabulous on her. The khaki capris were already on, covered, for the moment, by an oversized school sweatshirt. Her dark, wavy hair had been scrunched after an early evening shower and was pulled away from her face by a braided leather headband. She leaned against the closet door, biting her lower lip.

Her roommate, Robyn, came running into the bedroom they shared, wrapped in her blue fleece robe, towel turban sliding off her head as she slammed the door. She plopped onto her bed and sighed, then noticed Lizzie staring into the closet with uncharacteristic intensity.

"No matter how much you stare, Liz, the clothes will still be the same."

Lizzie turned around and sighed, then climbed onto her own bed on the opposite side of the room. She lay down and curled into a ball. "I was just debating on whether or not to go to the institute dance tonight."

Robyn looked surprised. "You? Dance? On a Friday night when there is homework to do? Who are you, and what have you done with my roommate?" Robyn darted across the room, pulling her hands into a fake gun position. She shook off the towel turban and tossed her wet hair in her best *Charlie's Angels* imitation, yelling, "Freeze! On the floor, buster! You aren't getting out of here till I've found Lizzie!"

Lizzie laughed at Robyn and shook her head. Was she really that antisocial?

Robyn smiled knowingly and said, "Okay, who is he?"

Lizzie felt a little cornered but tried to answer as casually as she could. "Will Pemberley."

"Are you kidding? Will Pemberley? He's hot. Good for you," Robyn whooped. "He's the most hunted, most untouchable man on campus. No girl can get more than one date with him since his big breakup."

"I ran into him on campus today," Lizzie explained. "He was wearing some hideous anti-BYU T-shirt, so I went up and teased him about it. He asked if I was going to the dance tonight, and I said no because the refreshments are always lacking."

Robyn burst out laughing. "I bet he liked that! His ex-fiancée is chair of the refreshment committee! You know Rochelle Rasmussen?"

"I think so." Lizzie racked her brain to come up with mental picture. "Tall, blond, ultrathin, perfect—the kind of girl who makes the rest of us look like hillbillies?"

"Exactly!" Robyn, who was in gossip mode now, began to comb out her wet hair as she talked. "They were minutes from the altar when she dumped him and then got engaged to some guy from BYU. I heard they were weeks away from the wedding when BYU Boy decides to break it off. She tried to get back together with Will, but he doesn't want anything to do with her now. I guess it's always a little chilly at council meetings now!"

Lizzie rolled her eyes. "Where do you hear this stuff?" She shook her head. "Never mind—I don't want to know. You shouldn't be talking about other girls, especially ones you don't even know. Go have fun tonight. I'll be waiting for your full and colorful report."

Robyn eyed Lizzie suspiciously. Lizzie never paid this much attention to guys, or their ex-girlfriends. And she certainly never asked for a full report on an institute dance. Something else was going on here. "Wait a minute! Did Will ask you to go or something?" Robyn asked.

Lizzie shrugged and tried to brush off Robyn's question. "He made some joke about bringing me some mint Milano cookies and a smoothie if I came and saved him a dance."

Robyn's eyes opened wide. "Liz, you have to go! This is *not* optional. When Will Pemberley asks you to come, you come!" She hopped up and started rummaging through Lizzie's closet. "Where is that blue twin set that looks so great on you?" She yanked it off the hanger and tossed it across the room. "You better put on some makeup too. We must take full advantage of this opportunity!"

"You sound just like Jana and my mom," Lizzie muttered as she walked toward the bedroom door, thinking of her finals.

Robyn turned to give her an admonishing look. "Liz, when a guy like Will wants to see you, it's your duty as a Mormon girl to comply. He's a total hottie—he's smart, talented, spiritual, rich . . . He's as close to Mormon royalty as you can get."

Lizzie cringed and cocked her head disapprovingly. "Mormon royalty? I don't even like the thought. And the only duty I have to anyone tonight is to my lit professor." She pondered her words as she checked herself carefully in the full-length mirror that hung on the back of their bedroom door, then shook her head. "Sorry, Rob, but tonight, I study. Go have enough fun for the both of us. For now, I'll settle for dreams of a dance with a total hottie and see where things go from there. *If* they go anywhere, *if* I ever see him again," she added as she shot Robyn a withering look. She paused in the doorway before going out in the living room to study. "One brief flirtation and a dance do not mean anything other than what they are. Besides, just being the institute president does not make a guy Mormon royalty, whatever that means!"

✳ ✳ ✳

To: jbenson47@email.byu.edu
From: Elizabeth.benson@uu.edu
Subject: The DANCE!

Dear Jana,

I know I could wait and tell you all of this Sunday on the way to Mom and Dad's house, but I can't, and therefore, I must tell you everything now. (And then we can rehash the entire thing all over again on Sunday.)

Tonight did not go as planned at all. I chose to stay home and study and sent Robyn off to flirt with the boys at the dance. But around 11:30 Robyn called me from the dance to come rescue her because she was having major stalker issues.

Poor Robyn—too many men, so little time. So I willingly surrendered my homework and went to rescue her in my little tin chariot. Not surprisingly, she wasn't standing on the corner waiting for me.

Knowing what I do about Robyn, I figured I may have to actually enter the dance to find her, so I wore the light blue sweater twin set just like you (and Robyn!) suggested, curled my hair, and wore makeup just for fun.

The dance was really full, and I'll give the deejay credit for playing some pretty good tunes. I couldn't see why Robyn would want to leave. I looked around but didn't see Will. It didn't matter, because I was having plenty of fun dancing as I worked the floor in search of Robyn. I eventually spotted Will by the refreshment tables talking to the tall basketball player guy I saw him with yesterday afternoon. (That guy couldn't hide if his life depended on it, he's so tall!) Anyway, I restrained myself from investigating the refreshment tables to see if he really did get Milano cookies and smoothies, but I couldn't help but walk strategically past him en route to the water fountain without so much as even a glance in his direction. I got all the way to the water fountain, and was almost back in the door, when he walked up to me, holding a smoothie. Well, what is a good Mormon girl to do when the perfect Mormon boy with gorgeous brown eyes walks up to her holding a smoothie just for her?

"Sister Benson, your smoothie idea has been a big hit. Thank you for the idea." He offered me the drink.

Inside my head my answer was something like, "Bedeeabbadabbayoobooboo." But somehow the words, "Really? And what about the mint Milano cookies?" found their way out of my mouth.

"The mint Milano, Nantucket, and chocolate caramel chip cookies were all well-received and consumed by 9:30, which is why we are now serving Oreos." He laughed. "So did you save me a dance?"

Right then, as if my guardian angel were running the show, my favorite slow song came on. Billy Joel's "To Make You Feel My Love" will make me swoon and melt in any man's arms, especially if that man has curly brown hair and dark brown eyes. Will offered me his arm, I accepted, and he led me to the center of the dance floor.

We made the appropriate small talk while we danced. I found out that he is from Olympia Heights, right here in Salt Lake, and graduated from Olympia High School. He's an international business major and interned in San Francisco for Huntsman Corporation last summer. He's planning to do another internship for them here this summer. And he served his mission in Russia. Oh, and Dad will love him—he played baseball in high school. The tall blond basketball player is his cousin Ryan. He just got out of the Air Force, and everyone calls him the Colonel.

But I digress! Will held me close, but not too close! We passed the Book of Mormon test, but were close enough to occasionally look in each other's eyes as we talked. As he led me nicely around the floor (and yes, the boy can dance very well), I noticed his tall, strong frame. He still has his pitcher's arm and baseball player's shoulders. (Not that I examined them too thoroughly. Ahem!)

When the song ended we talked for a minute more, and then went our separate ways. Robyn attacked me almost instantly to get the details. Funny how she found me instead of the other way around! I had to admit the dance was fun and I enjoyed myself. Okay, I REALLY enjoyed myself. I danced with a few more guys, including the Colonel, who is pretty fun himself. At about 12:30 I decided it was time to go home. I don't think Robyn was having much fun. She had a little stalker named Howard who kept following her around and asking her to dance, so it wasn't hard to convince her to leave. I looked around for Will before leaving but wasn't so sure I would say anything to him even if I saw him. But I did see him over by the water fountain, where he was talking yet again to the Colonel. I walked alongside the wall and not directly at him. I didn't want to be too obvious (obviously), and I am so glad I didn't! Wait till you hear what happened next! The guys didn't see me walking up to them. Thanks to a very fast song ending and a huge crowd running for the water fountain, the guys ended up getting pushed around a corner. I stopped to get a sip from the water fountain and overheard their conversation.

"There are a lot of good-looking girls here, Will. No wonder you didn't want to settle down with Rochelle so soon!" the Colonel said jokingly.

"Ah, I don't know about that. I haven't seen anything worth getting excited over," Will responded coolly. "I'm not into dating coeds. They are all too immature and just want to get married. That's not what I'm looking for."

"What are you talking about? The room is full of beautiful girls!" the Colonel exclaimed. "Who cares if they want to get married? Just go have fun. The more, the better, I say."

"Well, you can have them. I'm not interested."

"What about Liz, that girl you just danced with? She's pretty cute. And she looks interested in you," the Colonel teased. (How embarrassing!)

"College girls. They're all interested in everyone. If a guy has a nice car, or even just a heartbeat, they're interested," Will informed him bluntly.

"That is a bit harsh, don't you think? Liz doesn't seem that way to me." (Thank you, Colonel!)

"If there is anything I have learned, Ryan, it's that you can't trust a girl. They all have an agenda and a wedding to plan. When is the last time you went out with a girl who didn't bring up marriage on the first date?" Will asked.

Ryan laughed. "Brother, your problem is that there's just way too much talking on your dates! You gotta do something else with your lips!" Then his voice softened. "You have to start again sometime."

"Just give her time, Colonel. Just give her time," Will responded. He quickly changed the subject.

Can you even imagine? Well, that is the end of Will for me. I thought he was great right up till that point. Well, in order to hear this conversation I had to keep drinking from the water fountain. I thought my bladder was about to burst from staying there so long, so I ran right into the little girls' room. When I came back, the guys were gone, thankfully!

I grabbed Robyn and headed for the door. That's when I saw Will standing by the exit. I decided to just give him one little chance to redeem himself, although after his shirt earlier today and his comments this evening, I'm not sure he earned the chance. I will have you know that I followed Mother's advice. It may be the only time I ever have! You know how she always says to make sure you have a moment alone so the boys can approach you? Well, I made Robyn walk out the door ten feet ahead of me. I wanted—without being totally obvious—to give Will the innocent chance to say good-bye. It worked! Robyn went out the door, and Will came right up to me.

"Elizabeth Benson, thank you for gracing us with your company. Your refreshment ideas were a hit," Will said.

"Thank you. My consultation services are always available for a small fee or dinner and good conversation. Your free trial is over," I teased him. I couldn't help it. How dare he be all cute and flirty with me after his comments not five minutes earlier?

He laughed, then said, "Well, I was wondering what you are doing on the twenty-fifth. It's a Wednesday night."

My heart completely froze, and I couldn't speak! I decided to give him one last chance to talk to me, but only so I can let him know that his opinion on coeds is rather lame. I wanted to call him a liar, or a tease, but I just shrugged and smiled.

"I was hoping maybe you would like to join us at the Institute Council meeting. We could use some new ideas." He smiled hopefully.

"The Institute Council? Oh, I thought that was a ward calling or something. Are you sure I can just do that?" I was really surprised.

"I'm the president, and I can invite anyone I want to our meetings. Yours is not a calling—yet. It would just be for some fresh ideas."

"Oh, well, yes, I can do that. That might be fun. Where and when?" I only accepted so I could show him that not all women are carrying around MODERN BRIDE in their backpacks. The institute activities around here could use some help, and maybe a headstrong girl like me could do some good!

"Wednesday the twenty-fifth at the institute building, 9:00 p.m."

I was so surprised! I looked up at him, and he looked legitimately sincere—eyebrows raised and everything. I was still smarting over what he had said about me earlier, but I figured helping out the council couldn't hurt, so I said, "Sure, I'll be there." I gave him my phone number, and that was that.

We'll forget the part where I have an English lit class on Wednesday night. I completely forgot when I agreed to go! This means that I have some serious shopping to do. I've got to find smart new clothes that make it clear I don't need William Pemberley to make me happy. Want to go with me? We can get you a cute new outfit for Austen's homecoming!

I can't believe what a disappointment Will turned out to be. He showed such promise earlier. More proof that I am completely incapable of reading men correctly.

Okay, I'll see you Sunday, and let me know about shopping! But I must swear you to secrecy at Mom and Dad's house. I don't want Mom lecturing me about letting a man slip through my fingers. There is nothing for her to know right now! And you know what I mean!

See you soon.

Love, Lizzie

Lizzie turned off the computer, reached for the light switch, and noticed the light blinking on the answering machine. Who would have called so late? It was officially the wee hours of Saturday morning! She wondered to herself for only a moment and then remembered. There was only one person in the known universe who frequently called her at odd hours. Hitting the play button on the answering machine, Lizzie let out an exasperated sigh when she heard her mother's voice. It wasn't that she didn't love her mother, it was just that sometimes her mother tended to make a big deal over nothing.

"Lizzie dear, when you come up on Sunday I want you to make sure you wear that nice blue sweater set we got for you with your black skirt. We also need to start thinking of what you're going to wear to Austen's homecoming in a couple of weeks. My gracious! Can you believe he'll be home so soon? What a wonderful thing for our sweet Jana. Sister Young tells me that lots of Austen's cousins will be in town for his homecoming, and you want to look your best for them. Jana will be married soon enough, and we can't have you waiting too long, now can we? Your black skirt looks best with heels, so don't forget to wear heels. None of those clunky college girl sandals you like so much. And a little lipstick never hurt a girl any, so try to find some makeup. Okay, dear, that is all. Oh! Did we tell you that LeAnn went hiking with a boy today from the military base? Such a nice young man, and so tall! If you don't get a man soon, LeAnn will get married before you. Okay, dear, we will see you soon. Love you! Bye-bye."

Lizzie rolled her eyes, turned off the answering machine, and went to bed.

A Suitor Returns

JANALYN BENSON looked around the chapel and saw nothing but familiar faces. This was home. This was where she had been born and raised. The chapel was full of family and friends from throughout her life, but she had never felt as uncomfortable as she did at that moment.

She had been waiting for this day for two years. She was wearing a brand-new stylish dress, picked out by Robyn and Lizzie at the mall yesterday, and she even had gotten her hair trimmed, all because Austen had finally come home from his mission. She had waited as faithfully and devotedly as a girl could. Not a week had gone by without her writing him, encouraging him, praising him, and sending her love and support. She'd sent him packages for every major holiday and his birthday, and she had even made him a home video montage when he said he wished he could see home again. She had been the perfect girlfriend. And yet today was the scariest day of her life. It seemed as though all eyes rested on her, and most of the whispering in the chapel was about her and Austen. Jana did not appreciate the attention.

She had managed to pull some strings to get her unsympathetic professor to reschedule her exam and had gone to the airport with his family to welcome him home, waiting patiently at the luggage carousel for him to emerge from the terminal. In a case of Murphy's Law, the stake president had been out of town until last night, and Austen hadn't been released yet. She hadn't hugged him or been alone with him for five minutes. He had only been home forty-eight hours, but to her it felt like a month. She couldn't wait to run up and finally hug him, but she wouldn't be able to do it here, with all those eyes watching.

"Hey, sweetheart, how are you holding up?" Liz walked up and gave her twin sister a hug.

"Oh, Lizzie, I'm so glad you're finally here. Thank you so much. I feel like there's a huge spotlight on me and everyone is staring," Jana whispered almost breathlessly to her favorite sister.

"I hate to break it to you, but they are staring. They can't help it! You look beautiful. Where's Austen?" Liz's eyes panned the room but saw no sign of the man of the hour.

"He's in getting released by the stake president right now. He gave his report to the high council this morning. His sisters are sitting over there in front of Mom and Dad." Jana made no moves to go join them, mostly because she was paralyzed by nerves and fear.

Lizzie turned to give the Young family a friendly wave. She noticed with no small amount of irritation that Julie Smith sat with Austen's sisters, Erin and Natalie. The last person Liz wanted to spend any time with was Julie Smith. She turned back to her sister. "Jana, you waited faithfully for two years. The worst is over. You can relax," Liz said, but she could tell the anxiety was still building.

"I don't think I can play my piano piece. I'm too nervous. Look, my hands are shaking!" Jana nervously wrung her hands together, and Liz truly did wonder if her sister could play.

Just then, Austen walked through the chapel doors opposite them. Liz saw him search the room quickly and then spot Jana. A huge smile crossed his face, and he began to practically run across the room to her.

"Jana, don't look now, but I think he just got released," Liz teased.

Austen made a mad dash for the slender, blond, blue-eyed beauty anxiously standing across the room. A dozen different people must have tried to stop him to shake his hand, but he only had eyes for one girl at that moment. He didn't even stop to say hello before throwing his arms around Jana and hugging her right there in the chapel. Quiet, shy Jana smiled and giggled quietly into his shoulder as he held her in a tight embrace.

"Well, it looks like he's over all that missionary awkwardness. No kissing in the chapel, guys!" LeAnn Benson, Liz and Jana's youngest sister, blurted out loud enough that everyone in the chapel could hear her.

Liz shot her a dirty look. "LeAnn, that's not appropriate. Act a little more mature, please."

LeAnn smiled sweetly back at her sister. "You better chaperone those two, Lizzie. I have business to take care of." She skipped to the back of the chapel where the missionaries were taking a seat along the back bench. Lizzie made a mental note to chastise LeAnn for trying to embarrass Jana; a comment like that had the potential to scar Jana forever. But as Liz looked around the room, she realized *everyone* was staring at the couple. She was sure that if they weren't in the chapel that the congregation would burst into applause and cheer them on. Everyone, it seemed, except his sisters and their friend Julie. They whispered among themselves and shot disapproving glances at Jana and Liz. She ignored them and felt her heart burst with sheer joy for Jana's happiness. She realized, however, that although the couple was cute to watch, it was time someone broke them up.

"Austen, it is so great to have you back. How did you like Venezuela?" Liz interrupted.

Austen pulled back and grinned, looking like the cat that had caught the canary. Jana was shyly smiling and couldn't take her eyes off Austen. He turned to face Lizzie, but his hand was clamped tightly to Jana's. "I loved it, every minute of it. But how are you doing? You look great!"

He stepped forward to give Liz and the third Benson sister, Merry Bright, brotherly hugs. The organ prelude music began as ward members and possibly an extra hundred visitors filled the chapel quickly for the meeting. The Young family had come out in full force for Austen's return, not to mention dozens of friends from high school and Weber State University, where he had been a popular man on campus. The Benson sisters took their seats with their parents, in the pew under the clock, directly behind the Young family, as they had done for years. Austen took a seat on the stand, next to his father, who was also the bishop. Austen still couldn't take his eyes off Jana. Despite all the people from the ward coming up to Jana and Liz to greet them and welcome them back, Jana couldn't stop staring at Austen, relieved that he was home at last. He had changed so much, and he looked so different, so much more confident. But he was with her once again, and she could feel the strain of the last two years lifting from her heart. He seemed to read her thoughts and winked down at her from the stand. She smiled up in return, then tried very hard to find the opening hymn in the hymnbook.

As the organist played the introduction to the opening hymn, Lizzie noticed the Young sisters whispering conspiratorially with Julie Smith. She tried in vain to ignore them, but they kept glancing back at her and Jana, and Lizzie was starting to feel uneasy. Liz harmonized with the alto line, while Jana sang in her light, airy soprano, oblivious to the fact that she was being openly discussed by people just inches in front of her. Jana's mind and heart were focused on the man on the stand. Lizzie finally stopped to whisper at Erin and Natalie, "Is there something you need? A hymnbook, maybe?"

"No, we're fine, thank you," Erin whispered back, with a glaring smirk, barely glancing over her shoulder. Natalie offered a fake smile, while Julie pretended to ignore Lizzie and turned her gaze on Austen, tossing her hair and smiling. Erin continued, "We'll talk to you after the meeting. We have so much to catch up on."

Liz picked up the song again, but a nervous feeling flitted around in her stomach. She had always gotten along with the Young family and had grown up with both Erin and Natalie. Julie, however, had grown up in a different stake but had moved into their ward after high school, so Liz had never gotten to know her well. Jana had always admonished her to give Julie the benefit of the doubt—"since you never know where your next friend will come from"—but Julie had always rubbed Lizzie the wrong way.

Austen gave an amazing, spiritual talk, as expected. Lizzie stood in the foyer watching him shake hands with practically the entire ward after sacrament meeting. Everyone mobbed him, giving him hearty welcome-home hugs and handshakes. Sister Young, proud mother of the returned missionary and ever-patient wife of the bishop, approached Sister Benson and gave her a sideways hug as Lizzie and Jana moved into the fray in the foyer. The two mothers stood silently for a moment, watching all the young people chatting and waiting in line to talk to Austen. Sister Young beamed with that certain pride reserved only for mothers of returned missionaries.

"Louisa, I just wanted to let you know that Jana did such a marvelous job on her piano solo," she said as Sister Benson turned to look at her and return the sideways hug.

"Well, thank you, Nan!" Sister Benson replied happily. "Jana has always been such a good girl. I never had any reason to worry about her, although I must admit she did give my poor nerves a run for their money when she was twelve and kept sneaking off with your son!"

Sister Young laughed and nodded in agreement, dropping her arms and preparing to leave, but Sister Benson continued, "Now Jana, she has always been so gifted on the piano. I think Lizzie could have been as good, you know, since we started them in lessons at the same time, but she just wouldn't stick with it! She couldn't be bothered to practice and was always trying hard to be the intellect. If I told her once I told her a million times . . ."

Sister Young frowned. "Lizzie plays pretty well. She was nice enough to play for us in Relief Society a few weeks back when she was visiting and Sister Speed's arthritis acted up during the prelude. You should be proud of both girls. Of *all* your girls!"

"Oh, I am! I am!" Sister Benson declared. "The only one of my girls who ever gives me worry is Merry. You know, she's nineteen now, and she hasn't been on a single date! My gracious!"

"Yes, you've mentioned that, many times." Sister Young clasped a locket that hung around her neck. It was filled with baby pictures of her children, and she fiddled with it as she spoke. She loved Sister Benson dearly; she just happened to have had the same conversation with her on more than one occasion. Chances were excellent that rest of the ward had as well. A thought occurred to her suddenly, and she inquired, "That reminds me. Do you know Sister Evern in the Ogden River Eightieth Ward?"

Sister Benson thought a moment, and then nodded. "Didn't she give the workshop for Primary at auxiliary training two weeks ago?"

Sister Young nodded. "Yes, she did, and wasn't she wonderful? I learned so much! You'd never guess that she had recently suffered from a debilitating case of the stomach flu. Anyway, she mentioned that she has a son named Doug who never seems to date either. Maybe you two could put your heads together."

Sister Benson almost started clapping with excitement. "Oh, Nan, wouldn't that be wonderful! I love Merry dearly, but she really needs to get out and date. I'd hate to see her single at fifty-three and still living at home like my sisters Ellen and Sue." She glanced quickly over at Lizzie, who seemed very involved in conversation with members of the ward. She lowered her head and leaned toward Sister Young. "And, you know, I think Miss Lizzie might have a young man of interest too. I think I heard her mention a young man named Will Pemberley to her sister last night when they got home. She acted like it was no big deal, but I think she just might be interested! Wouldn't that be a wonderful thing, for all my girls to get married so soon?"

Sister Young looked thoughtful. "Pemberley? As in Pemberley Auto Mall?"

Sister Benson's eyes grew wide with elation. "I hadn't thought of that! I wonder . . ." Anyone passing by her at that moment would have thought she was holding a winning ticket from the Idaho lottery.

But Sister Young looked slightly more cautious. "I hope it's not the Pemberley I read about a while ago in the paper. There was a story in the society section about the merging of two business families as a Pemberley boy married into the Rasmussen family's restaurant chains. I'm almost certain it was a William and a . . . Michelle? No, that doesn't sound right. But I'm sure I read something about a William Pemberley." She brushed the thought aside. "But it couldn't possibly be the same people. Well, are you coming over for the big dinner?"

"You know I made my special Jell-O salad medley for the occasion!" Sister Benson exclaimed. "And we'll bring a casserole or two that Merry made for you. She found some recipes in an old pioneer cookbook that she wanted to try."

Sister Young gave her another hug. "You are simply wonderful, Louisa! I don't know what we'd do without your family. We'll be there all afternoon. In fact, I had better run. I'm sure people are waiting at the house already!" She jogged off as she waved her good-byes.

Liz watched Austen's mother push the glass doors open and exit the foyer as she stood to the side, watching Jana, Austen, and all his friends. As she waited to talk to him, she felt someone come up behind her and turned to see who it was. She groaned internally when she realized it was Erin, Natalie, and Julie, obviously there to finish their earlier conversation.

Erin and Natalie Young were strikingly pretty. Both had long blond hair, with just the right amount of curl to be the envy of every girl in their home stake. The Youngs were known for their trademark blue eyes, and both sisters knew how to accent those features. Despite their good looks and talent, Austen seemed to have all the charm and grace in their family. Liz couldn't help but wonder what went wrong with his sisters. Their friend Julie Smith was also a head turner, with a porcelain complexion and shining auburn curls, but she was definitely less sugar and more spice. The combination of the Young sisters, the Benson sisters, and Julie had often caused many people to call their ward the prettiest ward in the valley.

"Liz, so nice to see you once again," Julie said as Liz turned to face her, surprised that she even pretended she was happy to meet again. "Since I'm at BYU, I hardly ever get the chance to see my old friends from the home ward. Where are you going to school now? The tech school on Second Street in Ogden?"

Liz smarted at the tone of Julie's voice. The girl could pull off "fake polite" better than anyone she had ever met. She took a deep breath and reminded herself to turn the other cheek. "No, no, I'm still at the U on a full academic scholarship. After this semester I will be ready to graduate early if I can get the classes I need. Thanks for asking." She managed to muster a forced smile.

"Look at Austen," Natalie said, turning her attention to her older brother. "Doesn't he look amazing? The girls at Weber are going to go nuts over him when he gets back into school summer semester."

"That's actually why we wanted to talk to you, Liz," Erin began. "We've been watching Jana and noticed that she really seems to be clinging to Austen."

"Poor thing," Julie clucked with mock sympathy. She picked at an invisible fleck on her well-manicured fingernails, and under her breath she added, "She looks a little desperate. I guess I would be too if I were getting ready to graduate from the Y and still hadn't found a husband. Must be the extra ten pounds she's picked up over the last couple of years."

Erin tossed back her long blond locks unnecessarily and added, "We just thought, as Jana's friends, we should tell you to warn her that Austen plans to date a lot now that he's home from his mission. I hope she doesn't think they're going to get married or something."

"She's such a sweet girl," Julie agreed. She flashed a false expression of sympathy and straightened out her skirt. "We'd hate to see her end up with a broken heart. But I guess it hurts when you're as old as she is and you lose your first good chance at marriage. Poor thing!"

It was all Liz could do to maintain her composure. These girls were completely delusional! First of all, Austen and Jana were clearly in love. Second, Austen had always talked about marriage to Jana. Even if all of that weren't true, Jana was barely twenty-one, hardly a spinster! Lizzie wanted to bang her head against the wall. No, she wanted to bang Julie's head against the wall. Taking a deep breath, she looked over and saw Austen smiling, talking with old friends but keeping Jana firmly by his side. "They look pretty happy to be together right now," she replied as calmly as she could.

"Well, of course they do," Erin excused them. "I would never deny he likes hanging out with her. Why shouldn't he? They have been friends forever. I just don't want her to expect too much and get hurt. I want you to know I'm trying to protect my friend—and my brother, of course."

"That's so kind of you, Erin, but I think Austen is entitled to make that decision all by himself," Liz answered, a little more sharply than she intended. "What he wants and what you want for him may be two entirely different things."

"Whatever, Liz," Julie snapped back. "We just thought we'd let you warn Jana that Austen is fair game now!" She spun quickly, leading the perpetually perfect Young sisters over to the crowd surrounding the returned missionary. Lizzie wanted to shriek as she watched them go over to hug Jana, smiling and making small talk like dear old friends. "Girls are their own worst enemies sometimes. They'll stab you in the back and then offer you a Band-Aid," Liz muttered under her breath, hardly aware that her thoughts were slipping out her mouth. She noticed Julie sidle up between Jana and Austen, then turn her back to Jana and face Austen, forcing away others who were trying to talk with him. She shot Lizzie a triumphant look then smiled up at him and ran her hand along the arm of his suit. Before long, the Young sisters had Jana on the other side of the foyer, and Julie was leading Austen down the hall.

Lizzie took a deep breath as she approached Jana to take her home. They both needed to get home for dinner and head back south to get ready for Monday morning classes. As they walked through the parking lot and saw Julie and Austen pulling away in the Young's gigantic Suburban, she tried to fight the sick feeling in her stomach. She knew she had to tell Jana what had happened.

"They said what?" Jana asked in disbelief as they got in Lizzie's car.

"They wanted to make sure I passed along the message that you better not plan on anything happening with Austen now that he's home. They said he's fair game," Lizzie repeated as they pulled out of the parking lot and headed up Weber High Drive toward their house in Lakeview Heights. "Julie made that very clear."

"Julie said this to you? No, I can't believe it!" Jana exclaimed, shocked.

Lizzie nodded. "Believe me, I only wish I were making this up. They told me to warn you that he would be dating many, many girls now that he's home from his mission."

Jana shook her head. "I think you must have misunderstood what they said," she insisted. "I have always been such good friends with them. They would never say anything like that. They know how I feel about Austen, and we've always talked about how fun it would be to be sisters. Unless . . ." Her brow wrinkled with worry as she continued. "Unless he said something to them when he got back and they're just trying to put me on my guard so I don't get hurt. Oh, Lizzie, do you think he's changed his mind about me and is just too polite to say it?"

"No way!" Lizzie said vehemently. "You know that's not true. Anyone who sees how you two light up next to each other would know how you feel about each other. Julie is conniving to steal Austen from you, and somehow she has gotten Erin and Natalie on her side."

Jana shook her head again, her blond hair falling gracefully around her shoulders. Her natural beauty was so much more becoming than Julie's overly done style. "I don't think so. Julie would never do that to me. We've always been good friends. You must have just misunderstood them."

Lizzie laughed in disbelief as she pulled up to the curb in front of their parents' home. "I'm just telling you what they told me to pass on. You think what you want. But if I were a gambling woman, I would bet that Julie will find a way to go on the annual Young family camping trip to Yellowstone next month. Something tells me that Julie Smith epitomizes the phrase, 'All's fair in love and war.'"

"We'll see," Jana said, trying to smile but failing. "I think you just misunderstood them. I am willing to believe the best of them."

"I know you are, Jana, and that worries me," Lizzie warned her. "If you stay the sweet, trusting soul that you are, they are going to railroad you away from Austen."

"Lizzie," Jana sighed, stopping to face her on the front steps. "Why do you always expect the worst of people?"

Liz stopped in the middle of the path leading to the front steps, pondering her sister's words. "I guess I always expect the worst so I know what's coming. That way I'm rarely disappointed."

Jana opened the door, ushering Lizzie into the living room of their family's home. As she closed the door behind them she chided, "I think it was Neal A. Maxwell who said that it is better to always trust and sometimes be disappointed than to be forever mistrusting and be right occasionally."

Lizzie smiled at her sister and opened her arms to give her a hug. "That is why you are going to go straight to the celestial kingdom, and I will be passing out the hot dogs at the wienie roast in . . ."

"Jana! Lizzie!" Brother Benson greeted his daughters with a gigantic bear hug, squeezing both of his girls into his crushing grip. "My normal daughters are home at last. Are you staying for a while? Are you moving back in to save my sanity?"

"Goodness, Elray, what are you talking about?" Sister Benson howled as she stepped in behind him. The kitchen door swung shut behind her, nearly whacking her in the tail end. "All of our daughters are normal, and they're the envy of all the other mothers in the ward. You all looked so beautiful today, I'm sure everyone noticed. I know the elders sure did! But Merry Bright," she said, turning to her daughter who sat reading her scriptures on the couch, "you could have worn a nicer necklace. Oh, Lizzie, wasn't that the nicest sacrament meeting you have ever been to?"

LeAnn breezed into the living room from the kitchen, licking some chocolate pudding off a spoon. She dribbled a bit onto the front of the green dress she wore, then swiped it up with her index finger and licked it off as she plopped onto the couch next to Merry and opened a fashion magazine.

Merry Bright pursed her lips tightly and set her scriptures aside. "LeAnn, I am more than willing to share my clothes with you, but I would like you to ask next time instead of first raiding my closet." She pointed expectantly at the dress LeAnn wore.

LeAnn looked over and rolled her eyes. "You never wear it anyway," she commented as she dribbled more pudding on the front.

"Mother!" Merry cried. "LeAnn stole my dress and is in the process of ruining it. That's one of my nicest dresses!"

Sister Benson gave them a fleeting glance and waved her hand in their direction as she brushed the comment aside. Such antics between Merry and LeAnn were commonplace in the Benson home. "LeAnn, take off your sister's dress."

"Whatever!" LeAnn grumbled as she stomped up the stairs. "Merry doesn't have the body to fill it out, and she never wears it anyway . . ." She slammed the door to her room upstairs and in a few moments, the dress came flying halfway down the stairs before the door slammed shut again.

Merry gasped and ran up the steps to retrieve the dress, but Sister Benson did not seem to notice as she gushed on about the day's meeting. "Jana, your piano solo was absolutely beautiful, and Austen could not have been more clever or spiritual. Oh, to have that boy as my son-in-law!" She clasped her hands wistfully to her heart. "I think you were blessed with such beauty and strength of spirit so you could make a good match for someone like him. Are you going over to the dinner now?"

"I talked to Erin and Natalie about it, but I wasn't sure if we could make it. It starts pretty late," Jana replied, looking at Lizzie for confirmation. "We need to leave before then to get back to school. It's a two-hour drive back to Provo."

"Gracious, child, what do you mean?" Sister Benson exclaimed. "Sister Young told me it's going on all afternoon. Why aren't you there right now? If you aren't careful, some girl will snatch him away from you!" Jana looked at Lizzie in surprise, while Lizzie just raised her eyebrows knowingly. Lizzie didn't doubt that Julie, Erin, and Natalie had intentionally misinformed Jana to keep her away from Austen. Sister Benson continued, "We promised to take a casserole and a few gelatin salads over. I just dropped by to pick them up."

Brother Benson loosened his tie and kicked off his tasseled loafers, plopping down on the couch his youngest daughters had abandoned. He picked up the sports section of the Sunday paper, hiding behind the opened pages and pretending he hadn't heard his wife. When she went back into the kitchen, he quickly winked at Liz and Jana. He lay down on the couch and began to make pretend snoring sounds that could wake the dead.

Sister Benson walked back into the living room, her arms loaded with foil-covered dishes. "Lizzie and Jana, go upstairs and do something with your hair before going to the Youngs. There is hairspray and a curling iron in my bathroom. Elray, could you help me with— Oh, Lizzie, would you look at that? It happens every Sunday. He's not home from church two minutes and he's conked out on the couch.

Poor dear, I know how hard he works during the week, but he doesn't know what I've suffered with my poor nerves, trying to keep this house up while planning and preparing these dishes to help take some of the burden off Austen's mother. But you know me. I never complain."

Lizzie inwardly grinned as she lifted a casserole dish from her mother's arms, exchanging knowing glances with Jana. "No, Mom, you never would." Jana carried a couple of Jell-O dishes out the front door. Ignoring their mother's comments about their hair, they loaded everything into Sister Benson's minivan and headed down the road to the Young home.

Game Point

From time to time, a truly independent woman is born—a woman who knows her true value. She is talented, smart, opinionated, and worth getting to know. She will never let herself be stuck in a corner or put on display.

Knowing her worth, Liz approached the institute building. Will had called earlier that day and asked her to join him for dinner before the council meeting. She had agreed to meet Will for their dinner "get-together" but only to make it clear to him she was not like all other coeds. She wouldn't fawn all over him, and she had no desire to pretend she wanted to. She was smart, in control, and way too good for egotistical maniacs like Will Pemberley. So why did she have butterflies in her stomach at the thought of seeing him again? *It's business! We're just discussing institute business. This is not a date! Will Pemberley doesn't date coeds,* she reminded herself. *Not that I'm just a coed.*

She nervously reached down and adjusted her black, knee-length skirt. She normally wouldn't wear a skirt to something as informal as an institute council meeting, but she had to admit that she looked thinner and sassier in a skirt, and she loved the way her royal blue oxford shirt brought out her slate-blue eyes and trimmed her waist. This was the outfit for a career woman, not a coed only interested in marrying the first guy who comes along. She might not have much to add to the council meeting tonight, but at least she would look like she knew what she was talking about. With one last quick glance in the reflective glass of the door, Liz nervously tucked a piece of hair behind her ear. She took a deep breath and went inside.

The foyer was empty. Liz tried to shoo away the butterflies still fluttering in her stomach. She had expected Will to be in the foyer, but now she didn't know where to look for him. Was she early? Was she late? Did he forget? *I hate this!* Liz yelled in her head as she walked down the dark hallway to a lit room in the back of the building. As she got closer, she could hear male voices and the distinct noises of a Ping-Pong game.

When she stepped up to the doorway, she could see the back of Will's strong frame as he played a spirited game of table tennis against Brother Webb, the institute director. Neither noticed her, so she leaned against the door frame and watched the friendly competition.

Will was wearing dark olive-green pants, a white shirt, and a tie. Liz was immediately grateful she had gone with the skirt. She smiled as she noticed that Will's tie impeded his Ping-Pong performance. She also couldn't help but notice that Will cleaned up quite nicely. His hair had been trimmed since she last saw him at the dance. She smiled to herself again as the thought crossed her mind that she was about to have dinner with the most eligible LDS bachelor on campus.

Will whacked the Ping-Pong ball past Brother Webb and thrust his arms triumphantly in the air as he tied the game. "And that brings the score to 8–8. Only two points left to go!"

"What? We're only playing to ten? Or are you forfeiting when you realize that you'll never beat me?" Brother Webb taunted as he served the ball.

"Ha! You mean you'll forfeit to me!" Will returned the serve with a whack, and the ball never hit the table. Another point for Brother Webb.

As the institute director reached under the table for the ball, he finally noticed Liz in the doorway. She quickly raised a finger to her lips and shook her head.

An all-knowing look crossed Brother Webb's face as he raised one eyebrow. "The only reason Will Pemberley would forfeit a Ping-Pong game would be a girl. Do you, by any chance, have a date tonight?"

Liz winced when she heard the word date come out. But then she felt another little flip-flop in her stomach when she heard Will's reply.

"Yeah, we're going out to dinner and then the council meeting. I think she would make a good replacement for McKell when she leaves."

He just called it a date! Liz thought to herself, doing mental back-flips.

"Where did you meet her? What's her name? Is she pretty?" Brother Webb goaded him. Liz felt larger flip-flops in her stomach as she held her breath for Will's answer.

"Her name is Liz Benson, a political science major. I noticed her a few weeks ago when she spoke at a class debate on union rights. But I actually didn't meet her till Friday. She insulted my favorite T-shirt. I respect a girl who's not afraid to put me in my place." Will continued to focus on the game. Liz was surprised to hear about the class debate, since he had never mentioned it, and she didn't know what to think of the way his opinion of her flip-flopped around more than her nervous stomach. "And as far as being pretty goes, she's . . ."

"Hi, Will." Liz stepped into the room. She didn't need to hear his opinions on her appearance again.

Will missed the ball as it flew right past his paddle.

"That would be ten points, my game." Brother Webb smiled as he laid down his paddle and walked over to Liz. With typical institute director fashion, he reached out to shake her hand and made her feel welcome instantly. "And you must be Liz Benson."

Liz smiled at Brother Webb. She already liked him. "Yes, I am. Nice to meet you. So is Will always this good at Ping-Pong?"

"Nope, sometimes he's worse. He had a fairly good game." Brother Webb kept shaking her hand. He was clearly enjoying this. But Liz noticed that Will had deeply blushed and that he was still looking at her. What a compliment! The most eligible bachelor on campus had blushed over her!

* * *

DINNER that evening could not have been more perfect. Will told Liz about his parents, his career plans, his Church calling, and more. They didn't discuss "business" at all. She was impressed with the way he talked about his parents. He made it clear that he loved them very much, and he was very protective of his mother. Liz admired that protective quality and confessed her own mixed feelings about her lovably insane matriarch. Will was also a perfect gentleman throughout the evening, opening every door for her without making the gesture awkward or obvious. He just seemed to naturally be a gentleman. Lizzie enjoyed the chivalry, but couldn't help feeling confused about Will's intentions.

At the council meeting, she enjoyed watching Will at work and found something very attractive about a man in charge, especially one who made it look so easy. He had introduced her to the council, noting that she was just there to observe. At first Liz was content to sit back and just watch. But as the agenda turned to activities and raising attendance levels, she found it difficult to hold her thoughts. She would have liked to have better activities that appealed to more people, but she didn't feel it was her place to say anything. She noted in her mind that there were too many sports-related events and dances, but nothing in between. Liz rarely attended, because sports weren't her thing and she just didn't care to dance every Friday.

When the meeting concluded, she and Will walked out the front doors, away from the glare of the parking lot lights, and illuminated instead by the bright spring stars. The moon had not risen yet, and the April air still had a crisp winter bite to it. She clasped her arms together and rubbed them to push the goose bumps back down. For a moment, the only sound was their footsteps echoing on the cold concrete.

"Liz, thank you for coming tonight. I enjoyed having you here." Will smiled down at her. He was a perfect four inches taller than her. "If you'll let me walk you home, I'd like to hear what your thoughts are on the meeting tonight."

"You are welcome to walk me home, but I hardly have anything to say about the meeting," Liz fibbed, smiling back. A walk with Will sounded perfect. She didn't want to ruin it with her contrary opinion.

Will noticed her chill and helped Liz into her black leather jacket. For the thousandth time that night Liz admired his curly brown hair.

She was tempted to reach out and touch those curly locks, just to see if they were as soft as they looked.

"If there is one thing I am sure of, it is that the beautiful, unsinkable Liz Benson has an opinion on tonight's meeting."

She brought her gaze back to his deep brown eyes. Surprised at being called beautiful, and unsure of what to think of being called unsinkable, Liz didn't know what to say. Was her notorious stubbornness already apparent?

"You think you know me so well?" Liz raised her eyebrows and smiled innocently.

"If there is anything to know about Liz Benson, it is her legendary beauty and discriminating opinion." He kept steady eye contact with her as they stood facing each other on the institute building steps.

Liz quickly recovered from a brief moment of speechlessness. Will Pemberley had just called her a legendary beauty. Liz matched his steady gaze and smart little glare and smiled back at him. "The beauty is for all to enjoy. But the opinion is shared with a chosen few."

Will looked down at Liz with her perfect brown hair, beautiful blue eyes, and sassy little smile. He knew he had just met his match. For what felt like an eternity he looked into her eyes and wondered whether or not it was too soon to kiss her.

4

A Most Ardent Suitor

LIZZIE rolled over to smack off the blaring alarm and rubbed the sand from her eyes. Sunday morning. Who on earth decided it was a good idea to have a college ward meet at 8:00 a.m.? Liz dragged herself out of bed, quickly got ready, and grabbed Robyn, who was still primping in the bathroom.

They entered the foyer just as the prelude music came to an end and the bishop began conducting. They quickly took a spot on the back bench, in the center against the overflow curtain handles. Liz pretended she didn't know why she was so detached from the meeting that day, but as she watched Robyn doodling absentmindedly in her notebook, she realized that her mind was still on the steps of the institute building. Just a few feet away. She had a hard time erasing the mental image of Will on the steps. Will in that obnoxious T-shirt. Will in the gym at the dance, swaying in perfect sync with her, Billy Joel loud on the speakers but barely heard. She felt guilty that she couldn't focus.

Lizzie looked over at Robyn and tried to shake the daydreams of Will. Before meeting Robyn, Lizzie had never known a person who was so concerned about what other people might be thinking. Rarely did Robyn look serene or relaxed; she was always scanning the room with a worried but pretty look on her face. For a brief moment Lizzie wondered how long it took Robyn to do her eye makeup versus how long it took Lizzie to get totally ready in the morning. Maybe if there were more interesting boys around to get excited about, Lizzie would put forth more effort. Or maybe not. She always looked presentable, and her clothes were fashionable and always clean and ironed. She simply refused to spend hours fussing with makeup and hairspray, and she was a firm believer in natural beauty and a healthy glow. However, she did understand that sometimes a girl does have to go above and beyond her usual charms to snag a man.

"Holy cow, Lizzie, check this guy out!" Robyn blurted out in a loud whisper, rousing Lizzie from her silent contemplations. Others on the bench nearby looked over and gave Robyn a disapproving look.

"What?" Liz mumbled, directing her attention back to reality and the pulpit, at the man Robyn was oh-so-subtly pointing at.

"Check him out!"

Lizzie looked at the speaker, then back at Robyn, and repeated, "What?" She looked at her sacrament program and glanced quickly at the name of the speaker. Collin Light. He had been in the ward for several months and was working on a master's degree in English literature.

"Have you ever seen a skinnier guy in your life?"

Liz snorted but managed to swallow her laughter and retain her composure. "Honestly, Robyn," she whispered. "The guy is speaking about the power of the priesthood and you're worried about how skinny he is? This is sacrament meeting, not Muscle Beach."

Robyn's brow furrowed and Liz knew she wouldn't let it drop. "Just take a look at him. Really."

Lizzie sighed and looked back up, listening to his words. He had a commanding voice, and he had clearly spent a great deal of time preparing his talk, as he spoke powerfully with the Spirit. Despite all this, she still managed to become distracted by the bright red bow tie he wore. His round glasses and neatly trimmed goatee gave him the appearance of the ultimate beatnik intellectual, a look that was not foreign in the College of Humanities at the U. Still, he was really skinny. Not thin enough to make her poke someone else in the ribs and disrupt a church meeting, but disturbingly thin nevertheless.

"He's skinny," Lizzie conceded. "So?"

"Skinny doesn't cover it," Robyn pushed. "His thigh probably isn't as big as my forearm. Can you imagine dating him? I would hate to know that I outweighed my boyfriend by a good thirty pounds."

"Sssshhhhh!" someone on the same bench hissed in their direction.

Lizzie conjured up her best mother look and shot it at her friend, knowing they were disrupting sacrament meeting. "Focus on the talk," she advised, "and not so much on drawing attention to us. Please!"

"But . . ."

Lizzie held up her hand in silent protest. "The Spirit." Robyn's lips pouted, but she soon redirected herself back to her doodling. Lizzie shook her head and tried to listen to the talk again. She couldn't focus on the meeting, though, and started daydreaming once more. Will filtered back into her thoughts, except now he wore round glasses and a large, spinning red bow tie. She imperceptibly rattled her head to shake out the thought and silently vowed never to sit with Robyn in sacrament meeting again.

☆ ☆ ☆

"Sister Elizabeth Benson," a loud voice summoned over the noisy din of post-meeting flirtation in the foyer. Liz looked around, wondering who had called her name. She always tried to make a quick escape after Relief Society to protect herself from receiving a calling or being herded unnecessarily into another meeting. When she noticed the ultraskinny sacrament speaker waving at her, she stopped out of sheer surprise.

He approached her slowly as he forced his way through the crowd. He extended his hand and shook hers warmly. "Greetings, Sister Benson. Collin Light at your service." She gave him a confused look, but he ignored it and continued, "I have been awarded the privilege of serving you, since I have been called to home teach you and your roommate, Robyn Scott. I'd like to find a time this week to get my teaching done. What's your schedule like?"

Robyn, who had been standing nearby, bolted in the opposite direction when he mentioned her name. Liz knew as she drove Robyn home she would hear all sorts of complaints about not getting a cute home teacher. Still, Liz thought for a moment. "Well, I'm not sure this week is good. Finals start tomorrow, and we have pretty full schedules. Can you call us?"

"I would be more than happy to oblige you, gracious lady. However, I do like to get my service done at the first of the month," he replied. "I have finals myself and a thesis to work on. If you and Sister Scott are home for a few minutes some evening, I would be happy to bring some Chinese over in order to accommodate your busy schedules. How does that sound?"

Lizzie knew she must have been staring at him as though he had a severe abnormality. His manner of speaking could easily have come straight out of *Masterpiece Theatre*. She was a little surprised that he hadn't tipped a top hat toward her. Did he seriously call her "gracious lady"? Nevertheless, the offer of free Chinese food gradually won her over, and she figured whatever odd disease he had, it probably wasn't contagious. It might be fun to have a home teacher who probably could converse entirely in iambic pentameter. She heard Jana's voice echoing in her head: *"You never know where you'll find your next friend."*

Lizzie shrugged. "Sure, I guess that would be fine. I know we both have study groups tomorrow night at the library, but we should be home Tuesday. I'll make sure we're there, but just so you know, it's only because of the Chinese food."

Collin smiled. "Of course. My home teaching has always been 100 percent, and it is entirely due to the fact that I bring food."

"Then you and your chopsticks are always welcome at our humble little apartment." Lizzie looked around for Robyn, but she was nowhere in sight. "I thought Robyn was around here, but I don't see her. You'll just have to meet her Tuesday."

Collin nodded knowingly, shifting his weight from one leg to the other. He was exactly Lizzie's height, which she found a little distracting. He didn't seem to notice her distraction as he continued, "Yes, I've heard that Sister Scott is quite the social butterfly. She has her finger on the pulse of the ward."

"Maybe," Lizzie sighed. "I think it's more like she makes sure the ward gossip is alive and well. When the bishop gets up and lectures about the evils of gossip, he's really just talking to her."

He laughed. "Well, it should be an interesting evening then, Sister Benson. May I call you Elizabeth?"

"Sure."

"Elizabeth is such a beautiful, classic name," he said as he began to step away. He grasped her hand one more time in a farewell handshake, clasping his other hand on top of hers before planting a kiss on the top of her hand. "It suits you well." He locked eyes with her for one sharp, uncomfortable moment, then released her hand and turned to leave.

"Collin!" Liz called down the hall. He turned back around to face her in what could only be described as a gallant swirling motion. Lizzie stared at him oddly before remembering to speak. "Why are we getting new home teachers just before the semester ends?"

"We must trust that the Lord acts in mysterious ways that are beyond our comprehension. God bless you, dear sister!" And with that, he bowed and swirled gallantly back away.

Lizzie stood still as he disappeared down the hall, unsure of what to think. The Chinese food was starting to lose its appeal. There was nothing really inappropriate with the exchange that had just taken place, but somehow he managed to make her feel uneasy. She wasn't sure why. For some unexplainable reason, she felt like he had just marked her as his territory.

She tried to shake the feeling as she went to her car. Sure enough, Robyn was already sitting in the driver's seat of Lizzie's beat-up 1980 convertible Volkswagen Rabbit. The car was old, but it was vintage VW, metallic green with a white top and a white vinyl interior. She had locked the car before entering the chapel, but Robyn had broken in, as she always did, by popping open the triangular side window with a quick thrust from her elbow, then reaching in to unlock the door. She had pulled the top down and was leaning back in Lizzie's place, feet propped up on the fuzzy purple steering wheel cover, skirt wrapped around her legs.

"Of all the home teachers to get!" Robyn complained.

Lizzie rolled her eyes as she looked in her purse for her missing keys. "I don't think he's that bad, Robyn. He's going to bring Chinese food. Anyone who knows to bring us Chinese can't be all bad," she said, trying to convince herself just as much as Robyn. She yanked her keys from their hiding place, the zipped side pocket where she always left them, then motioned for Robyn to move out of the driver's seat.

"Chinese food isn't nearly enough to get me to stick around for that guy," Robyn told her as she scooted over into the passenger seat. "You wouldn't believe some of the things I've heard about him!"

Lizzie sat down and bounced into a comfortable position as she yanked the door closed, put the car in neutral, and started the engine. "I don't want to hear it, and you know it!"

"But you have to know what you're getting into with this guy!" Robyn insisted.

"Seat belt," Lizzie warned as they pulled out of the parking lot. She turned and headed left, toward their little one-bedroom basement apartment. "The way you acted today in sacrament, I thought you had no idea who he was."

"I'd never seen him before, but I've heard all sorts of horror stories about other girls he has home taught," Robyn explained as she buckled herself in. "He's so desperate that he works his way through a whole apartment of girls, asking them out one at a time until they all reject him, and then he moves on because they always request a new home teacher. So I won't be there when he shows. I don't have time to be stalked by some nerdy guy."

Lizzie burst out laughing. "You are so cocky! Why wouldn't he stalk me?"

"No offense, Liz, it's just that I'm the kind of girl that guys like."

"Or you're the kind of girl that attracts stalkers?"

Robyn lifted her chin defiantly. "I can't help it if guys like me. That's just the way I am. I can't take the chance of being associated with a guy like Collin."

"Why do I get the feeling that you would be willing to take that chance if you'd been assigned that guy from the football team to be our home teacher?"

Robyn gave her a sidelong grin. "Dave? Oh, baby! I think I might have to become his stalker. Isn't he yummy?" The cool, late spring breeze from the open top chapped Robyn's lips, so she reached into her purse for some lip gloss. She lowered the visor mirror and liberally smeared the sparkly gloss back and forth across her full lips. "So when is he coming so I know to be gone?"

Lizzie grinned wickedly to herself. "Thursday night at eight."

"Great, I'll make sure I have a date."

"Is it wise to make a date the night before a final?" Lizzie asked worriedly.

Robyn looked over at her concerned roomie. "Now, now, Mother, what's more important? A lower division final or a diversified social life?"

Lizzie shook her head. "Hmmm, I wonder why Robyn is a third-year sophomore? I can't think of one good reason . . ."

☆ ☆ ☆

THE next morning, Liz decided to walk to school instead of fight for a parking spot. The spring air felt invigorating as she trudged up the hill, and she relished the quiet opportunity to rehash the information she had studied as she walked. She was ready for this final. Math was not her strongest subject, but nobody else needed to know that.

She waited patiently at a crosswalk, thinking about all the citizen's arrests she could make of her fellow classmates who were jaywalking halfway down the block. She noticed that a Euro van had stopped for all the foot traffic and wondered to herself what kind of student would want to be seen on campus in a family van. Bikers and hikers were in abundance at the U; she thought the married folk with vans only went to Weber or BYU.

She shrugged off the thought as she headed across the street when the light changed. As she passed the van, she thought the driver looked familiar. Was that her new home teacher? He drove a van? Liz laughed to herself, thinking that Collin Light just might be the sort of man who came complete with the family van, ready to fill it to the brim as soon as he met Sister Right and married. Maybe he even had a marriage license in the glove compartment ready to go, and all she needed to do was sign on the dotted line. As she approached the building, however, she admonished herself for making fun of him. It probably wasn't Collin Light—her math-addled brain was taking her crazy places, trying to rid itself of all the problems, numbers, and equations. She turned and glanced at the street once more before going in. Sure enough, the Euro van was parked illegally at the curb, and Collin sat in the driver's seat. He rolled down his window and gave her a jaunty smile and wave. Liz quickly waved back and then rushed into her class. Never before in her life has she been so relieved to have a test to take.

Revealing Letters

SISTERS share a bond that no one can explain. They understand each other in a way not even a girlfriend can approach. Secrets, heartbreaks, codes, history, delights, and sheer happiness can be shared in a simple glance between sisters. Many have attempted to decipher the language between sisters, and many have failed. Sisters everywhere understand the importance of the bond and respect the relationship in other sisters. There is nothing more prized to a woman than the secrets she shares with her sisters.

☆ ☆ ☆

To: jbenson47@email.byu.edu
From: Elizabeth.benson@uu.edu
Subject: Bodyguards for missionaries?

Jana! My most beloved sister, how are you? It's been days since I heard from you. What's going on? Have you heard from Austen lately? Silly question! I guess I should be asking if you're engaged yet. You will call and tell me first, right? If you're too busy to write this week, I understand. Finals will be over soon, and then you graduate!!! Are you so nervous???

Also, did you happen to notice how LeAnn threw herself at the missionaries when Mom and Dad had them over for dinner last weekend? That was so embarrassing! That girl is headed for trouble if someone doesn't put a stopper in her soon. Does she think she'll get a prize if she snags a missionary while he's still in the field? Those poor guys need to be protected from her! I think we should mention it to Dad. He really should do something about her. She's going to make us all look bad and get herself in trouble in the process.

Love, Lizzie

✷ ✷ ✷

To: Elizabeth.benson@uu.edu
From: jbenson47@email.byu.edu
Subject: London, London, here I come!

Lizzie,

You'll never guess what! I got that study abroad scholarship to Oxford!!! Oh my goodness, can you believe it? I'm bouncing up and down! I promise to call tonight with all the details. I'm spending the summer in England! Yay!!!

Love, Jana

✷ ✷ ✷

To: Elizabeth.benson@uu.edu
From: jbenson47@email.byu.edu
Subject: I really am the evil twin

Lizzie,

I'm sorry! I really did mean to call last night. I'm not hiding from you, I promise. I've been beyond busy with finals. But then I graduate! Can you believe it? It will be such a relief. Then maybe I can devote a little more time to Austen before I go to Oxford. He hasn't complained. He never would—he's just too sweet to do that. I just feel like things aren't the same since he got back from Venezuela, and I haven't been able to spend any time getting to know him again. He's changed a lot in the last two years, and there are so many wonderful things to learn about each other.

The funniest thing happened at the Creamery. Not ha-ha funny, but odd. I ran into Erin there, and she was so cold to me. She was all smiles and sweetness at Austen's homecoming, which is the last time I saw her, but this time she acted so funny. I went up to her and gave her a hug, but she acted like she hardly knew me. After I talked to her for a moment, she and Julie, who she was with, turned from me and wouldn't even look at me, and I know they were talking about Austen because I heard his name several times. I was only a few feet away, but it's almost like they wanted me to know what they were saying. They said something about his true happiness and almost insinuated that they didn't think I could make him happy!

Do you think I misunderstood them? I just felt awful because I know I haven't been able to spend much time with him lately. Once graduation is over, I'm all his until I leave for England! If he still wants to be with me, I guess. Do you think I should be worried about leaving him for the summer? Do you think Austen is tired of me and they just didn't have the heart to say anything? AAUUUGGGHHHH!!!

Lizzie, I don't have time to stress out about this right now. I have so many other things to stress about. Austen is the one thing I have right now that brings me joy, except for you, of course. I'll be very glad to see you this weekend if you're still planning to come to dinner at the house. Are you bringing Will? I'd love to meet him, if he isn't wearing that awful BYU T-shirt.

Love, Jana

P.S. I agree that LeAnn was a little too flirty with the elders. Maybe we could talk to Dad when we see him.

* * *

To: jbenson47@email.byu.edu
From: Elizabeth.benson@uu.edu
Subject: Wicked stepsisters

Jana,

You know what I think of Erin and Julie. Please don't get me started! Julie has wanted to sink her hooks into Austen since you've known her! As for him not wanting you anymore, I think that's just insane! I always sort of laugh when I hear people talk about how they got engaged in the preexistence and vowed to find each other in this life, but I think if it were true of anyone, it would be true of you two. You are perfect for each other in every way. Erin just wants him to marry Julie, and I think it's because of Julie's brother James. I'm not one for gossip, but have you seen the way Erin looks at James whenever he's around? My goodness! She practically drools all over him.

Speaking of drooling crazy, are you serious about me bringing Will to dinner? First of all, I don't even know if like him. Second, if I did like him, I would never ask him out. Remember all of his comments about coeds wanting to get married? And you are forgetting that it would be nicer for Will if I dropped a T-bone down the back of his shirt and set a pit bull on him than to have him meet our mother. I am never taking him to meet the family.

I will see you very soon.

Love, Lizzie

✻ ✻ ✻

To: jbenson47@email.byu.edu, Elizabeth.benson@uu.edu
From: Isewlt4U@yahoo.com
Subject: A letter from your sister Merry

Dear Janalyn and Elizabeth,

This is your sister Merry Bright. I finally got my very own e-mail address, so I thought I would drop you a note. You both know that it's no great secret that Mother has been encouraging me to date. So I agreed to go on a blind date at her insistence, arranged by Sister Evern and Mother. His name is Doug, and he is Sister Evern's youngest son. Doug is a very sweet spirit, and I was pleased to learn that he was recently elected SLCC Chemistry Club president. It speaks well of his ambition.

We had a nice date on Saturday. He was very thoughtful! He picked me up in this father's Pontiac Bonneville, the hubcaps of which he had recently painted to match the silver blue paint on the car. It's a nice touch, really. Doug had obviously gone to great lengths to clean and vacuum out the car. I appreciated those small details—it shows great character. I could still see the vacuum stripes on the backseat and noted the three evergreen tree-scented deodorizers. It did smell very much like a forest in the car.

I finished my navy blue skirt in time for the date, and mother loaned me her pink sweater set. LeAnn was kind enough to lend me some gold earrings, which I didn't feel complemented my necklace, but I wore them out of gratitude for her generosity. Of course, I wore my favorite pearl necklace—I so rarely get the opportunity to wear my pearls out for a special occasion.

Doug was dressed very nicely in tan trousers and a white shirt with a periodic table of elements tie. He will be transferring soon into the chemical engineering program at the U. He's worried that he will not have the table memorized well enough, but we had a lot of fun quizzing each other on the elemental abbreviations in the car. Doug does not do himself credit—he's quite smart.

I tell you all of this to ask for your advice. The first half of the date was highly enjoyable, but the evening took an unfortunate turn, and I'm not sure what I should do next.

After the chemistry club awards banquet, where we enjoyed a lovely salmon dinner, we went for a drive up Parley's Canyon. I was a little concerned that he might try to get fresh on the dark road. After several minutes I noticed he became very quiet, and I wondered if I had done something wrong. I hoped my salmon breath wasn't too bad for him!

He began swerving around the road rather recklessly, and I couldn't understand what was wrong with him. He had a scary look in his eye! I asked him to pull over, telling him I was very uncomfortable with his erratic behavior. He suddenly yanked the car off the side of the road, but a little too far where we couldn't see the road anymore. It was very dark, and I was worried about what he would do next! No one knew where we were, and no one could see us from the road! I panicked and reached for the door handle.

Before I had a chance to get out of the car, or before Doug could get out of the car, he began to regurgitate his supper. It splattered all over the dashboard and windshield. I ran around to the other side of the car and pulled him out. He knelt down beside the car, so I did too, believing he intended to pray. He heaved again and again, so I offered the prayer for us.

I believe I was led to recall that there was a CB unit in the car. I had never used one before, but I somehow managed to reach someone on the radio and ask for help. The trucker who heard me contacted the police, and I ran to the road so I could flag them down. Both the trucker and the highway patrol showed up quickly. Within minutes the police had the medics en route. Doug was taken by ambulance to University Hospital. The highway patrolman was kind enough to take me there also. (It was not possible to drive the car due to poor visibility through the windshield.) While I waited at the hospital I changed clothes into scrubs provided by the nurses, since Mother's sweater set was rather filthy and my new skirt was ruined. Father arrived shortly and took me home.

In all of the hubbub, I never got a chance to thank him for the date. However, he did squeeze my hand before they rolled him away on the gurney. Is that a good sign? No one has ever held my hand before. What do you think I should do? I'd like to see him again.

With love,
Your sister Merry

* * *

To: Isewlt4U@yahoo.com
From: Elizabeth.Benson@uu.edu
Subject: Oh me, oh my!

Dear Merry,

It is so great to hear from you since we hardly ever talk anymore.
Congratulations on your entry into cyberspace! I was a little
shocked to hear about your experience. I can honestly say you
are treading uncharted waters in the dating pool. I have never
had that happen to me or anyone I know, although Robyn had a
pretty freaky run-in with a bullet bike and a garbage truck while
she was on the back (of the bike, not the truck, although it
wouldn't surprise me to see her on the back of either). :o) I guess
if you feel comfortable enough, you could call him and thank
him for the evening and ask about his recovery. But are you sure
you want to see him again? If it were me, I'd run the other direction, screaming and tearing my hair out. But you are a much
better soul than I will ever be. Let me know how it goes!

Lots of love, Lizzie

* * *

To: Isewlt4U@yahoo.com
From: jbenson47@email.byu.edu
Subject: I hope Doug feels better

Dearest Merry,

My goodness! You certainly had an awful time of it! Maybe you
could take Doug a nice pot of chicken soup when he's back on
solid food? Mom has a great recipe in her ward cookbook.

Love, Jana

An Incident That Would Be Well Forgotten

LIZZIE pulled the Rabbit next to the curb and saw a familiar vehicle parked in the driveway next to Robyn's red sports car. Was it the Euro van again? She glanced down at her watch, realizing that it was Tuesday evening and she was late for her home teaching appointment. She smiled to herself when she realized how surprised—and angry— Robyn would be—surprised at Collin for showing up two days earlier than she thought, and angry beyond measure at Lizzie. She bit her lip and hesitated at the door, pondering whether she was ready and willing to face Robyn's wrath, a frightening thing, really. She had always been grateful that she was on Robyn's good side. That would probably change after tonight.

Liz opened the door and saw Robyn and Collin sitting cross-legged at the ancient hand-me-down coffee table, eating Chinese food straight from the tub with chopsticks. An overwhelming look of relief crossed Robyn's face as she hopped up and bounded across the room to greet her.

"Hurray, Liz is home!" She dropped the chopsticks on the floor as she yanked Liz by the lapel and dragged her into the kitchen. "What happened to Thursday?" she hissed.

Liz couldn't hide the grin. "Oopsie, did I get the day wrong?" She almost laughed, but then grew serious. "I did tell you the wrong day, and I'm sorry. I just wanted to make sure you were here. I thought we should get home taught together and didn't think it was appropriate to be here alone with him."

"So you come home late and make me sit here with him by myself?" Robyn nearly shrieked. "What happened?" She looked down, her eyes resting on the bag in Lizzie's hands. "You ditched me to go shopping? I'm so wounded. I don't think I'll ever recover."

Liz looked guilty. "It's such a great outfit," she said lamely. "I'll let you borrow it."

Robyn held her hand up, turning her head aside. "Oh, no, I will not be bought. You, my dear, are on your own. I have listened to Collin Light for ten minutes—the *longest* ten minutes of my life, by the way—babbling about some random, bizarre things that I'm not sure are legal in the lower forty-eight states. He talks like that guy in Scrooge or whatever, and he wears too much aftershave, and I have a headache from trying to think of excuses to get him out of here." She weakly raised a hand to her temple, massaging it for effect.

"Ten minutes? That's it? Did you even give him a chance?" Lizzie asked, rolling her eyes.

"His chance was over when he told me I looked like a fate. What's a fate? Do I look like his fate? I think his fate may involve severe vandalism to his van if he tries to make me into his fate."

Liz swallowed her laughter hard, but she couldn't suppress her smile. "I think it was supposed to be a compliment. It's a reference to mythology. He meant that you have classic—"

"Classic beauty? Yeah, heard it already." Robyn nodded with finality as she picked up her backpack and threw it over her shoulders. "He's all yours, Liz. I'm going to the library to study."

"You? The library? *Alone?*" Her eyes opened wide in surprise. "That bad, huh?"

Robyn ignored her as she poked her head out the kitchen door and called out in her chipper social voice, "It was so great to meet you, Collin. I have to run to the library now, but Liz will take good care of you." She snatched her keys off the hook near the door and then turned to Liz, whispering, "I expect a batch of your famous chocolate chip cookies, hot and fresh, when I get back. Not the low-fat kind, either. With the nuts and everything. Plus, tomorrow I get to wear whatever is in that bag!"

Liz smiled. "Anything for my favorite roommate."

The door slammed behind Robyn, and Lizzie took a deep breath before heading into the living room to join Collin Light. She sat cross-legged at the coffee table, then pulled a pair of chopsticks from the wrapper and opened up one of the tubs on the table. "Sorry I'm a little late. What have we got?"

"Chicken and broccoli, General Tso's chicken, moo goo gai pan, egg rolls, and steamed rice," he told her, pointing to each container as he named them off. "What kept you? I was starting to think you had forgotten me entirely."

"Brother Light, something about you makes me think that there are few people who would forget you," Lizzie responded as she stabbed a chunk of General Tso's chicken with her chopstick. "Any man that speaks like Charles Dickens, as Robyn pointed out, is not easily forgotten."

He seemed pleased with her statement. "I try to make myself stand out. I am highly gratified to see that my efforts are not futile. From time to time, I rehearse what I might say should I encounter certain situations."

Liz had to clamp her lips together tightly to keep from asking if he actually practiced in a mirror, but she imagined that if he willingly admitted to thinking up conversations in advance, there was a high probability that he practiced the delivery as well.

He watched her chew, seemingly mesmerized with the simple act. Lizzie grew uncomfortable after a moment and looked down. It was quiet for several moments. "And why were you late, luscious one?" he asked, breaking the uncomfortable silence.

Lizzie nearly choked on her chicken. *Oh my goodness, he did not just call me luscious one!* her mind screamed in disbelief. "Luscious one?" she repeated incredulously, eyebrows raised.

"Of course, dear Elizabeth," he said. "Surely a lady as fair and lovely as you must be used to gentleman picking pet names for you."

She tried to smile politely, but her eyes were hard as flint as she tilted her head and tried to think of a gracious response. "Perhaps I said something to mislead you, Collin, so I do apologize. I am not the kind of girl who is used to being called pet names by anyone other than my family. I am a little surprised that you would be so forward with me, since we only met Sunday. I also think you should be aware that I am dating someone right now." She bit her lip as she said it, wondering where on earth she got the idea that it might even be remotely true. Was she dating Will? Did one date count?

His eyes narrowed, and she could tell that he heard the dating phrase quite a bit, whether it was true or not. "Really? Well, that's wonderful," he exclaimed a bit too cheerily. "It's so gratifying to see that the young single adult program works for some. And who is the lucky gentleman?"

Liz blushed a bit. She almost didn't want to jinx her relationship with Will by saying his name out loud. After all, if it hadn't started out as a date, it certainly ended as one. But it had only been one date, she reminded herself for the hundredth time. One fabulous, incredible, earth-shattering date, where two souls meet and they know their lives will never be the same for it, she thought with a sigh. Still, she argued to herself that superstition was for the uneducated and unfaithful. Saying his name would serve two purposes: she would affirm to herself that perhaps something really great could develop between her and Will, and at the same time she could let Collin Light know that someone had already staked his territory. "Will Pemberley," she said in a low voice.

"I'm sorry, what did you say?"

"William Pemberley," she repeated, louder and more clearly this time.

He sat back in surprise. "Really? William Pemberley! Well, isn't that marvelous?" He thought a moment. "For some odd reason, I thought he was engaged to Rochelle Rasmussen."

The tone of his voice grated on Lizzie. He thought she was making it up. "I was under the impression that they had broken up, but we just started dating. Our relationship is very new, and I would appreciate it if you would not pass the information along to anyone else." Even as she said it, she was flooded with self-doubt.

"I wish you and Brother Pemberley all the best in your friend-ship," Collin said graciously. "Your secret is safe with me, Elizabeth.

And if you ever need the male perspective in all the confusion of the dating world, I hope you won't hesitate to call upon me at any time. I am utterly and completely at your service."

Well, of course, Collin, Liz sarcastically thought to herself as she bit into an egg roll. *You're the first person I'll call for advice.* He took a large bite out of the other egg roll, after squirting in some soy sauce, and quickly changed the subject. "I must say that I am completely enamored of Robyn. She is positively enchanting. Is she dating anyone right now?"

Liz rolled her eyes. She was relieved to have changed the subject but still felt uneasy in his presence. She was also protective of Robyn and tried to think of how she could tell him, as politely as possible, that he didn't have a chance. "A better question might be who she hasn't dated! She makes the rounds pretty well. She's the kind of girl who needs a lot of excitement and fun, so she's always in the middle of something. She seems to have a different date every weekend."

"So she's looking for someone in particular, and she is so discerning that she continues to seek until she finds what she is looking for?" Collin mused. "Excellent, excellent." He sat back and continued to grill Lizzie about Robyn until the Chinese food had been completely consumed. And there was a substantial amount of food! Lizzie thought she was going to burst. Why does Chinese food always expand even further once it hits the stomach? She sat back, eyes closing from time to time, and listened to him speak, nodding her head politely every once in a while. He didn't seem to need any sort of response.

* * *

"Lizzie, wake up!" Robyn shook her shoulder gently, and Liz awoke to find herself on the couch. The green lights on the VCR clock glared 2:00 a.m. She was curled up in a ball on the sofa, a purple chenille throw that her mother had given her tucked carefully around her.

Lizzie sat up groggily and rubbed her eyes. "Did you just get home?"

Robyn nodded. "Yeah. I wanted to make sure I gave him enough time to clear out. When did he leave?"

Liz shrugged as she stood up and staggered down the hall. "I honestly have no idea. I must have fallen asleep. Did he tuck me in before he left? That was sort of thoughtful."

"You let him tuck you in?" Robyn demanded. "You didn't kick him out?"

Liz's brow furrowed. "I didn't want to be rude. I mean, he was a little forward with me at first, but I made it clear that he wasn't going to get anywhere, so he focused his attention on asking questions about you." She smiled gloatingly as Robyn moaned, and without changing her clothes, she collapsed into bed. "Now, if you had stayed here and stuck it out, we could have ganged up on him, had him out of here by nine, and spent the rest of the night giving each other pedicures while we studied. See what you missed out on? And now you officially have a new stalker."

Robyn groaned. "Did he even give you the month's message?"

"Ummm . . ." Lizzie thought for a moment. "I don't remember. He's like listening to Shakespeare. You know what you're hearing is English, but at the same time you have to focus on the words or you don't get a single thing out of it. I didn't focus clearly enough. I think he talked a little bit about the power of the priesthood, sort of retelling his talk from Sunday, but in the context of how he would need it in the home when he is married and presides over his family."

"Good grief, can you imagine being married to a guy like that?" Robyn muttered, plopping down on her bed.

Lizzie closed her eyes, and she hovered in that dimension between asleep and awake. She knew she was still having a conversation with Robyn, but she didn't have the strength or willpower to open her eyes. "His wife will be a very faithful, spiritual girl. And you know, despite everything, he's really not so bad. I think I could be his friend, maybe. If he promised not to stalk me or call me 'luscious one' ever again." As she drifted off to sleep, she promised Robyn, "I'll have a double batch of cookies for you in the morning . . ."

* * *

"Hey, you've reached Robyn and Liz. If this is our mothers calling, sorry, we're still single. If you're calling from church, we're at the meeting already! If you are a guy trying to impress us, hang up now and dial 1-800-FLOWERS and then call us back.

Thanks! Bye."

BEEP!

"Hi, Liz. This is Will. I just wondered if you wanted to celebrate the end of finals week by going up to Park City sometime this weekend. Let me know. I'll be at my parents' house this weekend, but you can reach me on my cell. Talk to you soon."

BEEP!

Robyn grinned with wicked delight as she listened to the message. "Oh, Lizzie, you have a message from someone."

Liz groaned as she came in and tossed her backpack down on their kitchen table. She had just finished her last final and had two weeks before her summer classes began and she wanted to play. "What did my mother want this time?"

Robyn smiled as she rewound the tape. "Oh, I think you'll like this message. It's from a guy."

"Our favorite home stalker?" Liz joked, while feeling slightly guilty at the same time for being unkind. She knew Robyn would understand though.

Robyn pushed the Replay button on the answering machine. *"Hi, Liz, this is Will calling. I just wondered if you wanted to celebrate the end of finals week by going up to Park City . . ."*

Robyn stuck the tip of her tongue out while she smiled with excited delight, and an incredulous smile spread across Liz's face. She picked up the cordless, unsure of what to do next. "Should I call him now? What should I do?"

Robyn laughed. "Did you forget how to dial? Call him now, girl!"

* * *

A girl can walk into a store, an eye single to the glory of finding the exact article of clothing that she is looking for, but it's the other eye that will spot the piece of clothing that will spark the daydream that will reveal what is in a girl's heart, whether she knows it yet or not. She enters the store a reasonable girl in search of the perfect white T-shirt to wear this upcoming spring. She will leave the store a lovesick romantic certain that the new rosebud pink dress in her bag will change her life for the better. It was a Wednesday afternoon, and Liz Benson was that girl.

The girl spots the dress and walks over to it cautiously. At first she looks at it longingly, almost regretfully. She shakes her head as she hears a voice tell her she has no need for such a dress. But she runs her fingers over it and contemplates whether the color of the dress will bring out the highlights in her long, chestnut brown hair.

She holds the dress up to herself and looks in the mirror. She doesn't see the reflection. She sees herself as she hopes Will Pemberley will see her. She pictures in her head what he will say to her in that dress. She imagines where they will go and what they will do. She hears the bells in her own laughter and the warmth of his touch as he holds her hand when he greets her at the door. She can picture his brown eyes as they gaze at her appreciatively in the rosebud dress.

Intuitively she knows how her new light pink purse will make her look clever, organized, smart, and feminine all at once. As they walk to the car they will discuss the latest events and trends. He will marvel at how well-rounded she is.

If she slips on a pair of high heals, wears her hair swept up high and off the neck, he will know what a romantic she is. He will want to take her to someplace cozy and intimate for dinner. Then they will take a long walk around a big fountain and hold hands under a dimmed streetlight.

But if she wears her hair in a simple ponytail, leaves the purse at home, and accessorizes only with a simple pair of slip-on shoes, he will recognize her for the sporty, carefree, outgoing girl she is. They will laugh all night long, and after dessert they will go mini-golfing. He'll let her win at mini-golf, and then he will take her to the high school parking lot and spin doughnuts for an hour, laughing the whole time, denying that they're dizzy.

However, if she wears the rosebud dress with a complementary silver necklace and matching dangling earrings, with her hair down and full of curls, he will take her to a trendy restaurant and pay for valet parking. He'll help her out of the car and notice the way her strappy sandals and pedicure, complete with toe ring, show off her long, lean, tanned legs. They will go dancing at the most popular club in town, and he'll whisper compliments in her ear as they dance slowly cheek to cheek.

He will wear khaki pants and a dark green shirt that will complement her rosebud dress. The green shirt will also highlight his brown eyes and curly brown hair. The CD player in his brand-new sports car will have a great collection of music in it. There will be, at least, Pearl Jam, Bon Jovi, Justin Timberlake, John Mayer, and Tony Bennett. He will keep Tony Bennett on softly in the background while they talk before saying good night.

No matter what, he walks her to the door and kisses her softly on the cheek. She'll brush her hand gently over his forearm as she says good night. And he'll take one long, last look at her in the light cotton rosebud dress with simple embroidery along the scoop neckline and its cap sleeves as he walks away. There is no question he'll call tomorrow. She would be surprised if he doesn't call when he gets home tonight just to say he misses her.

Yes, she must have the rosebud dress. The rosebud dress will answer all of her dating problems. She is sure her mother, sisters, roommate, and girlfriends would agree she should buy it. If the dress is on sale, her life will be complete. Even it's not on sale, she'll get it anyway. She walks out of the store wondering if he will call tonight, and checks the voicemail on her cell phone, just in case . . .

* * *

WILL and Liz sat in the Rabbit, the convertible top pulled down, enjoying the hard rush of the cool, early evening breeze in Parley's Canyon. Will had offered to drive, but Liz wanted to ride in her convertible on such a nice night. It was officially date number two and Liz had on her new, perfect rosebud dress. They had spent the afternoon wandering around Park City, laughing about the insane prices in some of the art galleries while checking out some of the finer specimens of western art on display. Liz couldn't remember the last time she had seen so many paintings of cowboys, bison, and kokopelli. As they drove home, they had to yell at each other over the roar of the wind to be heard, but it didn't matter. She was having such a great time, and she felt so comfortable and right with Will.

As they emerged from the canyon and entered evening rush-hour traffic on I-80, they grew silent for a brief time. Eventually, Will turned to her and said, "Two truths and a lie."

Liz raised her eyebrows as she lifted the hair off her neck and twisted it in a knot. "Excuse me?" she asked.

"It's a game," he explained as she inched the car forward. "You tell me three things about yourself. Two are true, one is a lie. I have to figure out which is the lie."

"I'm not sure I like this game," she said hesitantly. "I lie to you? I have to tell you stuff about me?"

"And then I do the same, and you figure out which is the lie."

"Okay . . ." Liz said with uncertainty, and then thought for a while. "Okay!" she repeated with finality, ready to go. "Three things about me that you did not know. A little Liz trivia, if you will." He smiled at her sarcasm. "One: I was arrested for vandalism for shopping-cart bombing at the grocery store in North Ogden. Two: ummm . . . my hair used to be red. Three: I met my first boyfriend dragging the 'Vard in Ogden."

Will was laughing so hard by this point that she wasn't sure she had done it right. "What?" she asked defensively. "I'm trying to make this as entertaining as possible!"

He nodded. "You did. I'll give you credit for that." He thought about what she has just said, and then systematically deconstructed her words. "You don't seem like the vandalism type, although I wouldn't put it past you." He held up his hand as she laughed. "Not done yet. Red hair on you? I'm not sure that would work, but you never know. And what is 'dragging the 'Vard'? It sounds painful."

Liz looked at him incredulously, but a knowing expression soon crossed her face. "You've never been to Ogden, have you?" She nodded in understanding when he shook his head. "It's Ogden's answer to the club scene. We don't have much clubbing in Ogden, so on weekend nights everyone gets in their cars and drives up and down Washington Boulevard between Twenty-first and Thirty-sixth Streets. When you get to the end, you turn around and do it again. It's where the underground element meets and greets in Weber County."

Will looked shocked. "Seriously? That's what you guys do in Ogden?"

"Yeah . . . but it's sort of like our dating service there," Liz explained with a shrug, attempting to defend the practice. "I had the Rabbit way back then, and it was our preferred dragging vehicle. Christy, one of my friends from Roy, actually used to jump out of the convertible and go hang out with guys on the corners. She said she kissed around sixty guys that she met dragging the 'Vard. She even met her husband on the corner of Twenty-fifth and Wall, across from Union Station."

"She actually married a guy she met on a street corner?" Will asked, seeming to have hard time processing the fact. A second later he cried, "She kissed *how* many guys?"

Liz laughed. "I'm putting the actual number closer to thirty. But with her, you never know. She was pretty wild then, but she's all settled down now," she assured him.

"I am learning so many things I did not want to know," Will muttered. He turned his thoughts back to the game. "I think you're making up all that stuff about 'dragging the 'Vard.' That's just a little too surreal. That's your lie."

Liz gasped in feigned shock. "You think I was arrested for vandalism? You think that's true?" She laughed as he gave her a side-long look. She winked at him slyly as she whispered, "I've never been caught, and they still can't prove it was me."

"I knew it!" Will declared triumphantly. "I knew you had an evil streak in you."

"I'm not so sure that's a good thing, though."

"And later you'll have to explain to me what shopping-cart bombing is."

"It's very dangerous. You're still a little young, William." Lizzie thought a moment. "You still don't believe me about dragging the 'Vard, do you?"

Will shook his head. "Come on, people actually do that for fun? Plus, I have a very hard time believing that someone as intelligent and interesting as you would have nothing better to do on a weekend than drive laps around Main Street."

Her cheeks flushed a bit at his compliment, but she continued, "Oh, honey, you really have never been to Ogden." She noticed an exit coming up, and she quickly changed lanes and sped up, cruising onto the ramp that would take them to I-15.

"Where are we going?" he asked.

"It's Friday night, Will. You want to go drag the 'Vard?"

"Are you kidding?" he exclaimed.

She looked a little worried as she glanced over at him. "I mean, if you want to. I can take you back to your car if you need to go. It's no big deal. Ogden really isn't—"

He smiled at her. "You know what? I'm having a great time." She could tell from the tone of his voice that he was rather surprised he was having such a good time with her. She was rather surprised to discover she felt the same. "Let's do it! Let's go drag the 'Vard." He reached over and took her hand. Although she was a little surprised, she willingly let him take it. She looked at him and their eyes met. She smiled shyly and bit her lower lip, returning her focus to the freeway, although she couldn't recall the last time she had been so distracted. Will continued, "I'm really having fun with you, Liz. Today has been great."

"I know." She looked at him again but couldn't bring herself to look him in the eye. "I'm having fun too."

"You're a little more impulsive than I expected you to be," he told her.

She raised her eyebrows questioningly. "Is that a good or bad thing?"

"It's a total plus, Liz. I love knowing we can just hop in the car, be crazy and still always have a great time together."

Liz wasn't quite sure how to respond. What was it about Will Pemberley that made her, the glib, self-assured Elizabeth Benson, blush and giggle like a thirteen-year-old at a slumber party? She suppressed her feelings and changed the subject. "Good thing you like impulsive, 'cause you ain't seen nothin' yet!" Lizzie smiled at him with a look that made his mind wonder. "Okay, your turn. Two truths and a lie."

"Okay, I'm good at this," he said confidently. "One: I pitched our team to a state baseball championship. Two: I didn't baptize anyone on my mission. Three: I failed English twice before I met all my general ed requirements."

Lizzie frowned as she thought. "You have an unfair advantage," she pointed out. "You already had those ready! Are those your standard-issue answers for this evil little game?"

He ignored her question and demanded, "Which is the lie?"

She hemmed and hawed. "Well, you seem pretty smart, so I doubt you failed any general ed classes. I don't doubt for a moment you led your baseball team to the state championship. I think you're lying about your mission. You had to have baptized someone, even in Russia."

He shook his head. "No, I actually never baptized anyone. I taught some wonderful people, but I never entered the waters with anyone. One companion and I taught the gospel to a woman in St. Petersburg, but my comp performed the baptism and I confirmed her."

Lizzie thought for a moment. "At least you were able to teach the gospel to one. You made a difference for her, and it altered her eternity." He nodded quietly, seeming to disappear into his thoughts until she asked, "So did you fail English twice? How is that possible? Isn't it your native language or something?"

He laughed. "No. Just once. I blame the professor."

"Yeah, blame the teacher," Liz teased. She noticed suddenly that they had talked through most of Fruit Heights and Layton and were going up the big hill before Highway 89 merged into Washington Boulevard.

"Are we close?" he asked

"Almost there."

He looked up and grabbed the top of the convertible's windshield, stretching his arms and arching his back, working out the kinks from being seated in the car for over an hour. "So you took this little dragster downtown and dragged the 'Vard with your friends on Friday night? That's really what you did for fun?"

Liz nodded, then explained, "Well, not really, not all the time. I just happened to be the one with the car, and when they wanted to go, sometimes I would drive them."

"Depending on what happens here tonight, I may lose all respect for you."

She laughed. "The driving up and down isn't the fun part. The best part is making fun of other people. What you want to do is find a guy in a really big truck and challenge him to a race."

Will's eyebrow raised, and he looked at her doubtfully. "You're going to race a big truck in this?"

Lizzie nodded, turning on the radio. "And the music is an essential component. We need to find a really bad AM station. See if you can find any Barry Manilow or Neil Diamond." Will fiddled with the dial for a moment, then found a station that was playing synthesized elevator music. "Perfect!" she cried, then cranked up the volume and let the music blare from her tin-can speakers.

"I can't believe you're doing this," Will laughed.

"Just watch."

They entered the middle lane as the heavy Friday-night traffic slowly rumbled through the streets of Ogden. They passed several low-riders with hydraulics, the deep bass resonating from inside their black tinted windows. She finally stopped in the front position at Twenty-sixth Street, her bumper right above the white line, waiting for a light to turn green. She noticed next to her in the left lane a large white pickup splattered with mud. The driver wore a dusty brown cowboy hat. He also had a gun rack, complete with rifle, hanging in the back window of the truck's cab.

"He's perfect. Watch this! I'm going to beat this guy across the intersection," she declared, revving her engine loudly—at least as loudly as she could for such a small, wimpy car. She leaned the cowboy's way, elbow hanging over the window's edge as she swayed toward him, eyes alive with the dare of a challenge.

The cowboy looked over at her little green convertible and scoffed. He gunned the big heavy engine, quickly drowning out the sound of her elevator music. Undaunted, Lizzie revved her engine again, the convertible's high-pitched squeal embarrassingly cute, while Will covered his face with his hands. "Hey, cowboy," she called, "what you got in there?"

"I got a V-8 and 360 horses under here, little girl," he said with a hint of West Weber twang. He revved his engine again for effect. "What you got in your little soup can, darlin'?"

"I have a Toro." She revved it again and beeped what sounded like a girl's bike horn. Will started to duck down lower so no one could see him. The light turned green, and the convertible sped through the intersection. The cowboy sat at the light for a moment, laughing. He quickly recovered and blew past the convertible with no problem, as Will peeked from under his hands and started laughing so hard he almost couldn't catch his breath.

"A Toro?" he asked when he could speak again. "Like the lawn mower?" He was incredulous. "I can't believe you did that. This is what you did growing up?"

She smiled and nodded. "Welcome to Ogden."

"I have new respect for you. I never would have guessed you had it in you."

Lizzie laughed. "So should I take you home now, or do you want to go up to North Ogden? There's this place that makes the best ice cream sundaes you'll ever taste."

"I'm not about to go home, Miss Elizabeth Benson," he said adamantly. "You have shown me a world I never knew existed. I see a whole new future for us here on the 'Vard."

"So much for your college education," she teased. "But I guess if it takes you three times to pass English . . ."

"Hey!" he protested as she laughed. He continued, a little more seriously, "I'm really glad we took the convertible, Liz. I can't remember the last time I was this spontaneous."

"You are quite welcome," she answered lightly.

He looked over at her as she drove, and then reached over and held her hand again—when it wasn't busy shifting gears—as the buildings and city lights gave way to shadowy pastures illuminated by the moon rising above the mountains to the east. She didn't seem to notice, but he could not take his eyes off her. She glanced at him quickly as she parked the car at Country Boy Dairy, then stopped, noticing that his gaze had changed somehow. Their eyes locked for one moment as each searched the other. Liz broke the gaze first, looking down nervously to pick up her purse. He hurried to open her door for her, reaching for her hand as they walked inside.

A Most Joyous Reunion

IN a soft-pink bedroom, with matching twin beds covered in hand-made white eyelet quilts, and walls adorned with the souvenirs and rites of passage of two sisters, stood Janalyn Benson, faithful girlfriend, devoted sister, and perfect daughter. She looked into the mirror at her reflection and wondered if she had changed much in two years.

Tonight would be her first date with Austen since his return. She had seen him a few times since he came home, but this would be their first official date. They had been together for five years, had known each other since they were six years old, and had lived less than three blocks from each other their entire lives. They held no secrets from each other and knew each other's past inside and out. Janalyn held few memories outside of her family that didn't include Austen Young.

A closer look in the mirror reminded Jana of the eight pounds she had gained over the past two years. She wondered if Austen would notice them. He had grown two inches during his mission, lost twenty pounds, and looked incredible. He hardly resembled the husky football player that had won her heart in high school, but he would always look good to Jana no matter what. She looked at her long blond hair and wondered if he would like it long, as she had never worn it this long before. She had never intended to grow it out, but she had been so preoccupied with school that she hadn't cut it in nearly a year. She liked the long hair and all the options it allowed her, but it did make her look older than the short, curly styles she had worn before Austen's mission.

Nervously, Jana twisted the CTR ring she wore on her left hand. Austen had given her the ring for her sixteenth birthday and she had worn it ever since. A few months after Austen had left for Venezuela, she moved it from her right hand to her left-hand ring finger. Now she wondered if she should move it back to her right. She didn't want Austen to think she was going to pressure him to get married right away. They hadn't even discussed their future in several months. She had thought about marriage and their future nearly every day for the last two years, and even more frequently these last few weeks. When would they get married? When would they start having children? She had hopes and answers for all of these questions. But did Austen feel the same? She wondered if he would bring any of it up tonight.

Keeping with an old tradition from their childhood, they planned to meet on the corner halfway between their houses. She smiled as she remembered the first time they had snuck out of their houses to meet. She wondered if he ever thought about their old memories together. Did guys do that?

Jana glanced at the clock and realized that she needed to get going. It was going to be chilly in the mountains tonight, and Jana knew exactly which sweatshirt she wanted to bring. She pulled it out of the overnight bag she had brought home with her for the weekend. It was well-worn, soft, and gray with a few small stains here and there, and a big blue Y on the front—just another BYU sweatshirt to anyone else. But to Jana it was a reminder of Austen's support of her choices. He had given her the sweatshirt back in high school when she had been accepted to BYU and he hadn't. He encouraged her to go to BYU while he stayed in Ogden and attended Weber State. They had wanted to go to school together, and Jana had been willing to attend Weber with him, but he insisted that BYU would be a wonderful experience for her. The sweatshirt was a gentle reminder of all the ways Austen had been the perfect boyfriend.

Wrapping the sweatshirt around her waist and tying the sleeves into a knot, Jana turned off the bedroom lights and attempted to quietly slip out of the house unnoticed. She quickly darted across the lawn and looked back to make sure no one had seen her leave.

She smiled to herself and let her excitement at seeing Austen take over. She started at a fast walk but then broke into a run down to the corner, where she could see Austen standing under the street-light. As she ran straight for him, she could see him laughing. And just as she did when she was a teenager, she hurdled a fire hydrant, just for fun, making him laugh even harder. She never missed a beat as she kept running right at him—and right into his arms for a big hug. Austen lifted Jana off her feet, hugging her tight and spinning her around in circles under the street lamp. They continued to laugh and swing, holding each other as tightly as possible. It wasn't until a car drove past and honked at them that Austen put Jana back down on her feet.

Laughing, flushed, and excited, Jana stepped back and looked at Austen. Her Austen. The Austen whom she had known forever. She silently chastised herself for having ever doubted that he still loved her. One look at his sparkling blue eyes glimmering in the darkness told her that he had waited just as breathlessly for this night as she had. She grabbed his hand, smiled conspiratorially, and said, "Let's go."

☆ ☆ ☆

Two best friends sat on a rock under the moonlight eating Twinkies and looking out at the valley below them. They could name nearly every street, recognize every family, and tell a story about each. They were surrounded by everything familiar, but tonight they were new to each other, discovering the changes that two years had wrought. They didn't touch or hold hands, but sat cross-legged facing each other, entranced with each other's face. Jana was looking at how Austen's hairline had receded just a bit at the temples, making him look more mature, and how he had started to lose his perpetual baby face. She still saw the boy she fell in love with, but she could also see the man he was becoming. Austen was looking at how Jana's blond hair had darkened and grown out, giving her a more distinct, mature beauty than she had before. She had always been the prettiest girl he had ever seen, but now she was the most beautiful girl in the world.

"Austen, do you remember the first time we ever snuck out to go see each other?" Jana asked him, her mouth full of Twinkie. The Twinkies were part of their tradition. They had climbed the mountain to this spot many times, always with a box of Twinkies and a six-pack of A&W root beer. They never left the mountain until both were all gone.

Austen laughed out loud, licked the filling out of his Twinkie, and chuckled again. "I thought my parents were going to kill me. The look on my mom's face when she found out that I had snuck out at midnight to go see a girl was priceless. I'm still surprised she didn't ground me for life."

Jana laughed. "I was grounded! Don't you remember that? And then they gave me that awful 'the birds and the bees' talk! Mom gave me that book, *Our Special Bodies.* Oh, that was so horrible! And I didn't have a clue what it was all about or why everyone was making such a big deal out of nothing!"

Austen laughed again, this time so hard he almost choked on his Twinkie. "All we wanted to do was look at the moon with my new tele-scope. We were just kids! I had never even imagined kissing you or even known how to try! And there were our parents, absolutely sure that we're going straight to H-E-double-hockey-sticks for . . . who knows what! What did they think we were going to do? We were just twelve!"

Jana couldn't stop laughing at the memory. "We were so innocent back then. Do you remember the look on your sister's face when she found us?"

Austen had been in the middle of taking a sip of root beer and laughed so hard he spit it out, nearly hitting Jana. "Oh my gosh! She was so furious. They had been looking for us for hours, and there we were, sitting in the tree fort in your backyard, asleep. She just yells, 'Mom! I found them! They're sleeping together!' And everyone comes running, thinking we had been doing something wrong, but all we had done is fallen asleep looking at the stars. Hadn't you even brought your teddy bear?"

"Oh! Mr. Cuddles! I remember that! I had forgotten about him. I did bring him. But in all the chaos, I left him in the tree fort, and it rained on him and he got ruined. I was so sad when I had to throw him away. I miss that bear. He was a great bear!" Jana laughed reminiscently.

"Wow, we were so young then. Do you think they could have ever imagined that ten years later our parents would be encouraging us to go out together?" Austen peered at Jana. He still smiled at her but had stopped laughing. Jana knew him well enough to know that he was trying to turn the conversation in a more serious direction.

"I doubt that back then they ever could have seen us here like this. I don't know when everyone else caught on," Jana said thoughtfully. The chilly mountain air started to blow, and she pulled her sweatshirt a little tighter around herself.

"You were always just my best friend; it never mattered to me that you were a girl. I realize now that most twelve-year-old boys don't like to hang out with girls. That probably was a little strange." Austen let his voice trail off as he looked up at the stars. The sky was clear and the stars were twinkling. It was a beautiful mountain night, complete with the sounds of the woods around them, as well as the distant noises from the valley below. But the couple sitting on the rock were oblivious to everything but each other.

"When did you start to think of me as a girl?" Jana asked curiously, scooting herself microscopically across the rock, a tiny bit closer to Austen.

"Oh, that one's easy. When I was seven. I thought you were the prettiest girl in the world. I remember I told my mom I was going to marry you. She said that was nice and to finish my peas," he joked. The night air was getting chilly, and he pulled a blanket out of his backpack and wrapped himself up in it.

"Very funny. Seriously, when did you change your opinion of me?" Jana asked impatiently, as she contemplated stealing his blanket away from him.

Austen paused for a long time. "We were in school. We were still just friends, and I never had thought about you as anything other than Jana who could burp root beer out of her nose—hey, can you still do that?"

"I'm not even going to try. Get back to your story!" Jana was horrified to think that she'd ever done that.

"Well, one day I'm in the hall at school, and I see this guy from the football team talking to you. I can tell he thinks you're pretty. You're talking to him and laughing, your short little curls bouncing everywhere, and all of a sudden I was jealous. It hit me out of nowhere. I realized I didn't want you smiling at other guys ever again. I wanted you to be mine," Austen said softly. He pulled one hand out of the blanket and up over his head to reach over and squeeze Jana's hand gently. It pleased her that he didn't pull away immediately.

Jana smiled down at the man sprawled across the rock. "You've never told me that before. I don't remember that. How old were we?"

"We were in first grade."

"Austen! Seriously, how old were we? Who was the guy?" Jana laughed at him. Austen couldn't be serious for long, but Jana knew how to keep him on topic.

He thought a moment. "Um, sophomore year of high school, and the guy was Steve Gresko," he replied, lifting one hand up to Jana's long blond hair and gently stroking the now-wavy locks.

She watched him play with her hair. "Steve Gresko?" she muttered absentmindedly. "Wow, I don't even remember that. I forgot that he used to like me. I can't believe you were jealous of him. Is that why you never liked him?" Jana inquired.

"Yep."

"But you didn't ask me out till our junior year!" Jana protested.

"I asked you out on your sixteenth birthday. I couldn't ask you out a minute before that. That was a part of the conditions after getting grounded the night of the tree-fort fiasco." Austen then attempted to put an entire Twinkie in his mouth at once. Jana had been hoping he had outgrown the disgusting habit over his mission, but she could see that his mouth had apparently expanded over two years because he could actually get it to fit now.

"I remember the first time I noticed you were a boy," Jana softly offered.

"Vrmeajfdlyy?" Austen mumbled through the Twinkie.

Taking that as a cue to tell her story, Jana continued, "It was my first Church dance. I was in the bathroom, and I heard Tina Kelly say that she thought you were the hottest guy in the stake. For some reason it bothered me that another girl would say something like that about you. So I went out and asked you to dance, just so she couldn't do it."

Austen rolled onto his side and laughed. "I remember that. You came out and practically dragged me out on the floor!"

"I did not!"

"You did too. You didn't even ask me to dance. You just grabbed my hand and pulled me out there," Austen accused her, still swallowing his Twinkie.

"That is an outright lie, Austen Young. I never pulled you anywhere. I walked over to you and suggested that you should dance with me." Jana faked indignation, but her giggles gave her away.

"Suggested?" he snorted. "You grabbed my hand and said, 'You have to dance with me first!'" Austen continued laughing.

"I don't know what you're talking about! I walked over to you and said, 'I think you should ask me to dance because this is my first dance!'" Jana exclaimed, and turned her chin up defiantly.

"You remember it your way; I'll remember it my way!" Austen proclaimed.

"Whatever! You know I'm right!" Jana rolled her eyes, but grinned back at him.

"Do you know what this means?" Austen said.

"No . . ." Jana said slowly.

"It means you have been in love with me longer than I have been with you. You wanted me first!" he declared triumphantly and put a fist into the air. "Ha ha!"

Jana blushed a little as he used the words "in love" so openly and freely. She squirmed a little. She looked down, not quite sure how to respond.

"I'm sorry. I didn't mean to make you feel uncomfortable," he said quickly, and Jana hesitated a moment too long. "Jana, if you don't love me anymore, please say so now," Austen pleaded, his voice sounding pained.

"Oh, Austen, that's not it. Of course I still love you. You know I love you. It's just hard for me to say that as freely and openly as you can. You could always say it better than I could." Jana could barely get the words out as they came in a soft whisper, barely audible.

Austen sat up and put his arm around Jana. "Jana, if something is wrong, please tell me now."

Jana sat back a little and turned so that she could face him, causing his arm to drop from her shoulders. "Austen, nothing is wrong. It's just been a long two years, and I wonder how well we know each other now. I've changed a lot, and you have too. I don't know that I am the same girl you left behind. You've been to another country, you speak another language, and you have this incredible testimony now. You are so grown up and have changed so much!" Jana's chin trembled a little as tears formed in her eyes. "I don't know how to relate to that. I haven't even left Utah yet. I haven't seen anything of the world. How could you want someone like that?"

"Jana, you are what I have always wanted." He paused. "Where is this coming from?" Austen's throat tightened as he spoke.

"Austen, wait. I am not breaking up with you. I'm just scared. I have changed a lot since you've been gone. But you are talking to me as if I am the same girl I have always been." Jana let the tears flow down her face.

Austen replied, "I know you have changed. I watched you change in your letters. You have grown up a lot, and so have I. And you are going to grow up a lot more when you go to Oxford. It's going to be a great experience for you. I can't wait to see how it's going to change you. You will love England." Austen tried desperately to console Jana, but he was still unsure of the cause of her tears.

She looked at the ground, unable to meet his eyes. "I'm not going to Oxford, Austen."

"What? Why not? When did this happen?"

"I don't think it's the best thing for me right now," Jana said quietly.

"What are you talking about? Is this about me? Are you staying here for me?" Austen pushed.

"My mother doesn't think I should leave you now. She wants me to stay here," Jana provided. "And I want to stay here too."

"Jana, you have been talking about this study abroad for over a year now. You need to go. I will be right here waiting for you when you get back. Heavens, you just waited for me for two years; I can wait for you for two small months. It's not too late, is it?" Austen paused, the unhappiness about her decision showing in his face. "I won't let you hold back because of me."

Jana was surprised at Austen's determination. She had expected him to be happy that she wasn't going to leave. "You want me to go? I thought you would be happy that I am staying here."

"Not if that isn't what you want. I want you to go and do what is best for you. I'll be here when you get back. Jana, you need to see the world. You need to know there's more to life than Utah and BYU. Get out and see how the rest of the world lives! I can't ask you to stay here and lose this opportunity. You earned that scholarship, and you should take it. Go!" Austen wasn't going to take no for an answer.

"Do you really think I should?" Jana asked.

"Did I just say that? Go!" Austen laughed. "Jana, you just told me how you've never left Utah, and this is your chance. You deserve to see the rest of the world! Go!"

"It means I leave in four days," she reminded him.

"That's all right. In two weeks my family leaves for the annual Young family Yellowstone camping trip. I guess we'll just have to stay pen pals a little bit longer," he said with comfort in his voice. "Jana, you waited for me. I will wait for you. This will be the best thing that ever happened to you—well, except for me, obviously!" He winked slyly at her. "I cannot ask you to miss it. This won't be like a mission. We can actually call each other and e-mail each other more often. Don't worry about me. Go to England to learn something and experience more."

A wave of relief crashed over her. "Thank you, Austen!" Jana cried, and wrapped her arms around his neck. "This really means a lot to me."

They held each other for a long time before slowly letting go. Jana leaned back reluctantly, scanning Austen's face for his thoughts. She could still see the little boy who gave her a black eye while playing T-ball. She saw the boy who had taken her to the prom. And she saw the young man who had sat on this rock two years ago and asked her if she would wait for him.

A small smile crept onto his face and a wicked little gleam appeared in his eye.

"Do you remember the last time we sat on this rock?" he asked, seeming to read her mind.

"Yes." Jana began to blush.

"Do you remember what I said?" Austen teased.

"Austen, knock it off. Of course I remember." She had turned a deep shade of crimson and began to push herself backward across the cold rock.

He let out a chuckle and pulled Jana to him. He wasn't about to let her sneak out of her promise so easily. "And what did I say?"

"Austen, please don't make me! Come on!" Jana laughed and tried to look away.

"I said that if you were still waiting for me when I got back that I would climb this mountain to this rock . . . and?" he teased.

"Austen, it's after midnight. You don't have to do this! I remember!" She kept laughing.

Austen jumped to his feet and let out a mighty roar. "JANALYN BENSON, I LOVE YOU!" Dogs in the valley below began to howl in response.

"Stop it! You will wake someone up!" Jana squealed, ducking under the blanket even though she knew no one could see her.

"I AM THE HAPPIEST MAN IN THE WORLD! SHE WAITED FOR ME! STICK THAT IN YOUR PIPE AND SMOKE IT, STEVE GRESKO!" Austen bellowed at the top of his lungs. He turned back to face her, placing his hands proudly on his hips and tilting his chin up. He sucked in a lungful of cold mountain air and let it out with a satisfied sigh.

She continued to hide under the blanket. "Are you done yet?" she squeaked.

"No," he answered shortly. Whirling back around to face the valley and the small, distant streetlights below, he hollered, "JANALYN BENSON, I WILL WAIT FOR YOU! GO TO ENGLAND!"

There was a brief moment of silence after Austen's exclamations echoed around the valley. She was absolutely certain the entire state of Utah had just heard his proclamation. She groaned softly under the blanket before pulling it down to peek out at him.

"Okay, now I'm done!" he told her, offering one hand to pull her up. She took his hand and hopped to her feet. "Now there is one other thing I said I would do on this rock, if you ever came up here again with me."

Jana hadn't forgotten that part either. She caught her breath as he pulled her tightly against him. On one hand she wanted to giggle uncontrollably, but on the other hand she wanted to melt in his arms, a feeling she had known ever since her first date with Austen. Years of emotions, feelings, and confusion came to the surface. Jana couldn't have been more scared or excited, and her hands trembled slightly. She wrapped her arms up around his neck, and again realized how much taller he was. She smiled up at him as he pushed the hair back from her forehead. He kissed her forehead softly and pulled back again to look at her. He smiled, revealing a soft dimple in his cheek. Jana knew that this was the smile he reserved just for her. She had waited a long time to see that dimple again. She didn't need any more encouragement. She stood on the tips of her toes and kissed Austen.

"WHOOOOOOOOOOOOOO-HOOOOOOOOOOOOO!" He tipped back his head and let out the loudest cowboy yelp ever heard in Weber County.

"AUSTEN IS HOME AND HE'S ALL MINE!" Jana yelled into the night sky, causing him to yelp again at her declaration. The two of them laughed and hugged each other more tightly.

"Austen is home," she repeated, her hand clasped around the back of his neck. "And he's all mine." She buried her face in his shoulder, convinced that she could stand there with him forever. And never be happier.

A Highly Significant Development

To: jbenson47@email.byu.edu
From: Elizabeth.benson@uu.edu
Subject: Home stalker strikes again

Jana,

You will never believe what happened to me on campus today! I was in line to register for summer semester when my new home teacher found me. I have no idea where he came from—he could have emerged from the trash can for all I know. Did I ever mention how interesting he is? "Interesting" is one of the nicest things you can say about him. He is my height, very skinny, lost in the nineteenth century somewhere, extremely intelligent, and desperate to get married. He was pretty fresh with me when he came home teaching, and I thought I made it clear I wasn't interested. He seemed to forget all that, though, as he pestered me while I stood in line. Have I mentioned that there were about a hundred other people in line observing us? I wanted to sink into a hole and disappear.

"Elizabeth Benson, so wonderful to see you. Lovely day. May I inquire what you're doing?" What did he think I was doing there in line?

"I'm here to register for summer classes, Collin." At that point I was about three people away from the front of the line, but it wasn't moving. It was like it was frozen in time! And since no one else in line had anything better to do, they all watched our exchange. The area pretty much fell silent.

"I happen to have a picnic lunch with me, Elizabeth. Would you care to join me outside?"

"You have a picnic, ready to go, right now?" I asked in disbelief. He pulled a basket out from behind his back, opened it up, and showed me fried chicken, pasta salad, apples with fruit dip, and sparkling cider, complete with plastic champagne flutes!

Who on this earth has a picnic lunch ready to go on the off chance that they might score an impromptu date??? I have two theories here: (A) he actually stalked me and planned this out, or (B) the man really does keep a picnic packed in case he finds a willing victim. From what I know of this guy, both are very real possibilities—and very frightening. And the whole line watched this!

I made it as clear as I could that I could not go frolic in the wildflowers with him because I had to register for summer classes. He acted very miffed that I wouldn't drop my number three spot in line after waiting an hour to claim it, so I told him the brutal truth—I have a date with Will tonight and am not interested in a picnic with him today, tomorrow, or ever.

He closed the picnic basket in a huff and informed me, "Fine, Sister Benson. Enjoy your evening with William Pemberley. Just remember his reputation as campus playboy and know that because I am a true disciple, I will be there to hold your hand and wipe your tears when he has ripped your heart from your chest and ground it into the dirt. That's the kind of good-hearted man that I am." (Yes, those were his exact words. Oh, how I wish I were kidding!) He took off, and I was in complete shock while everyone in line laughed at me. (Again, I'm not kidding.) Everyone. When I finally got to the window, the registrar apologized and said she didn't have a picnic lunch for me but she might be able to get me a class.

The moral of the story is this: utilize online and telephone registration! I may have to cancel my date with Will tonight and run Robyn to the emergency room. I think she may have popped a lung from laughing so hard.

Love, Lizzie

P.S. I just realized that you are reading this from an internet cafe in Oxford! I want to hear all the details of your flight, room, and classes when you have a free minute.

☆ ☆ ☆

LIZZIE was a little beside herself. She and Will had continued making plans together, and she found it a little difficult to believe that they still enjoyed each other's company and still had things to talk about. This type of relationship was new territory for her. Most guys she had dated until now fell far short of the mark she had set for herself—not that she had a rigorous judging scale like Robyn, the professional serial dater. But she usually found most guys lacking in intelligence, wit, testimony, common sense, or, devastatingly, all of the above. She thought with self-deprecating irk that she probably missed their marks as well, but she was grateful for that. Might as well lighten the dating load and not waste time. Dating, she thought, is supposed to be a fun sort of treasure hunt, not a dreaded burden, which, considering her social history, is how she had viewed it until she met Will. She was determined not to waste her time with those who had little potential and got on her nerves in the meantime.

Yet there she sat in Will's car, ready to go on a double date with the Colonel and his girlfriend in Ogden. She could hardly think straight, she was so distracted. They were *still* having fun, they *still* liked each other, and seemed to like each other more after every date. They now were doing official "couple" things together. She almost couldn't believe it.

"Okay, so where are we going?"

"Wildcat Lanes at Weber State," he replied. "The Colonel wants me to meet his new girlfriend at Weber. He can't stop talking about her. I haven't seen him for weeks, he spends so much time up here with her."

"He does? That's great," she answered, nodding. "I haven't been bowling up there since I was in high school. It was this big thing for all of us to come up here and pretend we were college girls and check out all the hot college guys. They spotted us from a mile away, though. We never fooled anyone." She laughed at herself.

"How many guys did Christy from Roy kiss up here?" he teased with raised eyebrows. She smiled ruefully and whacked his arm as he pulled into a parking spot by the student union building.

The vibration from the deafening music shook their bones as they entered the bowling alley. Ryan was nowhere to be found, so they put their names on the bowling waiting list and went into the adjacent arcade to play a little competitive pinball against each other. As they were playing, Liz looked up and noticed a group of girls squealing and laughing at one of the pool tables nearby. *Some things never change,* she thought. She sincerely hoped she had not been that obnoxious, but she knew deep down that she most likely had. She began to turn her head back to pay attention to Will and his brilliant run on the pinball machine but quickly spun back for a better look when she realized that LeAnn was among the girls.

"Will, my baby sister is here," she said, standing on tiptoe for a better view and pointing to the girls at the pool table.

Just as he whirled up and turned to see where she pointed, Ryan walked in and joined them. "Ryan, hey, where's the girlfriend?" Will asked.

"She's meeting me here," he said, looking around. "Hi, Liz. How are things going with you today?"

"Great, thanks, Ryan," she answered with a distracted smile. She made a mental note to chastise her sister later for the outfit she wore—a short blue linen skirt with a cropped white eyelet tank top that revealed her tanned (probably fake-baked) midriff. Liz knew she would have gotten her hide paddled if she had attempted to leave the house in an outfit like that when she was LeAnn's age. She wanted to go talk to her, but Ryan seemed determined to find his dream girl that very moment. Maybe she could catch her on the way out.

"I see her over there," Ryan said, leading them through the noise and the crowd, heading straight for the gaggle of high school girls. *Oh, no,* Liz thought, heart sinking somewhere between her toes. *Please let it be anyone other than—*

"Here she is, guys. LeAnn, I want you to meet my best friend and cousin, Will, and his date, Liz."

LeAnn, all smiles when she saw him, suddenly looked horrified to realize her big sister was about to ruin her date. She recovered quickly and extended her hand. "Hi! Great to meet you!"

Liz's jaw hit the floor. Was her sister really about to pretend that they had never met before?

"I got our name on the list for a lane," Will informed them. "They should call us pretty soon. So, LeAnn, you go to school here?" The four of them had moved away from they noise and were now standing in a circle outside the game room so they could hear each other a bit better while they talked.

She looked at Liz a little guiltily, but nodded her head pertly when she responded. "Yeah, I really love going to Weber. It's a great school."

Liz's eyes narrowed, and she folded her arms tightly and pursed her lips. She knew her body language screamed bitter shrew, but she did not care at that particular moment. She wanted to take LeAnn over her knee and give her a sound spanking. "So, LeAnn, is it? What's your major?"

"I'm just doing my generals now," she replied, avoiding eye contact with her sister.

Liz nodded, realizing that LeAnn had all her answers planned out. Obviously, she had been doing this charade for some time. She changed tactics and put on her brightest smile, although her eyes were hard as flint. "Well, I suddenly feel like I need to make a quick trip to the little girls' room. Would you like to join me, LeAnn?"

LeAnn shook her head vigorously. "No, I'm okay, thanks."

Liz laughed. "Oh, come on! Don't you know that rule about college girls? How we always have to leave our dates alone so we can discuss them in the restroom?" She pulled her sister by the arm, practically dragging her as she turned and waved. "We'll be right back, boys!" she called cheerfully.

Ryan winced and rattled his head as they disappeared into the ladies' room. "What was that all about?"

"One thing I have learned about girls is that sometimes you just don't know, and it's safer not to ask," Will replied.

Liz yanked her sister into the handicapped stall and clamped the lock shut before whirling around and turning into the Wicked Witch of the West on her turbo-powered broom. "LeAnn! What on earth are you doing dating a college guy? You are way too young for this. And you're lying about yourself? And don't even get me started on that shirt you're wearing!"

LeAnn rolled her eyes. "Mom saw me when I left, and she didn't say anything, *Grandma*. Why should you care if she doesn't?"

Liz raised her hand to her throbbing temples. "Did you tell her you were coming to the college for a date in that outfit?"

LeAnn shrugged. "She thinks I came here with friends, and that's not a lie! They're all over there playing pool. I'm just going to hang out with Ryan for a while."

Liz could not believe a word she was hearing! Trying to reason with her sister was about as fun as banging her head against a brick wall. "He thinks this is a date."

"It is."

"He thinks you're a college girl," Liz persisted. "Does he know you just barely turned sixteen?"

"He thinks I go to Weber, and I didn't lie about that!" she cried, defending herself. "I just never said it was Weber High School instead of Weber State University." She smiled, really seeming proud of herself.

"And that's a LIE!" Lizzie shrieked.

"Whatever, Liz," LeAnn rolled her eyes. "I'm just having fun. He's hot, he drives a nice car, and he's a great kisser."

LeAnn probably threw the last characteristic in just to make her sister go ballistic, and it worked. Lizzie had to take several deep breaths before she could respond without yelling. "Here's the deal, LeAnn. This is completely wrong on so many levels, so you have a choice. You go out and tell Ryan that you're sixteen, or I'll do it for you. If I do it for you, I call Dad and make him come get you. So what do you think, college girl?"

LeAnn looked like she could spew venom at any moment. "I'll go talk to Ryan," she spat in defeat, but her chin shot up in defiance. "This doesn't change anything, though. I'm old enough to date now, and I can date whatever guys I want!"

Liz's eyes narrowed. "Chances are excellent that once he knows how old you are, he'll tell you to call him in about two years."

LeAnn yanked the stall door open, ignoring the amused looks the girls at the mirror had on their faces. Lizzie stopped to rinse her face and collect her thoughts before returning to see LeAnn over on the far side of the lobby, near the stairs, having an earnest conversation with Ryan. Will gave her a questioning look as she returned, looking very exhausted.

"What was that all about?" he asked.

"LeAnn is my little sister, and I'm not so sure Ryan knows she just barely turned sixteen," she answered.

His eyebrows raised and expression darkened as he watched Ryan and LeAnn talk. He shook his head as he muttered, "You never know. Ryan has always liked them young."

After a few moments, LeAnn reached into her purse and pulled her keys out, casting an angry look at Liz before reaching up to kiss Ryan and walking off.

"Looks like something came up and LeAnn has to go," Ryan told them as he returned, "but we can still knock some pins down. I think they just called your name, Pemberley."

As they walked to the counter for shoes, Lizzie's mind raced. Had LeAnn told him anything? She struggled to contain her thoughts. They reached their lane and tied on their bowling shoes in mute silence. Will and Ryan commandeered the computer, adding their initials and secret codes that seemed to amuse them while Lizzie sat with a glazed expression. As Will went to choose a bowling ball, she knew she had to talk to Ryan.

"So LeAnn went home?"

"You know that call she got while you two were in the bathroom? Something came up and she had to go, but she said to call her when we're done bowling and she'll meet me at Jake's for a shake." Ryan gave her a funny look for a moment, debating whether or not to ask the question he could hardly contain. "So what did you two talk about in the bathroom?"

Lizzie was so angry she could hardly think coherently to formulate an answer. "Um, did she tell you she's only sixteen?"

He brushed it off. "I already knew that. I went to her house once to pick her up, and her sister told me when she gave me the third degree. She has this total prude of a sister with glasses. Ugliest girl I've ever seen, sewing and knitting her way to spinsterhood." He laughed. "She's just a sorry, sad girl!"

"Did she also mention that *I* am her sister?"

Nope, she guessed not. From Ryan's shocked, flushed expression, it became clear that LeAnn had failed to mention it. "I'll be straight up with you, Ryan. LeAnn is a very immature sixteen, and while you seem like a great guy, I really think the worst thing in the world for her is to date someone older than she is. And I can guarantee if my parents knew how old you were, she wouldn't be allowed to go out with you anyway."

He relaxed a bit, nodding knowingly. "You must be the sister she calls her grandmother. Look, Liz," he said, looking around to see if Will was anywhere in sight. He slid over on the bench and put his arm around her. His voice became smooth and svelte, morphing from embarrassed clod to gringo suave. "You just need to lighten up a little. You're really hot, and I think you and I could have some fun together.

But you need to chill a little, you know, just relax." His hands reached up to massage the tension from her tightened shoulders. "I can help you with that."

She shot up from her seat and looked at him incredulously, hardly knowing what to say next. Will, who had returned, had seen the exchange and stood rooted to the spot, holding his bowling ball in both hands, trying very hard not to hit Ryan in the head with it. It was most likely a good thing that he held the ball so tightly; Liz could offer no guarantees that she would exercise the same self-restraint.

She looked at him, then back at Ryan. "You aren't much of a best friend, are you?" She shook her head and reached down to get her purse from under the bench. Before turning to leave, she said, "Shame on you." She snatched her shoes from their cubby and walked away. Will appeared shocked, like he didn't know quite what to do. Ryan innocently shrugged his shoulders when he saw him, as if nothing had happened and he had no idea why Liz had left.

Will looked crushed. He handed the ball to Ryan and kicked off his bowling shoes. "I don't trust very many people, Ryan. This makes one less."

"Aw, man . . ." Ryan mumbled, leaning forward to put his head in his hands. Liz and Will met in the foyer, grasped each other's hands tightly for comfort, and walked away.

* * *

To: jbenson47@email.byu.edu
From: Elizabeth.benson@uu.edu
Subject: Home stalker needs a hobby

Dear Jana,

I was just up at the parents' house and the subject of what happened with LeAnn at Weber the other night came up. Can you believe they have not grounded her? All Mom said was that Ryan was a nice boy and looked like he treated LeAnn well. Dad said if he forbade her from seeing him, all she would do is sneak out to see him anyway! Am I the only person who thinks what she did is wrong? They are LeAnn's doormat! What do you think?

Love, Lizzie in a tizzy

✳ ✳ ✳

To: Elizabeth.benson@uu.edu
From: jbenson47@email.byu.edu
Subject: A lecture from your sister

Dear Lizzie,

I think you did the right thing to talk to them about it, but we have to remember they are the parents and that we should honor what they say and do. All we can do for her is set a good example and be there for her if she needs us. I haven't met this boy yet, but after what he said about Merry, I don't think I want to! Just remember, this is LeAnn we're talking about. She'll find another boy to fall madly in love with next week. It should all blow over soon.

Love, Jana

✳ ✳ ✳

"THE moment was never right, so no, I didn't kiss him." Lizzie kept her eyes right on Will to gauge his response. *Will he be glad I've never kissed another guy?* she thought to herself. She shifted a bit, hoping he hadn't heard the squeak she made as she moved around in the vinyl bench in their booth in a corner café just off Temple Square. The place was getting ready to close, and they were among the few patrons left.

"Excuse me, the *moment*?" The only emotions on Will's face were bland and quizzical. She knew him well enough now to know that he was pretending not to be too interested in her personal revelation. She wasn't sure why he was interested in her past relationships. The only serious relationship she ever had was with Mike, a guy in high school, and that had never amounted to much. But Will had been asking questions all night about him. Liz knew that Will had once been serious with Rochelle, but he wasn't saying much about their past, and it was driving Liz crazy. Why had their engagement ended? All she knew came from the gossip generator Robyn, and that was anything but reliable information. Will was a very inquisitive guy, always asking her questions. Lizzie had never been very good at opening up or sharing her feelings, but something about Will made her want to try harder. He had such a way of making her feel interesting and secure that she didn't mind opening up.

"I won't kiss if the moment isn't right. He tried, but I never let him." Lizzie remained the perfect picture of innocence and aloofness. Will liked to call it "playing naive." But how naive and innocent was Will? Lizzie determined to get to the bottom of the Rochelle mystery that evening.

"And exactly what makes the moment 'right'? The porch light has to be off or on? Your hair must be perfect? He needs a mint first?" Will had changed tactics and suddenly was having fun with her answer.

"None of the above," she responded. "I won't kiss anyone for the first time on a doorstep, or in the car. And never on the first date. Shows how much you know! I will only kiss in the 'moment'!" Lizzie smiled laughingly at Will. She had ulterior motives. She and Will had these sorts of "moments" all the time, but he didn't seem to know it. He still hadn't kissed her. She had never kissed a guy before, except for a bad experience when she was fourteen involving a boy with orange cheese crackers stuck in his braces and an impromptu round of Seven Minutes in the Closet—a game she would never forgive Natalie Young for starting. Years later, she still tried hard to forget that had happened. But now she was ready for the real thing. She had decided she wanted Will to be her first meaningful kiss. But somehow, as crazy about her as he seemed, he still hadn't made a move. Was she doing something wrong? Or was he still hung up on Rochelle?

"So exactly what constitutes a 'moment'? The perfect sunset, walks by the lake?" He gave her a strange smile, one she hadn't seen before and couldn't define, and it unnerved her. He leaned towards her over the table, his body language reading loud and clear that he was interested in her. But his face wasn't sending out the same message. What was he up to?

"No, nothing like that, even though it couldn't hurt." She wanted to bait him a little bit. "I'll make you a deal. I will tell you what constitutes a moment, if you will tell me what happened with Rochelle." Lizzie raised her eyebrows expectantly.

Will kept his blank stare for a solid thirty seconds, striking pure fear into Lizzie's heart. Had she said the wrong thing? Was he hiding something? Liz could tell he was trying really hard to hide his emotions—a little too hard.

Finally, Will raised his eyebrow, sat back, and said, "Deal. You first."

"Okay—a moment. I won't kiss a guy just because he took me out or paid for dinner. Kissing is not a repayment. A kiss is a token of affection. So for me to kiss a guy, it has to be a moment where I feel affection towards him—not just attraction . . . a little moment of twitterpation." Her voice started sounding dreamy, so she covered it with a little *humph* and tone of finality. The truth was, this conversation was scaring her to death. Was she really telling Will she wanted him to kiss her? For a girl who had never really been kissed, her explanation was not easy. She could feel herself holding her breath waiting for his answer.

"Twitterpation? And exactly what is twitterpation?" Will looked rather skeptical. Maybe Rochelle never made him feel twitterpated, Liz thought hopefully.

"You don't know what 'twitterpated' means? How old are you, anyway?" Liz replied, shocked. Boys could be dumb, but not that dumb. How could he not know what "twitterpated" meant?

"No, please enlighten me." He raised his eyebrow and leaned back further, putting his hands behind his head and ruffling his hair in his signature way. He looked like a CEO or chairman of the board the way he always had so much confidence in himself. He took in a deep breath, expanding his chest and showing off the fit stomach that reminded Lizzie of how this man had caught her eye in the first place.

"It's those moments when you are with someone and everything just clicks. You can't stop looking at each other and smiling. Everything just falls into place and you just *know*." With all her heart she wanted to add, "Like when we went biking yesterday, or when you smeared dirt on my face, or the night we tried watching a video but ended up talking all night instead." But she just couldn't bring herself to say the words out loud.

Will smiled and shrugged his shoulders as if her answer was all very cute but not believable. His voice was full of skepticism as he said, "So he has to be completely in love with you before you'll even kiss him? Sounds like you are a bit of a tease, Miss Benson."

Liz shook her head. "No, that's not what I said! A kiss should be an expression of what you are thinking or feeling. I just want it to mean something. Is that so bad?" Lizzie's voice revealed a bit of the passion she normally kept bottled up, and she knew she probably sounded like a naive little girl still waiting for Prince Charming to sweep her off her feet. For a strong-willed and stubborn girl like herself, it wasn't easy to let her guard down and allow a man to see who she really was. But she could tell Will recognized the sincerity in her voice, and she could see the wheels turning in his head as he mulled over her answer.

He changed the conversation and they finished off their desserts. The waitress brought by the check, and Will reached for the bill with a little too much vigor. "Now, just because I'm paying for this doesn't mean you have to kiss me at the door!" He smiled broadly and dodged the sugar packet Liz threw at him.

* * *

WILL drove Lizzie out to University Park, where they sat on the swings and talked late into the night. Right now, he was telling her about a baseball game he had played in high school. He had grown up in Olympic Heights, just a few minutes from where they sat. She knew it was a very affluent area and wondered what he thought of her humble hometown. North Ogden was very proud that it had not only two grocery stores and a genuine artesian well, but also several national fast-food establishments along with its pride and joy, Country Boy Dairy, home of the world's most delicious ice cream sundaes.

Will didn't seem to be pretentious, even if he did come from affluence. He continued on about his baseball team while she studied his facial features. She hoped he didn't quiz her at the end of his story, because she might not remember a word he had said. All she could focus on was his eyes, his dark brown eyes, with the slightest hint of crow's feet around the edges that she could see only when he smiled. But there was something about those little crinkles that she loved. They made him look older and wiser, and yet playful and fun all at the same time. His curly brown hair was always in need of a haircut, but she admitted to herself that she loved his moppish look. She had recently started wondering what it would be like to play with those curls—probably more times than she should.

Lizzie sat in the dark, gently swinging back and forth on the children's swing, wondering what it would be like to kiss Will Pemberley, while pretending for all she was worth to listen to him talk about baseball. By her count, there had been four dates so far, and he had been an absolute gentleman. While she respected that he was a gentleman, and was grateful for his diligence, she couldn't help but wonder if she was doing something wrong. Why hadn't he made a move yet? She knew he liked her—why else would they keep dating? Maybe he didn't think of her as a girlfriend and instead only saw her as a friend. She could live with that, albeit unhappily. She enjoyed his company, and being friends would be nice, but Lizzie really wanted to kiss Will Pemberley, and that meant friendship was out of the question.

Liz still was waiting to hear about Rochelle; she just hadn't found the nerve to bring up the topic again. And they were having such a good time that she didn't want to bring up a possibly sore subject. Besides, she didn't really want to talk about her boyfriend's ex-girlfriend. Okay, she did. Very much! And she knew she wasn't going to be able to relax fully until she knew their story.

When he finished his baseball story, they sat silently for a moment, swings creaking, until she summoned up all her courage. "Will, remember the deal we made earlier? I would tell you about a 'moment,' and you would tell me about Rochelle?" Liz quietly asked. She sat nervously on the swing and drew circles in the dirt with her foot. She had no idea what she was afraid of.

"Rochelle. And what would you like to know about Rochelle?" Will asked in a funny voice. Every time he said "Rochelle" he drew out the "ro" sound so that he said it all long and with a twang.

"I know you dated her for a long time. What happened?" Liz asked softly. She continued drawing circles with her foot.

Will paused and drew in a long breath. Liz could see this wouldn't be easy for him. "Rochelle and I have known each other for a long time," he began. "Our families have been friends for years. When I got off my mission, I didn't date anyone for over a year; I wasn't ready yet, I guess. Finally, one day my mom said she wanted me to take Rochelle out, so I called her and asked. Dad gave me fifty bucks and the good car, so I took her out. Rochelle was really friendly and easy to get along with. We hung out just as friends for a long time. Then one day she says she wants to define the relationship and that she wants more than just friendship from me. I wasn't opposed to that. I guess I knew she would want that sooner or later. She was always the leader of the relationship, planning things for us. And it was easy to like her. We were good friends."

Will's voice grew low and quiet. Liz could tell he was carefully choosing what to say, but she felt that he was being as honest as possible. She could see the pain in his eyes. "So after a few more months of dating, we started to get serious. Our families started hinting about us getting married. And I was in love with her by then. She was perfect as far as I could see. She was going to make the perfect wife and mother. She's smart, spiritual, beautiful, and funny.

So I proposed, we got engaged, our families were thrilled. I always got along great with her family, especially her brothers. I have always admired her family, you know. They are Church stalwarts, the kind of people that make the Church go 'round.

"We found a place to live, planned our wedding, and she bought a dress. But about three months before the wedding, she started acting funny. I just figured it was the stress of the wedding and school stuff. But one day she just showed up at my apartment unannounced, and I could tell she'd been crying. She started crying again and couldn't even talk to me for an hour; she just sat and cried. Finally she says that she can't go through with the wedding. She loved me, but she wasn't *in love* with me. She was in love with a guy named John, and she'd been seeing him too. She thought that she had fallen in love with me and that she could break up with him, but she couldn't do it after all."

Will's voice broke and he paused for a long time. He stared vacantly ahead, as if he could still see Rochelle in front of him. He let out a long breath and continued. "I was crushed. She was my friend, and I trusted her with everything. I trusted her with the rest of my life, with eternity. I could imagine seeing her at the end of every day, waking up with her. She was everything, my best friend. Basically she was my whole life."

Again Will stopped and stared into the darkness. "Trust isn't something I take lightly. I don't have many close friends or people I trust. But I trusted her, and for her to lie to me and keep something that huge from me really hurt. I wasn't mad that she broke up with me or that she didn't love me." He stopped and thought a moment, admitting, "Maybe a little. My pride was wounded, but what hurt most was that my best friend hadn't been honest with me."

Liz looked at Will in the softness from the distant streetlights. "I'm sorry you had to go through all that. I'm sure it must have been difficult."

"Difficult? Difficult doesn't even come close," Will snorted bitterly. "I hadn't taken lightly the decision to get married. I had prayed about it and felt that it was right and I knew I was making the right decision, so how could it happen? I knew she was the one I was supposed to marry. What went wrong? Was I the one who made the mistake? Had I misinterpreted the answers to my prayers? Her betrayal didn't just break my heart; it nearly broke my testimony too. I felt like the Lord had turned His back on me. I didn't know if I could trust my own feelings or beliefs anymore, especially when two months later she got engaged. Why were good things happening to her? She was the one who lied and cheated. So why was I the one in so much pain?"

"I'm sorry, Will," Lizzie said softly. She hardly dared speak. It broke her heart to see him reliving so much pain. "Are you okay?"

Will peered at her through the darkness with a surprised look on his face. "Yeah, I'm over it. I know there are a lot of rumors that she and I hate each other, but that isn't true. We're still friends in a way. We don't talk much, especially about her new fiancé. But she's still really close to my mom. I don't hate her anymore. I did for a while, but not anymore. Things happen, life goes on."

"But how did you reconcile your feelings with the Lord? How did you accept those issues?" Lizzie asked.

Will looked at her with a softer expression on his face. "My testimony was pretty shaken for a while there. But then one day I realized that not having the Spirit in my life was harder than accepting the truth. I realized that sometimes things like this happen. I started praying again and reading my scriptures, and one day I read the passage that says, 'These things will be for thy good.' And somehow that made me feel better."

He looked Lizzie in the eye. "Liz, I am over Rochelle, and I am over what happened. I learned a lot from her about commitment and honesty. I learned who I am, and I learned about what is important to me. I know now that I could have never been happy with Rochelle and all her 'perfect' qualities. I don't want picture-perfect anymore. I want fun and exciting, which I never had with her. I want someone who is better than me and challenges me to be a better person. I want someone who will stand up for herself and express her opinion and doesn't just say whatever she thinks I want to hear. But most of all, I want someone who will always walk beside me. Not in front of me, or one step behind, but an equal partner in all things. I see a couple as a jigsaw puzzle—two pieces that fit together perfectly and intertwine. I don't want someone just like me. I want someone who will complement me, and I complement her."

Will spoke with a passion Liz had never heard in him before. She knew that for the first time since they had met, he was being completely open and honest with her. Lizzie didn't know what to say next, but she knew what to do.

The best part of a kiss is the eternal seconds preceding the moment of contact. The breathlessness, anxiousness, hopefulness, anticipation, and longing, all just suspended in the air those last few seconds before the mystery is revealed. The first kiss—with all of its tension and butterflies as you make eye contact and just look at each other and wonder, "Is this really it? Is this finally going to be the moment I've been hoping for? The moment where our true feelings will be revealed? Does he feel the same? Is this what he really wants?"

Sitting on the squeaky old playground swings in the darkness, Liz discovered that the best part of a kiss was in those few seconds where she realized that once they touched, her relationship with Will Pemberley would never be the same again. The best part of a kiss was when their eyes met and they knew what the other wanted. Liz could smell the hydrangea bush nearby and could hear the soft, late-night sounds of cars going by, but she hardly noticed. Will quizzically looked at her and smiled self-consciously. He looked like he was afraid he would break her. He was both bashful and eager in the same instant, and Liz was scared and excited, nervous to reveal herself, and yet ready and willing to share her feelings. She felt her legs trembling and suddenly knew what it meant to go "weak in the knees," as Will gently pulled her swing over closer to him. She pulled his swing over to hers, and she held her breath in anticipation.

Will touched her face softly with his fingers and tilted her chin up to face him. They were so close that Liz could feel the softness of his breath on her face. Their eyes never lost each other until they slowly closed and he leaned over and softly brushed his lips against hers. She reached her arms around his neck, ran one hand through his curls, and hoped the moment would never end.

Two Destined Souls

A wise man once said that a mighty cockroach cannot be caught without perseverance. Collin Light had failed to catch Elizabeth Benson at home for three straight days, and he was growing perturbed that she had not returned his calls. He had done everything a diligent home teacher should. It's not as if he had shown up on the last day of the month and spent five minutes giving a quick synopsis of the month's message. He took great interest in the lives of those he taught. Since he couldn't catch her at home, he surmised that she might have gone to visit her family for the weekend and decided to look for her there. As he slowed down at the end of the off-ramp of the Pleasant View/Farr West exit, he glanced quickly down at the directions he had found on the Internet—directions to the Benson home in North Ogden.

He had felt a moment of inspiration earlier when he could not reach Elizabeth at home. With an ever-handy student directory he kept by his desk and the conveniences of the Internet, he would soon reach his flock. He felt strongly, as Elizabeth's home teacher, that he needed to warn her about dating Will Pemberley. There were men, including himself, who had so much more to offer than Pemberley ever could. Perhaps Collin didn't have the looks, the charm, or the friendly nature that made Pemberley as attractive as he seemed, but why should that hold a true gentleman like Collin Light back? He was certain that, with time, she would find similar qualities in him as well. *The Lord looks upon the heart,* he reasoned, *and my wife will be greatly rewarded for choosing me.* He was determined to let her know this.

He double-checked the address on his directions before parking the van on the side of the road and yanking up the emergency brake. He made certain his button-down plaid shirt looked crisp and clean, popped in a breath mint, then made his way to the front door.

Every girl dreams about a day when a handsome man appears on her doorstep, roses in hand, and is so taken with her that he asks her out right then and there. Moments later, they ride off on his steed into the sunset, her hair blowing in the breeze. Collin had a similar fantasy, in which he played the role of the handsome man, a fantasy he entertained as he rang the bell.

"Just a minute, I'm coming!" a voice strikingly similar to Liz's called out.

Good, he thought, *she's here.*

But when the door opened, it was not Elizabeth, but a shorter, slimmer version of her with longer, darker hair, wearing round glasses very similar to those he wore. He was so caught off guard that he was unsure of what to say.

The two stood there awkwardly for a moment until Merry finally asked, "May I help you with something?"

Quickly recovering, Collin cleared his throat. "Yes, fair lady. I am Collin Light, your sister Elizabeth's home teacher, and I was wondering if she were here today." He extended his hand and shook hers warmly.

Merry's brow furrowed in consternation. "Well, she's not here today. She doesn't live here. As her home teacher, surely you must know that. Shouldn't you look for her at *her* home?"

"Well, that's the thing, uhhh . . ." Collin began. He looked at her again, and his expression changed and softened. "I'm sorry. Elizabeth never mentioned any sisters, let alone sisters as beautiful as you. I'm quite distracted. You are . . . ?"

Merry blushed slightly, looking behind her to see if he was talking to her. "Me? I'm sorry, how inconsiderate of me. Merry Bright Benson, although only my mother calls me that." She held out her hand again, and he took it once more, closing his hand over hers as he shook it.

"Merry Bright. What a beautiful, enchanting name." He smiled at her, still holding her hand. "It suits such an enchanting, classic beauty."

They stood awkwardly for a few moments, Collin holding her hand in the handshake that would never end, Merry unsure of how to proceed. She finally told him, as she pulled her hand away, "Collin, I'm sorry that my sister isn't here for you today. She may come up here sometime this weekend, although it seems silly for you to come all the way back up here if you live in Salt Lake. Shall I leave a message for her?"

He shook his head. "No, no, fair lady, don't bother. Fate, it seems, has called me here today for another reason, although sometimes when listening to promptings, one does not know why until afterward." He gazed into her eyes with piercing intensity. "I realize this is incredibly short notice, Merry Bright, but I wondered if you would do me the honor of accompanying me to dinner this evening? If, of course, you have no other plans. I realize that it is Friday night and a girl as lovely as you must have several young men lined up to engage you for the weekend."

Merry laughed. "Me? Goodness, no. I was planning to spend the evening sewing." She looked behind her to make sure no one was listening, although she knew full well she was home alone, then continued, "My younger sister, LeAnn, has some outfits in her closet that are slightly inappropriate. I was just going to let some of her hems down to make them more modest."

Collin chuckled approvingly. "Really? That's marvelous."

Merry giggled a bit at her own brand of subterfuge. "I've been doing it since she was about twelve. She has no idea!"

"I hate to take you away from such important business, but might I beg of you to let down her hems some other time and spend the evening with me?" Collin inquired.

Merry was still taken aback, unsure of how to respond. Things like this never happened to her—men never showed up for her sisters and asked her out instead. He sensed her hesitation and said, "I certainly understand if you choose not to trust me. It shows great strength of character to avoid going out with any man who comes along and asks. It was lovely to meet you, and I hope I will meet you again soon in the future."

Merry watched as Collin shoved his hands in his pockets, gave a jaunty little bow, and whistled as he walked back toward his van at the curb. She hastily pulled the tape measure from around her neck and followed him down the front walkway. "Collin, wait!"

Surprised, he turned back to face her. She slowed down as she approached, putting her hand above her eyes to shield them from the bright afternoon sun. "I don't see any reason I can't go. I mean, after all, you are my sister's home teacher. That should be all right. If Lizzie trusts you enough to let you into her home, I think it would be fine if I allowed you to entertain me this evening. Maybe this once." She smiled up at him, then glanced at her watch. "May I have a few moments to change my clothes?"

"Of course." He looked very pleased, and more than a little surprised at the turn of events.

"Please come in, then," she said, leading him back into the house. She showed him to the living room and brought him a glass of water. "I promise I'll hurry."

Merry made sure he was settled comfortably on the couch with the latest issue of the *Ensign* before running up the stairs, trying to hold in her shrieks of surprise and delight. This was such a dream moment. She felt giddy and pretty, a new sensation for her, and she could not wipe the ridiculous smile from her face. Collin had called *her* a classic beauty.

She rummaged through her closet but was not satisfied with what she saw. Why do a girl's perfectly nice, acceptable clothes suddenly seem like secondhand-store rejects unfit for wear when she's looking for a date outfit? Her shoulders slumped, but then she peeked out her door and snuck across the hall to LeAnn's room. Where was that green dress Mother said looked so nice on her? She found her dress in the back of her sister's closet and ran back to her room. She tugged on some tan nylons, jammed her feet into her cream-colored pumps, and carefully put on her pearl necklace. She pulled her hair up into a French twist, dusted some blush on her ivory complexion, and swiped on some of LeAnn's sparkly pink lip gloss. *Date-ready in less than ten minutes*, she thought to herself. Many a good woman could learn a lesson in efficiency from Merry Bright.

Merry grabbed her purse and ran down the stairs, but she didn't want to appear too anxious. To some men, anxious might appear desperate. Merry didn't want him to know this was only her second date ever. At the foot of the stairs, she took a deep breath and smoothed the dress down. It had suddenly developed severe static cling, and she did not want him to think her immodest. She stood straight and tall, took in a deep breath, and held her shoulders back as she tried to walk nonchalantly into the living room, where Collin sat.

Just then, LeAnn opened the front door and threw her backpack down on the floor. She saw Merry, but she didn't see Collin, so she gave her sister a strange look. "Where the freak are you going?"

"LeAnn, watch your language!" Merry exclaimed. "I have a date."

LeAnn snorted. "You do? Who with? Is the throw-up guy out of the hospital?"

Collin stood just then, offering his hand. "Collin Light, if you please. I'm your sister's date for the evening."

LeAnn looked him as though he had leprosy, rudely ignoring the outstretched hand. "I guess you look like the kind of guy Merry would date."

Merry ran into the kitchen. "I'm leaving a note here for Mother so she won't worry about me. Will you make sure she gets it?"

LeAnn shrugged. "If I remember. I'm going to a party tonight."

Merry returned to the living room and gave Collin a cheerful smile. "Okay, I'm ready." She put her purse over her shoulder and allowed Collin to open the door for her.

"You two crazy kids be careful," LeAnn called sarcastically after them. "And when you're home, I want the dress back. You stole it from my closet."

"It's not stealing if I reclaim my own property," Merry hollered back, then slammed the door behind her. She smiled brightly, surprised and delighted when Collin offered her his arm and opened her car door. A little shocked by what had just happened, she sat back and crossed her ankles, just as her mother had taught her, then silently prayed that Collin would not be afflicted with food poisoning during the course of the evening.

A Most Unexpected Turn of Events

LIZZIE rubbed the sleep from her eyes and turned her head to the sound of the phone. *Goodness, who is crazy enough to call two single girls at 7:00 a.m. on a Saturday?* she thought. She was barely able to muster a sleepy hello when she realized it was her mother. Of course. Who else had that aggravating habit of calling early on Saturday mornings? After listening half-heartedly for a moment, she discovered that her mother was very excited about something. She sat up in bed when she heard the word *Merry.* Or was it *marry?*

"Mother, slow down. I don't understand what you are talking about. What did Merry do?" Lizzie yawned into the phone.

"I am thinking you, Janalyn, and LeAnn will wear pink dresses and carry white flowers. She loves daisies, and they'll be in season. How does that sound to you? Of course, pink never was your color, but Jana just radiates in it. LeAnn looks good no matter what she wears," her mother rattled excitedly.

Lizzie still had no idea what her mother was talking about. "Mom, I'm sorry, what about pink?"

"Oh, Elizabeth, aren't you excited for your sister? We'll have to have the reception at the stake center, of course, since it's such short notice. Now what other flowers should we have in her bouquet? Really, dear, I thought you would have more to say about this. It's not every day your sister gets married."

Lizzie almost rolled off her bed as she jerked up. "Jana's engaged?!"

Sister Benson sighed in exasperation. "Jana? No dear, I don't think so. I don't even think Austen has called her lately. Do you think we should do mums or carnations for the bridesmaids?" she continued.

"Neither, Mom! Both are cheap and tacky. Who is engaged? Which of my sisters is getting married? And why don't I have a clue what you are talking about?"

"Really, Lizzie, I know you must be a little jealous that your sister stole your beau, but you should be happy for her. Merry's never had a lot of beaus. But who would have thought she would be the first of my girls to get married?" Louisa Benson was so pleased, she was actually giggling like a schoolgirl.

"Mom, I am still very confused. Of course I'm happy for my sister. I just have no clue what you are talking about. Who is Merry marrying? I didn't even know she was dating someone. Oh my gosh, not the throw-up guy! Why would I be jealous? I've never met that guy. I didn't even know he was out of the hospital. Please, start from the beginning," she pleaded into the phone. All the information was a little too much for an early Saturday morning, but she was wide awake now—and completely bewildered.

"The throw-up guy?" Sister Benson repeated, momentarily lost. Then it struck her. "Oh, Doug Evern? No, don't be silly. Merry is engaged to Collin! He was worried you may not take the news well. He felt that he should be the one to break it to you, but I just couldn't contain myself! It is natural for you to be a little jealous, dear, and we want you to know we understand what you must be feeling. You are older than Merry, and you did have first crack at Collin. But once you see them together, you can't deny that they are a perfect match. Just don't let your sister know you are jealous. I think it may be too much for her to handle," she replied, being annoyingly short on details.

Lizzie thought and thought, but still came up blank. "Collin? Collin who? I don't know any Collins! Why would I be jealous of someone I don't even know?" She was so confused and frustrated at her mother that she couldn't even think straight.

"Collin Light. Merry does feel bad that she stole him away from you—"

"Collin Light?!" Lizzie shrieked, causing her sleeping roommate to jerk out of a deep slumber. "Merry is engaged to *Collin Light*? How does Merry even know Collin Light?" Then she realized something else her mother had said, and she went ballistic again. "And he's *not* my boyfriend. He's my home teacher! And I hardly even know the guy!"

"Lizzie, dear," her mother clucked sympathetically, "you don't have to pretend you don't have feelings for Collin. He was very honest with us about your history together. He hopes this won't cause any contention in our family. He is worried that he may come between you and Merry, but I assured him that nothing could be further from the truth. No man could ever come between my girls. Soon you will soon get over your feelings for him, and you will be truly happy for your sister."

Lizzie was on the verge of hyperventilating. When had she stepped into the Twilight Zone? How could she get out of this horrifying fifth dimension? "Mother, Collin is nothing but a home teacher to me. I don't know where anyone got the idea I have a history with him. My history with him involved one night of Chinese food and several unfortunate run-ins on campus. That is it! Collin is not my boyfriend. I have a boyfriend."

"Oh, Lizzie! Why didn't you tell me you have a boyfriend!"

"Mother, focus," Lizzie breathed impatiently. She wasn't ready for that conversation yet. "How did they meet? How long have they been dating?"

"Last Friday he stopped by here looking for you," Sister Benson began. "You weren't here, of course, and I don't know where he got the idea that you would be. It was love at first sight for both of them. He's been coming up here every day for the past week to see her. They got engaged last night."

"Merry is engaged to someone she has only known a week!" Lizzie shouted into the phone. She looked up to see a very sleepy and irritated Robyn looking at her strangely. She waved her roommate over and scooted over to make room for her on the bed. She wanted Robyn to hear this conversation; otherwise, it was quite possible that no one would ever believe her. Robyn curled up on the bed next to Lizzie and continued to look at her strangely.

"Don't sound so alarmed, dear," Sister Benson chided. "When it's right, it's right. Collin is such a lovely young man."

Did she really just call Collin "lovely"? How irritating, Lizzie thought. "Mom, when is the wedding?"

"In August. We don't have an exact date picked yet."

"August?" Lizzie howled in reply. "They met last week, and they want to get married in less than three months?"

Robyn rolled over and laughed into her pillow.

"They want to get married before school starts. He needs to focus on school, and Merry wants to look for a job at Primary Children's Hospital. It's just so fortunate she took that CNA course so she can get a good job with benefits while he's finishing school. Isn't it just amazing how we can be led in these decisions?" Sister Benson sighed dreamily before she continued. "Listen, dear, I have so many phone calls to make and a zillion things to do. I need to let you go. Just please make sure you get up here sometime this weekend so I can get your measurements for the bridesmaid dress. So we're settled on the pink dresses? It's not your color, but we can do some wonderful things with makeup to hide all that. Love you, bye-bye." And with that, she was gone, replaced with a dial tone and leaving a drop-jawed Lizzie.

Lizzie slowly placed the phone back in its cradle and thought for a long time as she stared blankly at Robyn, who looked at her expectantly. Instead of filling her in, she silently walked across the room, stopped decidedly in front of her closet, pulled out her favorite Ute T-shirt, and said, "Get up and put your clothes on. We're going out for breakfast."

"Why?" Robyn said sleepily.

"Because what I am about to tell you will go down much better with large amounts of hot chocolate and Krispy Kreme donuts." She paused for a moment, swirled around, looked her roommate squarely in the eye, and announced, "My little sister is engaged to *Collin Light.*"

"What?!" Robyn's jaw joined Lizzie's on the floor as she laughed. She was laughing so hard, in fact, that she rolled off the bed and landed on her tailbone with a resounding thud. "Okay, just give me a minute." She grabbed some shorts and a baby-T from her dresser, then raced down the hall to the bathroom, slamming the door behind her.

"Hurry . . ." Lizzie said in a distant voice. Her head was spinning, and she had no idea what to make of everything that had just happened. She tried not to fall over as she pulled on her clothes.

She shook her head and tried to focus. As she pulled her hair up into a high ponytail, she called out, "Yeah, apparently he's not as in love with us as we once thought. He's been dating my sister for a whole week! One big, long . . . apparently blissfully glorious week in which they have fallen madly in love and think they should get married. Why would they think that after a week? I never thought Merry had it in her to be so reckless." She sighed. "At least that explains why he hasn't been stalking us all week. I wondered where he disappeared to . . . but I never thought . . . And now they are getting married . . . Is it normal to have your head pound so hard it feels like your brain is trying to come out your eyeballs?" Lizzie sat back on the bed and just stared at the wall for a minute.

"Calm down, sweetie! You're babbling." Robyn brought her laughter under control as she opened the door. She walked over to rub Liz's back to comfort her—then burst out laughing again. "I'm sorry!" she giggled. "I can't help it! Collin Light is going to be your brother-in-law? This is the funniest thing that has ever happened. You will be stuck with Collin for *eternity*! I can't stop laughing! How did this happen?"

Then it really hit Lizzie. "Oh my gosh. You are right. Collin Light will be my brother-in-law. I'll have to see him everywhere—for the rest of my life! I can't believe this. But how did they ever meet? Merry lives in North Ogden! What was he thinking going up there? And she's only nineteen! She's not even old enough to get married! And they've only known each other one lousy week! This must be a practical joke. I just don't believe it!" Lizzie wailed bewilderedly at the wall. She froze suddenly and stared at Robyn with the most horrified expression her roommate had seen in two years of sharing a room with her. "Robyn, they are going to have children together. Collin Light, the Shakespeare-spouting, bow-tie-wearing, Euro-van-driving home teacher, is going to be the father of my little sister's children!"

Robyn swallowed hard, faked a serious expression, and placed her hands squarely on Lizzie's shoulders. With the somberness of a four-star general, she looked in Lizzie's blue eyes. "Let's not think about things like that right now. Baby steps. Let's get you through this with a little chocolate therapy, one step at a time, and then we can focus on the little Lightlings that soon will be crawling all over the place." She steered her toward the door and picked up both their purses.

"Lightlings," Lizzie repeated, her voice again coming from a far-off place. She grabbed her keys off the hook near the front door, then thought a moment and handed them to Robyn. "You should probably take these. I don't think it's safe for me to drive right now. We should walk instead."

Robyn nodded in agreement. "You're right," she said, taking the keys from Lizzie's limp hand. "And you should probably avoid taking cold medicines and operating heavy machinery too."

Suddenly, Lizzie stopped and grabbed Robyn by the arm. "Robyn! My sister's name is going to be Merry Bright Light!" Lizzie wailed. "She sounds like a bad Christmas carol!"

Robyn patted her sympathetically on the arm and steered her out the door.

"Merry Bright Light? This can't be happening!" Liz mumbled to herself as she followed Robyn out the door. She hoped that all she would need to make sense of her world was a good friend and some glazed chocolate doughnuts.

☆ ☆ ☆

To: Elizabeth.benson@uu.edu
From: jbenson47@email.byu.edu
Subject: Merry's big dinner

Liz,

Are you inviting Will to Merry's big dinner on Saturday? I want a full report of how everything goes—right down to the shoes you wear and what Dad says to him. But no engagements until

I have inspected him and made sure he's good enough for my darling little sister. Remember, everyone knows about him now, so you don't have to hide him from the family anymore. Besides, with all the attention on Merry, Collin, and Collin's family, Mother will hardly have any time to humiliate you in front of Will. Bless her heart, she doesn't mean to, but she's just so anxious to make sure we don't end up like Aunt Ellen and Aunt Sue that she gets a little crazy in the head trying to make sure her girls are all perfect for the boys. That's one reason I'm so glad I found Austen and don't have to worry about her trying to find someone for me!

That reminds me. Did I tell you Austen and his whole family will be there as well? Mother insisted on inviting them, even though I won't be there. I hope Merry can handle all this pressure. She's never disappointed before, but I am wondering how she is planning to make dinner for our family (5), the Youngs (8), the Lights (4 including Collin), and Will (because you will be bringing him). That is 18 people, not including whatever friends LeAnn may bring as well. And I think Mother mentioned inviting the missionaries over too! That could easily put the party over 25 people! Maybe you should go early to help cook. I don't think Merry, as capable as she is, has ever pulled off something so big!

Good luck!

Love, Janalyn

P.S. BRING WILL! ASK HIM!

* * *

To: jbenson47@email.byu.edu
From: Elizabeth.benson@uu.edu
Subject: I need serious therapy

Jana Banana,

You know how terrified I am to ask Will. I'm not sure why I'm
so hesitant for him to meet the family. I guess I just feel like I
am going to jinx this whole relationship by making it out to be
more serious than it is. It's just a few dates, right? No big deal.
Plus he has mentioned that he's not looking for anything
serious. We're just having fun together!

But when I am with him I am confident and sure of where we
are and what is going on between us—which is wonderful, I
must add. I really am starting to fall in love with him—I think!
But how do I know what love is? He's my first serious
boyfriend! If our relationship is serious. I never am sure! But
I'm crazy about him, and I look forward to every minute with
him. And I am pretty sure he feels the same way about me. But
how do I know this isn't what all relationships are like?

Love, Me

P.S. Did I tell you he left daisies on my doorstep this morning?
He's so cute!

P.P.S. Yes, I'll go up early to help with the cooking. I have no
idea how Merry thinks she can do this all by herself. That's
what sisters are for, right?

* * *

To: Elizabeth.benson@uu.edu
From: jbenson47@email.byu.edu
Subject: Personalized news flash for Liz Benson

You are in love, Liz. Get over it, and bring him.

* * *

THE young woman rolled over onto her back and looked up at the puffy white clouds above her. The purple majestic peaks of the mountains were accented by the brilliant blue sky behind them, and the trees gracefully reached up towards the bright sun as if to soak up every last ray on this beautiful summer afternoon. Next to her lay a napping young man, his beautiful brown eyes shielded from the sun by a red baseball hat pulled down low. His brown hair curled gently from under the hat, and his female admirer toyed with the idea of slowly pulling the hat off his head and running her fingers through the curls, without waking up their owner. The young woman slowly sat up and quietly reached her hand towards the tempting curls.

"You wouldn't be trying to steal my hat now, would you, Sister Benson?" Will said softly, startling Lizzie and causing her to yelp.

"No! Will! Oh my gosh! Don't scare me like that!" Lizzie jumped and slapped him playfully.

Will chuckled and opened one eye, squinting from under the brim of his hat. "Then what were you doing?"

"Nothing," Lizzie said a little guiltily.

Will raised his trademark eyebrow at her, lifting his hat a little in the process. "What were you doing?" His tone was slightly accusatory but slightly curious.

"Swatting at a fly?" Liz said a little too hopefully, too shy and sheepish to admit the truth. She raised her eyebrows in expectation, hoping he bought her pasted-on innocent expression.

Will looked at her questioningly and unbelievingly. He didn't know what she had been up to, but she sure looked guilty over it. And Will recognized the opportunity to tease when one came his way. "Swatting at a fly? Really? Where did it go?"

"Um, it just flew away?" She didn't even sound convincing. "That's why they call them flies, Will. They fly," she said, knowing she sounded ridiculous.

"The fly flew away? Hmm . . . interesting." Will pretended to mull over her reply and kept a deadpan face and serious tone.

She couldn't tell what he was up to. Was he serious? Did he believe the fly thing?

"Sister Benson, I think of all the conversations we have ever had, this one ranks up there as the most pathetic."

"Oh, Will! Good grief!" Lizzie said in mock disgust. She knew she had just fallen for nothing and laughed at herself.

"So what were you doing?" Will laughed with her.

"Nothing. I was just thinking about playing with your curls. I didn't want to wake you up though. You looked so peaceful lying there like that." Lizzie smiled sweetly at him.

Will tipped his hat back to get a good look at her. He smiled his broad grin and reached one arm out towards Lizzie to pull her to him. She accepted the invitation and snuggled up to him on the old green quilt.

Lizzie enjoyed the comfort of his arm and soaked up the warmth of the sun. But deep down she knew she had to ask him; the family gathering was in two days and she was running out of time. They had gone on countless dates by this point, and he called her nearly every day, but the truth was, she had never called him or asked him out on a date. Inviting him to meet her family made her so nervous she could feel her legs trembling. She wasn't sure she was up to the daunting task.

"Will?" Lizzie squeaked nervously. She looked up at him, his eyes closed, the brim of his hat pulled down low to block his face from the sun.

"Whatever it is, the answer is yes," Will said sleepily.

Lizzie giggled. "How did you know I was going to ask you a question?"

Will stretched his legs, yawned, wrapped his arm tighter around Lizzie, and never batted an eye. "Because you just have that tone in your voice."

"Well, how do you know it's something you want to do?" she asked suspiciously.

Will paused and appeared to have fallen asleep. Reaching up to pull his cap down tighter, without ever opening his eyes, he finally said, "Because whatever it is, it's obviously important to you, so I'll do it. That's just the kind of guy I am. I do whatever the woman I love wants."

Lizzie stared at him wide-eyed. Her jaw dropped down and she gaped at him. She couldn't believe he just said "love" so casually. He didn't even seem to be stressed about it. He said *LOVE*! The man who wasn't looking for love had just told her he loved her. She was more than a little confused and shocked and not sure how to respond.

"Liz?"

"Um, yeah?" Lizzie replied, still startled.

"What did I just agree to?" Will asked groggily.

Lizzie still wasn't sure she could ask him, but somehow the words came out of her mouth. "To go to a picnic on Saturday to meet my whole family," she said as sweetly and innocently as possible, never taking her eyes off him. Will didn't wince, flinch, or even blink.

"Cool. Sounds fun," Will said through a yawn. He wasn't even fazed by her invitation! He didn't even look nervous! *Wow,* Lizzie thought to herself.

"That sounds great, then." Lizzie heard the words come out calmly, but inside she was terrified and elated at the same time. She relaxed and looked back up at the puffy white clouds in the sky and felt her heavy eyelids begin to close. The stress of asking him was finally over, and it was so much easier than she had ever expected. *Maybe this relationship is as serious as I think it is,* Lizzie thought to herself. *I guess these things don't have to be so complicated after all.*

"Liz?" Will nearly whispered. He was just seconds away from falling asleep. "Is this what you have been so nervous about today?"

How was he able to read her so well? Liz smiled sheepishly, even though Will wasn't looking at her. "Yes."

"Liz, you don't have to worry so much. You are way beyond perfection in my eyes. I love you," Will whispered into her ear as he drifted off to sleep right there on Lizzie's favorite old quilt on the side

of the mountain in the middle of the week in the middle of the afternoon, just as if he hadn't just said something that changed the whole
world as Lizzie knew it.

When Nothing Goes as Planned

NORTH OGDEN. The sleepy little town of thousands that closed down by 10:00 p.m., home to the Benson clan. Lizzie made the right-hand turn onto the street full of familiar houses, her mind wandering as she made the drive she could probably make in her sleep. This was the street where she had spent the first eighteen years of her life. She knew the names of every person in every house she could see. But there was a white house, with a white porch, and a white porch swing, in the middle of the street that held her childhood memories, her past, and for today, her present. She had made the trip home dozens of times since leaving for college, but today was different. Today would mark the first time Elizabeth Benson would bring home a boyfriend to introduce to her family.

As she pulled up at the house, Lizzie took a deep breath and checked her outfit one last time. She knew better than to show up on such a monumental day without looking her best. She could already hear her mother's appraisal ringing in her head like an overzealous drill sergeant. In honor of the occasion, she had made an emergency trip to the mall and bought new lavender capri pants and a cute, matching, short-sleeved lavender gingham shirt, complete with a white tank top underneath. She was the epitome of a summer picnic, sporting matching flip-flops with little lavender bows at the toes. Lizzie smoothed down her long brown locks, blow-dried and combed into unwilling submission, and adjusted her matching headband. She took one last look in the vanity mirror and thought one last time about what the day ahead would hold for her.

Lizzie pictured inside the little white house. Merry Bright would be efficiently running the kitchen and preparing her famous apple-raisin-cinnamon pies. LeAnn would most likely hide out in her room, playing her stereo loud enough that the walls to the stairwell would ripple and thump along with the beat. Her father would be found in the backyard, firing up the grill for the chicken and hamburgers, yelling occasionally at LeAnn to "turn that racket down!" And, most predictably, her mother would be frantically running around in her bathrobe, her hair up in curlers, complaining that the house was a mess and the food wouldn't be ready in time. Not wanting Will to witness this inevitable scene, Lizzie had arranged for Will to drive up on his own later. Lizzie had wanted a few minutes with her family alone before the inevitable attack on Will began.

She walked up the stone path and opened the door, fully expecting to see a house hard at work. She was surprised to see only Merry through the propped-open kitchen door and no one else in sight. Merry was furiously rushing about the kitchen, looking more stressed than Lizzie had ever seen her.

"Merry, what are you doing? Honey, you are a mess!" Lizzie exclaimed as she walked in. She hurried across the kitchen and gave her younger sister a big hug.

"Elizabeth, I am so glad you are here. I fear I may not have everything under control. Would you mind making a salad?" Merry said in a strangely shrill, disconnected tone. Her normally low, calm voice was exceptionally high-pitched, almost strangulated.

"Sure, Merry. Anything for my favorite engaged sister." Lizzie steered her younger sister into a kitchen chair and turned to face the mess on the counters. She grabbed an apron and tied it securely around her waist, not wanting to risk getting anything on her cute new outfit. "Where is everyone? Relax, sit down; you look like you need a break!"

"Collin is at the store buying more napkins. He should be back soon. Father is taking a short nap, which is well deserved. He spent most of the morning weed-whacking and cutting the grass until the lawn mower broke. It took him over an hour to fix it, but it still didn't work, so he had to borrow the Youngs'. Thankfully the back-yard is all finished now. The heat was killing him, so I told him not to worry about the front yard. Collin offered to help, but I don't think he is really built for manual labor. He says he grew up on a farm, but somehow I just don't see it." Lizzie almost choked on her tongue, trying not to laugh at the thought of Collin out milking cows and haying. She raised her eyebrows and nodded instead.

Merry continued, "Mother is at the beauty salon getting her hair done. I haven't seen LeAnn all day, but I'm grateful that at least she hasn't been around to snitch the dough and make new messes." She sighed, then tried to continue in a positive voice, "I am sure everyone will be back soon. But look, here you are! We'll have everything finished in no time." Merry let out a long sigh. She was trying to place a positive spin on things, but Lizzie doubted they would accom-plish everything in "no time."

"So what is the final head count? Who is coming?" Lizzie asked, trying to cover the anxiousness in her voice.

"Collin, Will, eight Youngs, three Lights, perhaps Collin's favorite cousin, if he can get off work—and the five of us. That makes eigh-teen or nineteen, right? I hope so, because I have only prepared enough chicken for twenty. Speaking of chicken, I should probably go start the grill for Father." Merry spoke mostly to herself. She walked out of the kitchen and out the patio door to light the grill.

Lizzie looked around the kitchen and took a mental inventory of everything that needed to be done. A quick glance in the refrigerator revealed the ingredients for a large garden salad and a large fruit salad. On the counter there were a several lemons, which brought a quick smile to Lizzie's face. Merry must be planning to make her homemade lemonade, a family favorite. Lizzie also spotted two dozen peeled apples in the sink and rolled-out pie crusts on the kitchen table. The Benson family recipe for apple-cinnamon-raisin pie had been handed down for several generations, and nobody made it better than Merry. If Merry could pull this off, they would all be in for a gourmet delight. Lizzie pulled out the fruit and got to work making a salad. Moments later, Merry came back in and started on the pies. The two sisters worked side by side rushing to get everything done. Lizzie finished the salads and turned to help Merry with the pies. They had just finished pouring the filling into the last pie tin when the doorbell rang.

"I'll get it, Merry; you finish the pies," Lizzie said sweetly, heading for the door. The picnic was still an hour away, and she couldn't imagine who would be dropping by mid-afternoon.

Through the screen door, Lizzie could see three people she did not recognize: a man, a slim teenage girl, and a woman holding a large bowl. The woman was wearing hot-pink stretch pants and a long T-shirt knotted at the hip. She had big blond hair, brown roots showing at the crown, and bangs a good two inches tall; she clearly needed to get her perm refreshed. But the most noticeable thing about her was her garish pink lipstick that matched her stretch pants.

The man was wearing a plaid flannel shirt, in spite of the hot summer weather outside. As she drew closer she saw a hand-sewn name tag on the shirt as well, but she wasn't close enough to read the cursive writing on it yet. He had on a pair of dark blue work pants, with black work boots. He was balding badly on top, which not even his trucker hat could cover. He had a big, broad smile, and a big broad belly to go along with it.

The girl looked to be about fourteen or fifteen, but stood back behind her parents, so Lizzie couldn't get a good look at her. There was something strangely familiar about the family, but Lizzie couldn't place just what it was. She opened the screen door and greeted the guests, "Hi, can I help you?"

The man, whose stitched-on name tag indicated that his name was Buddy, pulled her out of the door and enveloped her into a gigantic bear hug. "It's a real treat to meet you, Merry! Welcome to the family! You are every bit as beautiful as Collin told us!" He pulled her off her feet and bounced her up and down a few times. He hugged her so tightly that Lizzie could hardly breathe. He placed her back on her feet, and she quickly stepped back, slightly surprised.

"I—I'm, uh, I'm not Merry. I'm Liz, her sister." She smoothed her hair down and quickly checked her outfit. "I'm sorry, you are?" she asked, thinking, *You can't possibly be related to Collin!*

"We're the Lights, Liz! I'm Buddy, and this is my wife, Lola, and our baby girl, Starr. It sure is nice to meet you!" Buddy took Lizzie's hand and pumped it vigorously up and down. Lizzie just stood there, stunned. This was Collin's family? Lizzie had no words, no words at all.

"We brought you a Jell-O salad. I hope you don't have one already. But then again, there's always room for Jell-O, right?" Lola Light said with a thick drawl. She tipped the bowl so Lizzie could get a look at the green gelatin with carrots floating in it.

"Oh, that's just lovely. Well, please come in." Lizzie didn't know what else to say, so she turned to the kitchen and called out for Merry. "Merry, the Lights are here."

The Lights were already at the kitchen door. Merry turned around, looking like a deer caught in the headlights. She hastily shoved the pie she was holding into the oven, failing to notice that the kitchen towel on her hand was still stuck under the pie tin as she slammed the oven door shut. She stepped forward to meet the Lights, looking very nervous and checking to see if Collin was with them. As Lizzie watched, she knew nothing could have prepared Merry for the sight of her future in-laws.

Buddy picked up Merry and enveloped her into a gigantic bear hug, just like he had done with Lizzie. "It's a real treat to meet you, Merry! Welcome to the family! You are every bit as beautiful as Collin told us!" he repeated. He pulled her off her feet and bounced her up and down a few times. Lizzie stood back and tried not to laugh.

When Buddy put her down, Lola took her turn with Merry, hugging her just as fiercely. "Hi, baby doll. You can just call me Momma!"

Merry looked desperately over Lola's shoulder at Lizzie, her eyes begging Lizzie for a clue what to do. Lizzie repressed a laugh and helped take over the situation.

"Merry, why don't you take the Lights into the backyard and get to know them? I'll finish up in here. And look! Sister Light—"

"Lola!"

Glancing at Sister Light quickly, Lizzie continued, "*Lola* brought a Jell-O salad. Wasn't that so nice? Why don't you go put that on the picnic table," Lizzie directed.

"Oh, I can't wait to see your yard. Let's go take a peek!" Sister Light put her arm around a still-reeling Merry, and they all walked to the backyard.

Lizzie sat down on a kitchen chair and laughed out loud. She never would have guessed that Collin would be related to this group of people. Thoughts of the Lights finding an abandoned six-month-old crawling through the gutters as he recited sonnets for cash filled her head, and she quickly tried to shake the distraction away. *Must focus on the salad!*

Lizzie hopped up, still incredulous. She needed to check one more time to make sure she hadn't just let her imagination play tricks on her. She looked out the back window onto the deck, where she could see Lola Light's backside. Lizzie couldn't help but notice that her stretch pants were getting old and worn, complete with the little nubby and nappy parts. Lizzie shook her head, laughed to herself, and turned back to the mess in the kitchen. The Lights had arrived nearly an hour early, and nothing was ready yet. The table in the back hadn't even been set yet. Lizzie pulled down the dishes and headed to join the group in the backyard.

". . . so I've been working the farm during the summers, and then I work winters as a plumber. Been doing that for about ten years now, to try and make ends meet. I always thought Collin would join me and we could have a father-and-son outfit, but he's always had other ideas," Lizzie could hear Buddy telling Merry. A glance at Merry told Lizzie that she was handling the Lights better, but was still in complete shock.

"Now Collin has always been the black sheep in the family," Lola interjected, wrapping her arm around Merry's shoulder and pulling her into a sideways hug. "I don't know how many times we tried to get him to show an interest in sports and whatnot, but he decided when he was little that he liked books a whole lot more." She beamed with pride as she added, "He takes after me. I was an English teacher once upon a time!"

Lizzie glanced over with mild interest as Lola continued, "My little boy knew from the start that he couldn't outrun the boys or beat them at other games, so he decided to outsmart them instead!"

"He is very smart," Merry agreed, relaxing a bit as she warmed up to them. "It's one of the things I love best about him."

"Oh, now aren't you just too sweet?" Lola squealed as she squeezed Merry tightly from the side and kept going—something about Collin starting a chess club at their tiny, twenty-strong high school in Southern Utah and being its only member for a year. Lizzie tuned them out as she quickly set the table and went back in the house. LeAnn had finally appeared and was standing over the fruit salad, snitching strawberries off the top.

"LeAnn! Stop that! Where have you been?" Lizzie reprimanded her.

"I was out shopping. Got these great sandals, what do you think?" LeAnn stuck out a well-manicured foot in an expensive-looking pair of tan Prada sandals.

Lizzie looked at her incredulously. "Oh . . . my . . . gosh! How much did those cost you?"

LeAnn rolled her eyes. "I don't know. I used Mom's credit card." LeAnn looked out the window. "Oh my gosh! Who is Merry talking to?"

"That's Collin's family," Lizzie said simply.

LeAnn choked on her strawberry and spit it out in the sink. "You have got to be kidding me! Oh, that's, like, so funny! She's wearing hot pink stretch pants! Does she know what decade we're in?"

"Be nice, LeAnn. And keep your voice down," Lizzie reprimanded again. "Here, take these salads outside and put them on the table."

The doorbell rang and Lizzie ran to get it again. She could see the entire Young clan standing outside. What were they doing here so early? Lizzie wiped her hands off on her apron and looked at her watch. Oh, dear . . . they were right on time!

"Hi, everyone! Come on in! It's good to see you all! Go on to the backyard. We're just putting on the final touches!" Lizzie said cheerily while ushering the Youngs through the house. She nearly grimaced when she noticed that Julie Smith had joined them, but she shot the most friendly smile she could muster. As soon as the Youngs were all out the back door, Lizzie quickly ran up the stairs to find her father.

"Dad! Wake up! Everyone is here!" Lizzie shook her heavily snoring father several times. When he rolled over and lifted his arms, she took a huge step backwards. He smelled horrible! He obviously hadn't bathed since mowing the yard that morning.

With a grunt and snort, Elray Benson opened one eye. "Lizzie, when did you get here? Good to see you, girlie. What's going on?"

How quickly could she sum up the chaos? "Dad! The Lights and the Youngs are downstairs waiting, and we haven't even put the chicken on the grill yet! Hurry up and get downstairs! And please take a shower! Oh goodness!" Lizzie dashed back out of the bedroom and downstairs. Where was her mother? And Collin for that matter? She paused quickly and ran to find her cell phone in her purse. She was about to dial her mother's cell phone when Will walked through the door.

"Hey!" He walked up to her and kissed her on the cheek. She was very glad to see him and scolded herself for not noticing he hadn't arrived yet. She hugged him back and told him quickly what was going on. "My mother is MIA, and LeAnn is the only one entertaining people. My dad stinks, and all of the other guests are here. Oh, and the food isn't cooked yet! Welcome to the Bensons, where we specialize in chaos!"

Will just laughed. "What can I do to help?"

Lizzie put her head on his shoulder. "Stay right here and keep hugging me."

Will hugged her tighter, when suddenly Merry Bright came bursting into the kitchen.

"Merry, is something wrong?" Lizzie asked.

"Sister Light, I mean Momma, just informed me that their entire family is allergic to raisins! I have to dig the raisins out of all the pies!" Merry said frantically as she grabbed a hot pad and opened the oven door.

"Merry, relax, I'll help you. Will, do you mind hanging out for a few minutes in the back without me? I'll be there in a second!" Lizzie gave him her most charming smile, and Will obediently went out the patio door.

Lizzie grabbed a spoon and started fishing raisins out of the pies. When she glanced out the window she saw Will and Bishop Young checking out the grill. She quickly remembered that the chicken hadn't been started yet. "Merry, I'm going to take the chicken out to Will to put on the grill. I'll be back in a second."

Lizzie couldn't tell if Merry had heard her, but she picked up the platter of chicken from the refrigerator and went out back. No sooner had she stepped onto the patio when Julie, Natalie, and Erin accosted her.

"So Liz, *who* is the hottie over there?" Natalie said with anything but subtlety.

"That is my boyfriend, Will," Lizzie said, with as much possession she could muster.

"He looks familiar. I wonder if I've been out with him before," Julie mused.

Lizzie wanted to dump the whole plate of raw chicken on her, but refrained—only for the benefit of the other guests. Who would want to eat chicken covered in Julie? "Oh, I doubt you have met him, Julie. But maybe you have seen his picture somewhere. He's the institute president at the U." Lizzie tried to sound pleasant and unimpressed, but she knew she was failing.

"He's from the U?" Julie sniffed with disdain. "Well, that can't be it then. I would never date someone from the U. He just has one of those faces and looks like everybody. Know what I mean? Nothing special, just an average Joe."

"So how long have you been dating? Any ring yet?" Erin asked, and all three girls looked instantly to Lizzie's left hand.

"Whatever, girls. I have chicken. Excuse me." Lizzie pushed past them and walked over to Will and Bishop Young. "Would you gentlemen mind throwing these on the fire? My dad will be down in just a minute to help." Lizzie shot them her best smile.

"No problem. I'm just interviewing this fine young man here to see if he's good enough for our little Lizzie," Bishop Young teased. "We'll see if he passes the manly grilling test."

"Don't disappoint me, Will!" Lizzie encouraged as she turned back to the kitchen. But on her way in she noticed that Merry had just brought out more food, so she went over to help her set it out. Dinner was starting to come together. Finally!

"Merry, where's Collin?" Lizzie asked while stacking the cups.

"I sent him to the store to buy napkins and ice. I can't put the lemonade out until we have ice, but Collin has been gone for over two hours! What happened to him?" Merry was still talking mostly to herself.

"Merry, does Collin have a cell? Give him a call."

"Well, no, he doesn't," Merry informed her. "Neither of us believe in the trappings of modern society."

Liz took in a deep breath and tried not to roll her eyes. "I'll tell you what. I'll go bring out some water for everyone. In the meantime, go mingle! Look gracious! This party is to celebrate your engagement!" She turned to the sliding glass patio door, pulled out her own cell phone—thankful for the trappings of modern society—and tried to get hold of her mother again. She had just hit Send when she realized there were swirls of gray coming out of the sliding glass door.

Lizzie threw open the door and ran into the kitchen. Merry was hot on her heels. Deeper inside the house the smoke had turned black and was billowing from the oven. Lizzie grabbed the fire extinguisher from the pantry and aimed it at the oven while Merry reached for the pitchers of warm lemonade sitting on the counter. She grabbed the oven door and jumped back as she yanked it open while Lizzie shot the contents of the extinguisher inside and Merry threw in the contents of a lemonade pitcher. The fire flared up out of the oven, scorching the ceiling. The two sisters screamed and ran out of the kitchen, but Lizzie turned back and kept firing the extinguisher foam on the blaze.

White dusty foam filled the air. The fire died down as quickly as it had flared up, and Lizzie began to cough. Anxious to get some fresh air, she turned to go outside and saw Merry standing there, tears in her big blue eyes.

"Oh, Merry, are you okay?" Lizzie put down the extinguisher and put her arms around her sister.

"Well, we don't have to worry about the raisins in the pie now, do we?" Merry said before breaking down and crying on her sister's shoulder.

"My gracious! What happened in here?" Sister Benson's shrill voice rang through the kitchen as she emerged from the smoke, waving her hands in front of her face and coughing dramatically. The kitchen looked awful. The smoke detectors were going off, and the air was still smoky and full of fog from the fire extinguisher. In the bottom of the oven, still smoldering, sat one very charred, black kitchen towel, sparks still glowing.

"It's okay now, Mom. There was a fire in the top oven, but we put it out. There shouldn't be any damage, except to some pies," Lizzie said, still holding Merry.

"What? What fire? What is going on? Why is Merry crying?" Sister Benson demanded worriedly.

"Mom, we put it out. It's okay. Merry is upset that all of her hard work just, well, went up in flames. This whole picnic has barely started, and it is already a disaster," Lizzie said as Merry began sobbing loudly.

"Merry, my precious darling, what has happened? Are you all right?" A panicked Collin appeared out of nowhere and darted across the kitchen, stepping into a puddle of ashy lemonade, slipping, and skidding toward them before landing on his knees at their feet. Merry lifted her head to see what had happened and bent down hurriedly to see if he was all right.

"There was a small oven fire, Collin. It is okay now," Lizzie said kindly, patting Merry's back. "We were starting to worry about you. You have been gone over two hours!"

"We needed ice. She sent me for ice. Is my precious okay?" Collin pleaded, sounding bewildered that he may have done the wrong thing and looking a bit like a wounded puppy. He pointed at the front door, where Lizzie could see ten bags of party ice and possibly twenty bags of napkins haphazardly dropped in the front hallway. What on earth was he doing with that much ice? *Never send a man for such a simple job,* Lizzie thought silently to herself.

"What is going on in here? Why doesn't someone turn off that freaking lame smoke detector?" LeAnn burst into the kitchen. "Oh my gosh! What happened to him?" She pointed at the slippery Collin on the floor. "Where's the pie?"

Merry started to whimper again as she turned her attention back to the charred, blackened oven.

"Are you okay in here?" Brother Benson came in behind LeAnn and looked at Collin. "Is he hurt?"

"There was an oven fire. He's okay," Lizzie said. She tilted her head to point at Merry. "She's just a little upset."

"Collin, honey, what are you doing on the floor?" Sister Light's drawl joined the loud din of the kitchen. The smoke detector was still beeping, Merry was crying, and people had to shout to be heard.

"Mother, a pleasure to see you. I am quite all right!" Collin reached for a kitchen chair to steady himself and instead pulled it down on top of himself.

"Here, I'll fix that!" Brother Light walked across the sticky, wet kitchen floor, reached up with one hand, and pulled the smoke detector down. It stopped beeping, and Merry stopped crying.

"Thank you!" Lizzie cried out.

For one quick moment the kitchen was silent, and then the beeping started back up.

Suddenly, everyone came in from the backyard, and the house was in complete confusion. Sister Benson was yelling about how the smoke was bad for her nerves and that she might faint, a threat no one took seriously. LeAnn was laughing at Collin, who was still sliding around on the floor; Sister Light was attempting to help Collin up, almost falling down herself; the Youngs were all asking what had happened; Brother Benson was banging on the incessantly beeping smoke detector; and Merry's quiet cry became a plaintive wail that could hardly be heard above the rest of the din.

Lizzie couldn't take it anymore. Someone had to take charge!

"How about we all go back to the backyard?" she yelled, herding people back out the sliding glass door. "LeAnn, can you open some windows in here? And Dad, why don't you grab the ice by the front door? Austen, would you mind running down to the store and grabbing a few pies and a couple liters of Sprite for me? Thank you." Lizzie commanded the situation, and most of the troops went out back. She deposited Merry on the nearest picnic bench next to a sticky and wet Collin, then looked around for Will, who seemed rather bored standing by the grill.

"Hi, what was going on in there? Did you burn the house down?" Will laughed as she approached. He looked at the white dust from the extinguisher in her hair and on her clothes. He reached out to pull her in for a hug.

"Little pie disaster followed by the usual family hysterics," Lizzie explained as she sighed and leaned against him.

"Sorry I couldn't come in. Someone had to watch this fire out here." Will laughed and pointed at the grill. "If it makes you feel any better, the chicken will be done in about twenty minutes."

"Twenty minutes? What's taking so long?" Lizzie asked.

"Well, there was a little issue with the propane tank being empty, and then we couldn't find enough charcoal! But never fear, Bishop Young has run home to get some." Will laughed again.

"Oh my goodness. Well, let's just keep that between you and me and not tell Merry. I don't think she could handle any more mistakes today." Lizzie sighed. And to think she used to believe Merry could plan anything!

"Well, we used what we could find, just to get it warmed up. At least we can start a few pieces," Will offered helpfully.

"Lizzie! Who is this young man over here?" Sister Benson called loudly from across the yard.

"Brace yourself," Lizzie whispered to Will. "Mom, this is my . . ." Lizzie froze as her mother approached, and no matter how hard she tried, she couldn't get the word *boyfriend* out of her mouth.

"Hi, Sister Benson, I'm Will Pemberley, Lizzie's boyfriend." Will extended his hand for a generous handshake. Sister Benson, offering her hand lightly for the requisite limp-fish handshake, seemed unimpressed.

"William Pemberley." Her lips pursed together tightly as she assessed him much more closely than was reasonable. The three of them stood awkwardly for a moment.

Lizzie expected her mother to launch into an embarrassing speech about Lizzie's finest qualities, followed by an even worse interrogation of Will. But instead her mother just stood there and looked disapprovingly at Will.

Lizzie was puzzled. She was the one who always made light of dating, the one who kept her social and love life—or in most cases, the tragic lack thereof—private, and she always felt that if she were to tell anybody about her life, she would do it when the time was right. So here she was, at the right time, she thought, presenting her boyfriend to her mother. This was the moment for which her mother had been praying for years, and somehow Lizzie expected this moment to be accompanied by the Tabernacle Choir singing the "Hallelujah" chorus in the background. She had actually brought a promising young man home to meet the family, one with money, no less—the mark of success and perfection in her mother's marriage-addled brain—and instead of pinching his cheek and yanking him into some sort of embarrassing mother hug, she stood there appraising him with disdain.

"William Pemberley," she repeated slowly. "Are you one of the Pemberleys with the Pemberley Auto Mall?"

"Uh, yes, ma'am." Will seemed keenly aware that something was not quite right. He raised his eyes and noticed the hat on his head, then snatched it quickly and twisted it in his hands. Cool, collected William Pemberley, the boy used to charming the socks off all women he met, seemed unsure of how to proceed.

"Sister Young in our ward showed me an article that ran in the paper about your family a few months back," she said sharply, though she smiled at him a bit—always polite no matter what. "Something about your family and the Rasmussens merging?"

Will raised his eyebrow and nodded. "It's possible. Since I've been in school I've devoted most of my time to finishing my degree, and I have chosen to intern with Huntsman instead of with my Dad. But you may have seen a story in the business section. We do a lot of business with the Rasmussens, and stories run on that from time to time."

Sister Benson shook her head as her eyes narrowed.

Lizzie couldn't tell what she was thinking, but his response to her question seemed to confirm in her mother's mind whatever misgivings she had. Apparently young William had given the wrong answer.

Did her mother have a problem with the Rasmussen and Pemberley business merger?

"No, no, this story ran in the society section," Sister Benson said.

Will shrugged. "I don't read the society section." His expression glazed over as a brief flicker of recognition lit his eyes.

Liz still had no idea what was going on. "Mom, what are you doing?" she hissed.

Sister Benson sighed as she turned away, but as she turned back, her old self instantly returned. "Well, William, this is most embarrassing. Lizzie did not tell me you were coming, so I made other arrangements for her. Lizzie, there is a young man here I would like you to meet. Will, there are plenty of young people around for you to meet. Have you met the Young girls and their friend Julie? They are such delightful girls. Julie is such a pretty thing. You should get to know her." She smiled at him once more before excusing herself and leaving both of them there speechless.

Lizzie's head spun as she followed her mother back to the table. "Mom, I did too tell you!" she insisted. "What's going on here? Why do you care about his dad's business dealings?" She pulled her mother aside, hoping no one else noticed the interchange. Lowering her voice, she looked her mother squarely in the eye and said, "Other arrangements, Mom? Are you kidding me? You always bug me constantly about not having a boyfriend, not dating, and when I finally do bring someone that I think is really great to meet my family, you treat him like this?"

"Lizzie, I don't think you know everything there is to know about this young man," she informed her condescendingly. She patted her daughter's flushed, hot cheek and reassured her, "Mothers know best. Trust me; you'll love Collin's cousin Karl."

"Mom, what are you not telling me?" Lizzie insisted.

"I asked Collin to bring his cousin Karl over to meet you. Wouldn't that be fun if you and Merry married into the same family? The Lights do seem so nice!" Sister Benson said innocently, but Liz knew her mother's ploy too well; her forced innocence told Lizzie that she was covering something. Before Liz could argue anymore, her

mother walked away and over to the Lights. In the interest of not
making Merry's day any worse, Lizzie dropped the subject.

She walked back to Will, ignoring the amused, pitying looks Erin,
Natalie, and Julie were tossing her way. *Yes, enjoy it, girls,* she thought
to herself. *What else am I good for but to give you something to laugh
about for the next month?* When she reached Will, she just shook her
head in embarrassment. What could she possibly say? "I am so sorry
about that. I don't know what got into her. This is just crazy. She's
invited some guy to come over today to meet me! And after she
demanded I bring you today! I don't get it!"

Lizzie was so humiliated that she wanted to cry. She was holding
back tears as her father walked up to them.

"Lizzie, is this the young man you've been hiding from us all
summer?" he said jokingly.

"Dad, this is Will Pemberley. Will, this is my father." The two
men and shook hands vigorously.

"Nice to meet you, sir," Will said politely.

"Good to meet you too. I hear you are a ballplayer."

Lizzie smiled, knowing her father would be a much easier sell
than her mother.

"Yes, sir. Played in high school and walked on my freshman year
at the U. Lost my pitcher's arm on my mission, though. I hear you
were quite the pitcher back at the Y!" Will knew where to steer this
conversation, and soon the two men were quickly engrossed in
comparing the statistics of BYU and U baseball teams, enlivened by
the rivalry. Lizzie saw her chance to sneak away. Bishop Young had
appeared with more charcoal, and Austen had returned with some
store-bought pies. With a little luck, the afternoon picnic might be a
salvaged. Within minutes, chicken was roasting on the grill, everyone
had a cold drink, and Collin had cleaned up respectably.

Lizzie looked around the yard and could see LeAnn flirting with
Austen's younger brothers. Erin, Natalie, and Julie had seemingly
disappeared, and Lizzie wasn't complaining. Her mother was on the
other side of the yard talking to a young man she didn't recognize.
She feared it was Karl. Her mother spotted her and waved her over.

Lizzie decided to be polite and go over, but only to prevent her mother from saying something embarrassing and making the situation worse.

"Lizzie, this is Karl. He just got here. He's Collin's cousin. He's single!" Karl looked like the sort of guy Collin would hang out with. He had mousy brown hair feathered back over his pointed ears—a sort of gothic Spock look. He wore thick glasses that were just a tad too large for his long, thin face, and a long-sleeved black shirt with baggy black cargo pants tucked into freshly shined combat boots. His attire was completely inappropriate for an outdoor summer party; the sweat dripping from his brow and making perfect wet circles at his armpits indicated that he knew this. He also had the most calloused thumbs she had ever seen, most likely from strenuous workout sessions with the Play Station controller. Lizzie was so angry at her mother for bringing him she could hardly see straight.

"Karl, it's nice to meet you," Lizzie offered politely, extending her hand. Instead of shaking it, he quickly took her hand and kissed it. *Yep, definitely Collin's cousin,* Lizzie thought to herself.

"Pleasure to meet you, Lisa," Karl said. "I'm enchanted to meet you. I've heard a ton of stuff about you." *Oh dear . . . Collin's sidekick needs a bit more coaching on his delivery,* Lizzie thought. *Did they sit around together and think this stuff up?*

"Karl, would you excuse my mother and me for a moment? Thank you." Lizzie retracted her hand from his sweaty iron grip.

She attempted to not roll her eyes as he told her breathlessly, "I'll be here, waiting." Lizzie hoped it wasn't her appearance that made him breathless; it was entirely possible that he had heat stroke from his outfit and was about to pass out.

"Why don't you run and get yourself some water?" She would hate to be responsible if he passed out at Merry's already disastrous picnic. She took her mother's elbow and walked toward the back fence.

"What is it, dear?" her mother asked innocently. "Isn't Karl lovely?"

"Mother, I think you owe Will an apology. He is my guest, not to mention my boyfriend," Lizzie scolded.

Her mother stopped and turned. "Elizabeth, listen to me. I don't think he's told you everything about himself. Sister Young's article gave me an idea, so I Googled Will's name last night. I found an article from the Salt Lake paper on his engagement to someone else!" Rubbing Lizzie's hand reassuringly, she continued, "I know this must be quite a shock to you, dear, but I'm sure you had no idea. It must have been so exciting to you, to be with a handsome young man with so much money, but he's just toying with you! I have a right mind to call his bishop and let him know what's going on!"

"Oh my gosh! Mother! He's not engaged! He broke up with that girl ages ago! Trust me, he's only dating *me*!" Lizzie said, relieved and exasperated at the same time.

"Are you sure? I didn't find anything about that on the Internet!"

"Well, why would you? Good grief!" Lizzie rolled her eyes. "Mom, I think you need to apologize for the way you spoke to Will earlier. He was really offended."

A light suddenly popped on in Sister Benson's head. A smile spread across her face, and she grabbed Lizzie's shoulders. "Lizzie! Do you know what this means? You are dating a very wealthy young man!"

"Oh, Mom, don't even go there. Will is a lot more things than just wealthy. He's smart, charming, interesting, spiritual, talented, and a dozen other things. He is going to be a great businessman some day too. He's interning with . . ."

Her mother cut her off. "Well, of course he'll do well in business. He's a Pemberley, and they have considerably well-known business holdings in Utah! Oh, and he is good-looking too. You two will have beautiful children. His curls and your complexion. Oh, and what a fine couple you will make. You look like wedding cake toppers. Of course, we'll probably want to use the temple cake topper that we are buying for Merry's cake on yours as well. Why spend money when you don't have to? Oh, listen to me! Like we'll have to be frugal with your wedding! He's a Pemberley!"

"Mom! Stop it!" Lizzie hissed.

Will was sitting just ten feet away and could hear the entire conversation. Lizzie caught his eye and gave him an apologetic look.

Will shot her back an understanding look and smiled lovingly at her.

"Oh, look who just got here! LeAnn's boyfriend is the nicest young man. You should meet him, Lizzie. Bring Will over and I'll introduce the two of you to him." Sister Benson gleamed. It was pure bliss to see 75 percent of her daughters taken, with reasonable assurance that the other would go at any moment.

Lizzie followed her mother's gaze across the yard and suddenly spotted Ryan standing with his arm around LeAnn. "What is he doing here?" Lizzie wondered out loud. Sister Benson didn't even notice. She was halfway across the yard and hugging Ryan before Lizzie could say anything.

"You've got to be kidding me. He's got some nerve!" Will said from behind Lizzie as he put his arm around her shoulder.

Liz thought for a moment, then recalled Jana's advice and sighed as she told Will, "I don't want to get involved. He knows her age. It's none of our business. Let's just leave it alone."

"I know him better than you do, Liz. We should talk to your parents. He's not to be trusted," Will said with anger in his voice, and yet Lizzie thought she also detected some disappointment.

"I thought you were friends. What do you know that I don't know?" Lizzie asked while quietly steering Will away to the corner of the yard.

"We grew up together. He's not just my friend, he's my cousin. We did everything together as kids, and he was one of my best friends in high school. I was the baseball star; he was the basketball star. He loved the attention and used it to get girls. He really liked girls," Will said disapprovingly, still not taking his eyes off Ryan.

"So what? There's nothing wrong with that, is there? What normal high school boy doesn't like girls?" Lizzie was confused. Looking around the yard at all the people milling about, she suddenly missed Jana, who would have been a big help today. And something in Will's voice told Liz that there was going to be a late-night phone call to Jana tonight. "Is this about what happened at Wildcat Lanes? The night we went bowling?"

"Trust me, Lizzie," he continued, ignoring her question. "There are not a lot of good things to say about him. I really thought he had changed. I was willing to believe that he had, but I guess he hasn't." Will's disappointment etched lines into his face as he stared at Ryan.

"Will, please tell me what is so awful about him! He's a creep, yes, but I'm over what happened."

Will let out a sigh and turned to face Lizzie. Kissing her quickly on the forehead he said, "Let's go someplace more private."

Confused, Lizzie agreed. They went to the front porch and sat down on the porch swing, away from the onlookers in the backyard. Her mother looked pleased that they appeared to be sneaking off on their own. Lizzie felt embarrassed for her entire family.

Will rocked the swing back and forth a few times and looked off into the distance. Whatever he had to say wasn't going to be easy for him, Lizzie realized. "Back in high school, Ryan used his popularity to get a lot of girls. It wasn't hard for him. Girls chased him all over the place, and he loved it. Girls even came from other schools to watch him play basketball and cheer for him. There was one girl in particular who tried really hard to get his attention. He played her for a while but never cared about her. But she really liked him, and he really liked the attention. She came from a pretty affluent family, it turns out. She would buy him these nice gifts and let him drive her car. Well, one day, the two of them went out after a game and didn't come home. Everybody was worried sick about them. We called the police, searched the hills, everything. And then three days later they came home and acted like nothing was wrong. And that was it. They got punished and all, but they offered no excuses for why they disappeared like that."

Lizzie noticed a sinking sensation starting to form in the pit of her stomach. "Oh, wow. Where were they? What happened?" she asked.

"They had run off to Vegas to get married and maxed out her dad's credit cards. Ryan thought that her rich family or his dad would support them. Her parents managed to pay everything off and get the marriage annulled, but he acted like nothing big had happened, like it was no big deal to ratchet up all this debt and not be held responsible for what happened. I never heard much from him after high school, until I was on my mission.

"I got a letter one day from him. Get this: I'm on my mission in Russia, and I get this letter from him asking me for money. He tells me how everything in his life was messed up and that he wants to start living the right way; he tells me he's a changed man. He needs the money to get his life together and really make things right with the girl and try to get her back. I believed him. I figured if he was desperate enough to ask me for help, he must've really needed it. So I get my dad to send some money to him. He starts sending me letters all the time, telling me about how much he has changed. He got discharged from the Air Force and decided to go to the U. I really hoped he had changed."

"Maybe he has, Will. My parents seem to trust him," Lizzie offered hopefully.

"I doubt he's changed. And quite frankly, your mother doesn't execute the greatest judgment. He's twenty-three years old. Is this really the guy you want dating your sixteen-year-old sister? You saw the way he treated you! He's a womanizer! He sees all women as a conquest. And from what I see, LeAnn is the exactly the type of girl he likes to conquer," Will said with disappointment.

Suddenly, Ryan appeared around the corner. "What are you two doing out here? The party is back there!"

"Ryan, what are you doing here? She's sixteen!" Will burst out, unable to contain his anger.

"Dude, relax! It's nothing. She's a nice kid. That is all there is to it!" Ryan laughed and sat down on the porch railing. "Nice evening, isn't it?"

"Ryan, look me in the eye and tell me I have nothing to worry about," Will said firmly. Lizzie could hear the love as well as the fear in his voice.

Ryan turned and looked angrily at Will, but then his face quickly changed and he laughed a little too loudly. "Dude, trust me. She is just a nice kid, and mature for sixteen. There's nothing to worry about. I came here for the pie. LeAnn makes killer apple-raisin pies. Speaking of which," he continued, anxious to change the subject, "I hear I missed Miss Lizzie playing the hero firefighter. Good job!"

Lizzie rolled her eyes. "Yes, I'm quite the little firefighter. I seem to be getting better at stamping out fires wherever LeAnn goes." Ryan obviously missed her potshot aimed directly at his head, so she continued with narrowed eyes, "You might want to know that LeAnn has never made one of those pies in her life. Merry, the one I believe you previously called the ugly sister, is the domestic goddess who makes the pies around here."

Right on cue, LeAnn popped out of the front door and went straight over to Ryan, wrapping his arm around her shoulder like a mink stole. "Making friends, are we, Ryan?"

"Will and Ryan are cousins, LeAnn. And he and I have met several times," Liz reminded her, not trying at all to mask the annoyance in her voice.

"Oh, yeah, right. Bowling. I forgot. Whatever. Anyway, so Ry-Ry, let's jet. I want to go to this party at my friend's house. And then we should totally go to the mall. I've got my mom's credit card." LeAnn poured herself all over Ryan, and Lizzie could hardly take the way she hung all over him.

"Sure, let's go! You two be good!" Ryan said, and with a backwards wave, they were off.

Watching them drive away, Lizzie turned to Will with a heavy sigh and said, "I sure hope he's changed."

"Let's go back to the party. I heard there's a Jell-O salad with carrots in it," Will said with a wink at Lizzie.

"As is proper with all truly Mormon functions," she replied with a smile.

Taking her hand, Will led Lizzie to the backyard. Suddenly, Lizzie felt very nervous about holding hands with him in front of everyone. And while she would have loved to make a statement in front of Erin, Natalie, and Julie, she let go of his hand anyway.

Looking around the yard, Lizzie could see that the picnic finally seemed to be going right. Everyone was eating chicken, talking to each other, and enjoying themselves. The Lights were playing checkers with Bishop and Sister Young. Erin, Natalie, and Julie had separated themselves from the crowd. Starr Light was talking to several of the Young children. Merry and Collin were holding hands and talking to Brother Benson under the big oak tree. And Karl was playing his Game Boy by himself. The only person Lizzie couldn't see was her mother.

"Lizzie, there you are! I was wondering where you two snuck off to!" her mother said with far too many implications in her voice.

"We were just talking on the front porch," Lizzie said indifferently.

"So, Will, Lizzie tells me you work for your father!" Sister Benson beamed.

"No, actually I work for Huntsman Corporation," Will corrected her.

"Oh, why not your father?" Sister Benson suddenly looked very worried.

"Convenience. And I am getting a much better experience working for Huntsman," Will tried to explain.

"But you see your parents often, don't you? How many siblings do you have? What does your father do?" she interrogated him with the determined nature of a veteran spy.

"Um, sure, I see my parents all the time. Lizzie and I are having dinner at their house tomorrow, actually. I have one sister. And, as we discussed earlier, my dad works in car sales," he responded simply.

"Oh, is he a salesman?" Sister Benson asked, disappointment evident in her voice.

"Not really a salesman, no. But yes, he does sell cars," Will dodged and began to look flustered.

"What do you mean, not really? What is his job title then?" she pushed further.

"For heaven's sake, Mom, what is this?" Lizzie knew full well what her mother was trying to do.

"His job title would be owner, I guess," Will said plainly.

"Oh, really? So do you think you will inherit one someday? Do you want to be a car dealer as well?"

"Mom! Really!" Liz scolded her. She was so embarrassed she wanted to crawl under a rock.

"I think Dad would give me a job if I asked for one. But I'm studying international business. I'm not really interested in car sales,"

Will stated simply. "Sister Benson, it was nice meeting you and your lovely family, but I have to leave now. Thank you for having me."

Lizzie was caught off guard by Will's abrupt announcement. "Oh, okay. Where do you have to go?"

His blank expression caught her off guard as he said, "I just remembered something. I'll call you later. Have a good night!" Will quickly left the backyard, not giving her the opportunity to walk him out to his car. He didn't even look back.

"Okay, bye!" Lizzie called out, confused.

"Oh, Lizzie, he's a wonderful young man. You two will make a beautiful couple!" Sister Benson squeezed her daughter tight.

"Thanks, Mom," Lizzie said, watching Will drive off.

* * *

Liz stepped outside after the post-party cleanup, grateful all the guests had gone and happy to be done with the chaos. After all that had happened, she just wanted to be alone. She plopped down in her favorite spot in the world, the porch swing overlooking the valley, soaking in the orange horizon melting seamlessly into the deep violet above. The first stars had already appeared, and the air was growing cool. She loved to see the night sky from here. She folded her arms and rested them on her stomach, then let her head fall back to watch the stars.

She looked up, wiping away a few tears, when the door opened and someone came out and asked, "Would it be all right if I join you?"

"Merry!" she exclaimed. "Sure, have a seat." Lizzie scooted over and patted the cushion next to her. "You know you're always a welcome sight."

Merry smiled. "I know this is your special get-away-from-the-matriarch hideout. Plus, with all that just happened, I wasn't sure if it was okay to bother you out here."

Lizzie grinned, though her eyes were still a little red. "I'm that transparent, huh? My underground railroad is always open and willing to accept more refugees."

Merry looked down nervously at her hands, the light from the house behind them glinting off the modest diamond on her finger. "I wanted to talk to you about Collin. I just wanted to make sure you're fine with everything that's happening." Lizzie thought hard for a moment, trying to find a safe response, but Merry mistook her hesitation and rambled, "I just want you to know if I had known about the two of you, I never would have gone out with him. It's just so odd that things happened as they did, and I really feel like this is right, and . . . I mean, I'm glad you have Will now, but I don't want this to come between us."

Lizzie bit her lip. "Well, I'm not so sure that I have Will anymore, but believe me when I say that Collin never can come between us, Merry," Lizzie assured her. She wanted to tell her that anything Collin had said was pure fantasy, but she held her tongue. He was, after all, her future brother-in-law, and she needed to get used to it. "Collin's reality and mine are very different," she said in an effort to be diplomatic. "I never viewed him as anything other than an interesting home teacher, and if I said anything to mislead him, I apologize. I really want the best for you two. I want each of you to be happy, I truly do. But this brings me to my question for you, Merry Bright 'Pookie-Doo' Benson," she teased, using Merry's childhood nickname. She wrapped her arms around Merry's neck in a sideways hug, growing serious. "Do you really love this man enough, after only a week, to want to marry him in the temple? Forever is a long, long time, and one mistake now can mess up your eternity. The way you were crying today made me wonder if you were having second thoughts."

Merry rested her head on her older sister's shoulder. "You know, I'm not really all that romantic. I never believed in love at first sight. I'm far too pragmatic for that. But there is something magic about the way he speaks, the way he looks at me." She kicked her legs back and forth, and the swing began to sway as she continued, "On our second date, when we went hiking, he started saying things about me being a queen and how I deserved to be treated as one. At first I thought he was insane. *Me*, a queen? How hokey can you get! That should be a top-ten Mormon pickup line." She laughed at the memory. "But I started to realize that he was right. I am a daughter of our Heavenly Father, with a royal legacy, and I deserve to be treated like a queen. And he does that. He is such a gentleman."

"It takes more than being a gentleman to make a marriage work," Lizzie chided her gently. "This isn't just about getting married. A wedding is one day of what can be a very long life. No one really stops to think about what happens after that."

Merry sat up and pulled away. "Collin is a good person, Lizzie. I am in love with him. People fall in and out of love every day, in a day or a moment or in the blink of an eye. It will take a long time to learn to love him like Mom and Dad love each other. I think my chances of loving him and being happy in the eternities are just as good with him as with any other man I might meet in the future. My chance is now, and I have to take it." She smiled and looked up at the sky. "You know my nature, Lizzie. This might be the only chance I get."

Liz hopped up and put her hands on her hips, staring at her younger sister in consternation. "How can you say that? Merry, you have so much to offer! If you're marrying Collin just because you think you won't get another chance—"

Merry cut her off. "I'm not saying that, Liz. I said I have as good a chance as being happy with him as with anyone. This is right for me, and he says it's right for him. We both have prayed about this, and we both feel this is where the Lord wants us to go. You can't fight the Lord when it's right. Even when it feels crazy, like marrying some man you've known only a week, the Lord will bless you for your righteous effort and unblinking faith."

Lizzie sat back down, mulling over her sister's words. "You're very wise for one so young," she said. They began rocking together again, enjoying the gentle sway and the silence. After a long time, Lizzie leaned over and rested her head against her sister's. "Then I wish you all the happiness in the world, Merry. I think if anyone deserves it, you do." Her eyes twinkled as she added, "And you will be greatly blessed in the next life for being able to live with a man like Collin Light."

Merry smiled again. "I'm glad you're fine with all this, Liz. I was really worried when mother told me how you reacted to the news."

"You know me when I get no sleep. Completely irrational. I would have been much better able to handle the news if she had called me at two in the afternoon and told me my younger sister was getting married to some guy she had only known a week. It's all in the timing."

Merry laughed a bit. "Lizzie, I'm sorry for what Mom did this afternoon. She had no right to say those things in front of Will," she said softly. Lizzie looked in her sister's eyes and saw true sympathy.

"Thank you, Merry. That means a lot."

A World Falls Apart

LIZZIE felt the summer heat with a little more intensity than she usually did. Her classrooms felt like saunas, and she wondered to herself, a little bitterly, if some of her summer-school tuition money should have been used to pay the air-conditioning bill.

Two weeks had passed since the incident at her parents' house. Her relationship was different with Will now. She couldn't define the difference, but she was emotionally distraught over her mother's behavior and his sudden reaction to it and she was still fuming over it all. Will had seemed to vanish afterward, and she hadn't seen or spoken with him in several days. Jana was still in Oxford, and Robyn was away at the beach with her family. Lizzie had no one to vent, whine, or cry to. She felt all alone in the desert.

She trudged down the steps from her final class of the day, ready to hike back to the convertible. She debated about whether or not she should try to contact Will at the Huntsman Corporation. He had given her the phone number, but he was only an intern, and she didn't want him to get in trouble for taking personal calls. Besides, she thought, if he wanted to speak with her, he knew where to find her! Just as the thought crossed her mind, she noticed a tall figure standing next to the glass door near the exit of the building. She stopped and squinted for a moment despite the dark sunglasses she had just put on and realized that Will was standing next to the door, waiting for her. As she approached, he shifted his weight uneasily, his hands in his jeans pockets, shoulders hunched, rocking from side to side. He looked uncomfortable, but gave her a confident smile and a warm hug when she reached him and said hello.

"Hey, it's been a while," he said lamely, shoving his hands back into his pockets. "Can I walk you back to your car?"

Liz nodded mutely and waited for him to say something enlightening. After a few moments of pointless chitchat, they reached the convertible. As she pulled the top down on her car and tossed her backpack inside, she quickly decided to change tactics and be as cheerful as possible. "I guess you've been busy lately. How do you like it at Huntsman this time around?"

"I love it," he told her enthusiastically. She could tell he really meant it. "How are things with you?"

She shrugged as she tried to lean back nonchalantly on the car, then yelped at the heat of it and jumped away. "Aye! That's hot!"

He smiled. "I was hoping we could do something together," he said suddenly. He looked down but raised his eyes to look at her. "I kind of miss you."

She raised her eyebrows. "Kind of?" she teased. "Not desperately?"

Will grinned at her, putting his arm around her and pulling her closer to him. "I really missed you. Are you busy tonight? I was hoping we could go play mini-golf and get some pie at Cherry Hill."

Liz debated internally for one long moment. She resented that he would show up out of nowhere after disappearing for over a week and expect her to drop everything to do something with him. As she looked up into his gorgeous brown eyes and saw the sincerity and hope as he awaited her answer, she melted. And it wasn't just from the dry summer heat. "I think we could do that. What time?"

"I'll pick you up around seven. Does that sound good?"

"Perfect," she replied with a smile, and began planning her outfit and accessories.

He leaned down to give her a gentle kiss on her forehead before pulling away and opening her door for her. "I'll see you then."

✳ ✳ ✳

"Oh, no. No you don't!" Liz scolded as they set their golf clubs back on the counter after the eighteenth hole at Cherry Hill's mini-golf course. "I don't believe for a minute that you threw the game for me. I won fair and square! You just need to admit it. Get over it, boy. You just got your tail whipped by a girl! Your business-school buddies would die of shame."

"I admit nothing," he said. "I was trying to be gallant." They had walked from the counter past the snack bar, where the water slides snaked above the walkway down to the exit pool at the bottom. As someone slid past on the curve just above them, a large splash of water sailed over the edge and soundly drenched Will as he made his excuses.

Liz burst out laughing. "You look very gallant when you're all wet. You know what I think? I think that's your punishment for refusing to tell the truth and admitting that I kicked your hind end on the golf course."

He looked at her through the water dripping from his hair and into his eyes and sputtered as he wiped his face with his hand. Liz ran back up to the snack bar to grab some napkins.

"Thank you," he said as she handed them to him.

She smiled at him indulgently as she patted his shoulder dry. "You are adorable when you're wet."

He took her hand, grasping it tightly as they walked back under the slides and past the camping spaces to get to the Pie Pantry. "I'm so glad we could get together tonight, Liz. I really missed you. I don't want us to go that long without seeing each other again." She was silent as he ordered a slice of apple pie with some vanilla-bean ice cream. They found an unoccupied picnic table and sat across from each other, each with a spoon, sharing the slice. They were quiet for a moment as they savored the warm pie à la mode. Liz finally found the courage to ask, "So why did we go that long without speaking?"

Will thought for a moment. "Honestly?"

"Yeah, honestly," Liz responded. "What happened?"

"I realized that you haven't learned how to love yet, and it's because of your family."

The blunt force of his words nearly knocked the wind out of her. She tried to catch her breath. "Excuse me?" she asked incredulously, the expression on her face begging for clarification, hoping that he would alter his words or make them sound better than they just did.

"After meeting your family and seeing how they behave, I realized that you haven't really learned how to love anyone, and it scares me. You are dating because that is what you think you are supposed to do. You aren't with me because you are in love. You have just met a guy that fits the formula. I wasn't sure if I wanted to continue in a relationship with you," Will said calmly and evenly.

Shocked and humiliated, Lizzie stared silently at Will. She didn't know how to respond. How could the only person she had been in love with sit there and tell her that she didn't know how to love? If he had said that her mother was rude and offensive, she could understand. If he had ranted about what a spoiled brat LeAnn was, she could have taken that. But to say she couldn't love? Lizzie felt the world closing in around her and her chest tightening. She fought back the tears building up in her eyes.

"Excuse me?" Lizzie managed to repeat in a strangulated whisper.

"It's not your fault. It is just the way you were raised. I think you have always felt secretly insignificant because you didn't have a boyfriend. Your mom made you feel that way. Your upbringing is the reason you are so jaded and tough around the edges," he said simply. His tone was so inconsequential, and he couldn't see the anguish his brutal opinion caused her.

"I'm insignificant? I'm tough around the edges?" Lizzie said, defiance building in her voice. "What did I ever do to you?"

Will looked inside the blue eyes that were glaring back at him and began to realize he had just made a mistake. "Liz, it's okay now. It doesn't bother me."

Full of indignation, her voice rising, Lizzie said icily, "I don't know how to love, but it's okay because it doesn't bother you now? I'm sorry, Will, but I don't quite follow your logic! Care to elaborate?"

"Honey, let me explain . . ." Will began.

"Honey? I don't think so, William I'm-so-smart-and-humble Pemberley. How about you just tell me exactly what it is that makes you so smart about my upbringing, especially considering that you spent about one hour of your life with my family? The picnic was a total catastrophe; is it really fair to judge us based on that day? And I would like to point out that you have never seen or met Jana. You don't know anything about us." Lizzie slapped back the arm he attempted to put around her shoulder.

Taking a deep breath and a big step back, Will tried to explain. "After meeting your mother and seeing what your other two sisters are like, I realized that you hold your emotions in because there is no one around who understands them. After seeing you all together, I realized why you are slow to love . . ."

"Okay, first I don't know how to love, and now I just can't share my emotions? Care to enlighten me on just how that works, all-knowing love guru?" Lizzie snapped. She had never been so hurt or offended in her whole life and her defenses were at an all-time high. When had she ever not loved Will? When had she ever held back her feelings for him? Why was he doing this to her?

"Lizzie, please. This is what I mean. The sarcasm."

"The sarcasm?" she repeated, taken aback. "What do you mean?"

"I love you. I love you for all your strengths, and I love you for your weaknesses. You just use this protective shell of intelligence and sarcasm to shield you from whatever you can't deal with." Will took in a deep breath. "Merry and Collin live in their own world, oblivious to how the real world works. They think they know so much more than everyone else, but their superior attitudes keep them from getting very far. They aren't actually in love yet, but they believe that they are both equally superior to the rest of the world and therefore good enough to marry each other. Your mother lives in a fantasy world where she ignores reality and the problems around her. She thinks if she pretends she doesn't see the problems then they must not exist. And I liked your dad, but he ignores the world. Yet who can blame him? If he were to acknowledge what is going on in his family he would have to tackle it alone. And LeAnn . . ." He blew out a puff of air, searching internally for the right words. "LeAnn thinks she owns the world. And because no one has the guts to try and confront her and set her straight, she's on a collision course with herself."

Lizzie's eyes narrowed. "Will, there is no way you can know anything about us, let alone be so prejudicial after meeting them only once. Getting an A in freshman psych doesn't make you qualified to analyze the rest of us."

Lizzie's voice began to rise, so Will pulled her away from the people going into the Pie Pantry. "Your mother can't see a thing wrong with what LeAnn does," he persisted. "If someone doesn't stop your sister, I can almost guarantee that she is going to end up in trouble. Your parents are lucky that you and Merry are such good girls, but I can tell LeAnn walks all over them. I'd hate to see anything bad happen to her, because those situations can rip a family apart, and if they aren't careful she's going to cause them a whole bunch of grief."

"Yeah, like your cousin Ryan?" she challenged, arms folded tightly across her chest.

For the first time, she saw a flicker of anger beneath his normally composed facade. "That's exactly my point!" His words exploded angrily.

"What does any of this have to do with my ability to love?" Liz asked coldly. Will hadn't said one thing about her family that she didn't already know, and she felt a little guilty for bringing up Ryan, an obvious sore spot. Despite that, she didn't see where he got off thinking he had the right to talk about her family like that. Each family was entitled to its own issues and the chance to work them out without the glaring eyes of unfair judgment.

Taking another deep breath, Will looked into Lizzie's eyes and saw the hurt and pain he had caused. "Liz, you have never known what it means to be loved."

"What do you mean?" she demanded as her throat tightened, using all her inner reserve to keep from yelling. "My mother may not be exactly what you think a perfect mother should be, and my family may be different than your perfect family Christmas picture, but I never once suffered from a lack of affection. My family loves me, and I love them.

We just show it differently. How can you even begin to tell me that I wasn't loved? And, yes, it was hard for me to admit that I cared about you, but I never once held back any feelings of affection for you."

"Most of your family is so concerned with themselves that you don't know what it is like to be unconditionally loved," he pressed, trying to clarify his words. "You know you love them, and you know that they love you. But you all love each other for the wrong reasons. Your family operates like a business. You do what you are told, and you are told that families love each other, so you do just that. You love each other, but you don't actually *feel* love. You have been slow to show your feelings to me because you have spent your whole life hiding your real emotions. Now that you feel something real, something sincere and strong, you don't know what to do with yourself."

Liz almost couldn't move and could not believe what had just come so easily out of Will's mouth. She stood up angrily, trying very hard not to hyperventilate. "Will, like it or not, my family is mine forever. We are definitely far from perfect, but part of who they are makes me who I am. And if you think they're so terrible, well, then I must be terrible too. Making a blanket judgment won't change anything about them. It won't change anything about me, except you." She stood quietly for a moment, looking into his eyes. She squared her shoulders and tossed her head back, full of quiet, pained dignity. "I think it's time to say good-bye," she said, almost in a whisper.

He sighed and ran his fingers through his short curls. Liz noticed he had recently gotten a trim and she tried very hard to forget how she loved to run her hands through his hair and play with those curls. She wished she could forget what her mother had said to him. She wished all of this had never happened. "Lizzie, you are taking this all wrong. You know how I feel about you."

"Do I?" She looked down, finding her keys in the zipped side pocket of her purse. "I'm new to this. If you truly love someone, do you say things like this and not care that it hurts them? My family is mine forever, Will, and I have to be loyal to them no matter what. So if you can't live with them, I can't live with you." She locked eyes with him for one moment, then smiled wryly at herself. Tears ran down her cheeks, and for the first time in her life, she was not ashamed of them. "But I guess this is no big deal. You'll get over it, right? You aren't into dating coeds anyway." Smiling one more time behind her tears, she whispered, "Good-bye, Will." Then she walked away. This time she was the one who didn't look back.

✳ ✳ ✳

To: Elizabeth.benson@uu.edu
From: jbenson47@email.byu.edu
Subject: I can't believe it!

Dearest Lizzie,

How are you holding up? I'm really surprised to hear what happened with Will. Of all the guys you have liked over the years, I liked him the best, even though I never met him. He seemed to make you so happy! I really thought the two of you were perfect for each other. When I get back we may have to dust off the ninja costumes and go polka-dot his car. Would that make you feel better?

I am trying very hard to enjoy the beauty and history here. I am learning so much in my classes and the people here are friendly enough, but I have not heard a thing from Austen. I hope you won't gloat too much when I tell you that I found out last week that Julie did end up going camping with the Youngs. Erin e-mailed me all about the trip, and it sounds like they had a blast. I hope you won't say "I told you so." You were so right! I can't believe the signs were right in front of me like that and I missed them. I guess you and I can be miserable together, even though we're thousands of miles apart. What else can I say? She's there with him now, and I'm here without him.

I can't believe I haven't heard from him once the whole time I've been gone. Not a single phone call, not even a lousy one-line e-mail. I feel very deceived by Erin and Natalie. I always thought we were good friends. I guess all I can do is wish them the best, if that's what he really wants. I never imagined that we would ever be with anyone but each other, but I love him enough to want the best for him. If she's it, then so be it. I truly want him to find happiness and joy, and I guess I didn't do that for him. But I just can't figure out where I went wrong.

I'm sorry this e-mail is so long and depressing! I should have told you something funny and made you feel better. Why don't you call me? I think we would both feel much better if we could just talk everything out.

Love, Jana

※ ※ ※

To: jbenson47@email.byu.edu
From: Elizabeth.benson@uu.edu
Subject: Stuck in an alternative universe

Dear Jana,

It was so nice to hear from you. I've been so wrapped up in my own little melodrama that I didn't even realize what was happening with you! I can't believe Austen hasn't written or called even once. This is one time when I don't like being right, so yes, you and I can be miserable together. Where's the double-fudge brownie ice cream when we need it?

I do have a very funny story to tell you, though. It is in perfect line with my love life in general; basically, it's unbelievable! But then, when I really think about it, this is more like what my love life was like before I met Will. Maybe I should have known things with him were too good to be true.

I went back to my own ward today for the first time in several weeks and arrived at the chapel about 20 minutes early for sacrament meeting. I found a nice, cushy, floral-covered chair in the foyer and settled down for a little light reading with some of the twenty flyers available on a nearby table. I probably should have been reading my scriptures. Maybe what happened next was my punishment for NOT reading them! I was halfway through a pink piece of propaganda pushing the summer sock hop, when a man I took to be about forty years old approached me. He had brown hair and an untrimmed goatee with flecks of gray in it. He had a few wrinkles around his eyes and a bad haircut that looked like a home job done with the #3 guard and an unsteady hand. His clothing was frumpy and wrinkled but more for a lack of attention to detail than anything else.

"Are you in this ward?" he asked while pointing to the empty chapel.

"Yes. I'm in the singles ward that starts next," I said politely, and returned to my pink propaganda.

His deep voice was just a little raspy, which added a few years to his appearance. "I'm going to the singles ward too. You've never seen me before. This is my first time." I remember that he did say his name, but I don't recall what it was, since I was surprised by his forceful way of saying "you've never seen me before."

I responded as nicely as possible. "Hi, I'm Liz Benson. I've been sort of MIA this summer, so I didn't realize you've never been here before. Nice to meet you."

At this point I could see he was giving me a thorough, head-to-toe, complete checkout. He looked at me the way a doctor examines a patient or possibly the way a potential buyer approaches a race horse. I felt like he might ask me to open wide so he could inspect my teeth. Instead he crossed the room and pulled one of the large mint-green armchairs across the foyer so that he was sitting directly in front of me, with his back to the center of the room. He gave me the once-over one more time. It was more than a little unnerving.

His inspection complete, he looked back up at my face, seemed to be contemplating something for a moment, then asked, "So how come you aren't married yet?"

Excuse me? Am I eighty? How did I not know that twenty-one was over the hill, except maybe at BYU? I thought about if and how I should respond, as a rather shocked look crossed my face. He continued, "I'm twenty-three and I want to get married before I'm twenty-four so I can move to Montana." And then he looked at me expectantly.

What's more surprising: that a man with wrinkles and gray facial hair was only twenty-three, or that to move to Montana you have to be married? Is there a law against being single in Montana? I wasn't sure what polite conversation required of me to say next, so as I was afraid of asking what kind of girl he was looking for, I went with Montana. "So you want to live in Montana?"

"Yes. They have nice people there," he replied very simply. And then he asked a truly frightening question, "Do you want to live in Montana?"

Terrified of where this conversation may lead, I faked an innocent reply and said, "I like it here. I want to live here."

He seemed intrigued, as if I were the first person ever to want to live in Salt Lake City. "Why?"

"I'm still finishing school." A safe answer, and true until December, right?

Suddenly he shifted in his chair so that he was leaning over and looked at me accusingly. "Do you have a dead-end job?"

"No, I'm on scholarship right now . . ."

He interrupted me harshly. "Do you have one of those dead-end jobs working for a fast-food place, flipping burgers and dropping fries or something?"

"No, I . . ."

"Because I won't marry a girl who wants a job like that. They say you can work at a job like that forever, but not if you go to Montana." He seemed very upset that fast-food joints don't allow job transfers to Montana.

"Oh," is all I said. How does one appropriately respond to something like that?

"Do you think I can find someone to marry today?" He looked at me as if he truly expected that I knew the answer, but I was afraid to say anything. Was he asking if I thought he could he meet someone today who would want to marry him eventually? Or did he mean to find someone to meet and marry today? Thankfully, I didn't have to answer him.

"Do you want to get married?" he asked bluntly.

Okay, maybe I would rather answer the other questions!

Was this "Will you marry me?" Or was this "Are you interested in the general concept of marriage?" Either way, I really didn't want to get into this topic with him.

"Elizabeth, my fair future sister-in-law, how does the world greet you this beautiful Sabbath day?" Collin called from across the foyer. I have never been so grateful to see that skinny little man in my life!

"Collin, hi! I'm good. How are you?" I introduced the two, and the guy kept giving Collin the look of doom. The usual friendly chatter began, and I kept it running smoothly. We got as far as the weather when Mr. Montana stood up abruptly. He looked upset. "Well, if you're not interested in marrying me, you could have just said so!" And off he stomped.

Bless Collin's little heart, he has never looked more confused. I'm sure this incident has cemented my reputation with him as the most determined flirt in the world, unrivaled even by our dear sister LeAnn. Maybe now he'll be convinced that I really, truly am over him. Ha! But if that's what it takes . . .

I must say I'm a little disappointed. I really had hoped that my first proposal would be more romantic than that. I'm not demanding Antelope Island sunsets, but outside the church foyer would be nice. Maybe you have to move to Montana to get that, though. I hear the people there are very nice.

Love, Lizzie

* * *

To: Elizabeth.benson@uu.edu
From: jbenson47@email.byu.edu
Subject: You rock!

Dearest Lizzie,

How can anyone stay sad with you around? Thank you, thank
you, thank you! I haven't smiled this much for a while.

Love, Jana

P.S. That didn't really happen, did it???

* * *

To: jbenson47@email.byu.edu
From: Elizabeth.benson@uu.edu
Subject: The tragic life that is my own

Wish it hadn't. See how many guys I have lined up to marry
me and whisk me away to a magical dream life of happily ever
after in Montana? Write me when you hear from Austen. I bet
an e-mail from him apologizing profusely and declaring his
undying love will beat mine into your inbox.

Who says I need Will? I am so over him. I'm feeling better
already.

Love, Lizzie

Some Time to Reflect

To an honest heart, finding love after losing it is far more complicated than just finding a new Friday-night companion. Roommates, sisters, and mothers can fill the social void. But a soul cannot be expected to not long for the happiness it once felt. And a soul that had found its match, a match nearly magnetic in longing, may never fully forget its attachment. To go from everything seeming so right to losing that in one unforeseen moment is not an easy thing to recover from. It can take days, weeks, years, or, for the truly lucky, minutes. Liz was not so lucky, though. She sat on the front stoop of her little one-bedroom apartment. A cool, late-evening breeze blew over her, and she gave an involuntary shudder as she sat and thought. She pulled her favorite old quilt around her more tightly and tried to clear her mind of all thoughts of Will. Okay, so she had fibbed to Jana. She was not over him; she was not feeling better. She was wallowing in her misery like a pig in the mire. And with all the chocolate she had consumed, she was starting to feel like one as well.

Behind her the screen door squeaked open and slapped shut, but she hardly noticed. Her roomie came outside and sat next to her, putting her arm around her protectively, resting her perfectly coiffed, blond, highlighted head on Lizzie's shoulder.

"I'm heading out now," Robyn quietly said, glancing quickly at her watch.

Liz looked surprised to see Robyn sitting next to her. She looked at the watch too. "It's pretty late, isn't it?" The face of Robyn's silver charm-bracelet watch showed the time at just past 10:30 p.m.

"The evening is young, Liz! There's a dance tonight at the institute. I don't suppose I could persuade you to come," Robyn offered hopefully.

Lizzie snorted and shook her head bitterly. "No thank you! That's the last place I need to be right now."

Robyn looked at her gravely and admonished her, "Please don't sit out here and mope all night. Go rent a movie, or use my home spa kit and give yourself a facial and a pedicure."

Liz smiled at her and gave her a hug. "I will, I promise. I won't sit here all night. I'm just enjoying the twilight. This is the best time of night, when the sky turns purple and all the stars come out. I just need a quiet night."

"But that's all you've had lately, sweetie," Robyn told her quietly.

Liz turned to look in the driveway as a black SUV with tinted windows pulled up. The horn honked. She stared back at Robyn with irritation. "Who is that? Can't that brainless idiot see you're sitting right here?"

Robyn grinned excitedly as she hopped up and clutched her little purse tightly. "It's Dave, so we don't care so much about the brain department. We just care that he's here."

Liz smiled at her in surprise and delight. "Football-team Dave?"

Robyn nodded, unable to contain her exhilaration. "We've been talking at church a lot, going out after FHE, and talking on the phone and stuff, but this is our first official public appearance together. How do I look?"

"Fabulous! Have fun tonight!" Lizzie smiled, noticing her roommate's sparkling earrings and new blouse. Robyn had a kick in her step and a glow in her face that she usually didn't have. Lizzie was happy for Robyn and yet instantly stung by her own sadness at the same time. What had happened to her Romeo?

"If I see Will at the dance, I'll make sure I spill something on his pants," Robyn called to Lizzie as she hopped into the SUV. Dave waved at Lizzie as he tried to redeem himself for honking by opening Robyn's door for her. He jogged back to the driver's side and revved the engine before backing out.

Lizzie laughed and shook her head. "Not necessary!" she called back, a little too late. Robyn cheerily waved good-bye as they sped away. She shrugged. Why did she care if Will got spilled on? She was no longer a part of his life. *And here I am again,* she thought angrily to herself. *Why do I always end up back at this miserable spot? Why can't I forget about him?*

Lizzie walked back in the house, wrapping her quilt tighter around her, and crashed down on the couch. All the lights were off in the living room, leaving an empty feeling to the little house. The sad brunette pulled herself into a ball under the blanket, staring into the empty darkness around her. No matter how hard she tried, her thoughts always turned back to Will and what he said about her not being able to love. She still didn't know if he was right or not.

Lizzie rolled onto her back and let the tears roll down her face. Was she that bad of a girlfriend? Was she that difficult to get along with? What had she done to make him think she didn't know how to love?

"Grrr! Who says it has to be my fault? This is stupid! He was my boyfriend for hardly any time at all! It couldn't have been love. We hardly knew each other. I need to get over this! Moping about what happened will not solve anything!" Only the darkness could hear her, but somehow the sentiments seemed more real said out loud and not just in her head. "So then why do I miss him?"

It's not as if he was a huge part of my life, she told herself. She had been alive for twenty-one years now, and Will had been a very small part of those twenty-one years, a very small part of what hopefully would be many, many more years to come. So why was everything associated with him now? She had thoughts and memories of many places, but now those memories were gone, replaced by images of Will and memories of what they had done together. The steps of the institute building were no longer just steps—they were the first date, where Liz was sure he would have kissed her. Her car. Her favorite park, where he had kissed her. It was all about him now, and she wanted so much to erase it all from her mind, but it seemed like her timeline was now Before Will and After Will.

Will's monologue continued to run through Lizzie's head. She convinced herself that she had misjudged him. She had always thought he was understanding and caring, but now that she had seen the real Will, she knew the truth. Maybe the Will she had seen at the water fountain at the dance was the real William Pemberley and he had decided to have a little fun toying with one of those despised coeds for a fun extracurricular summer project. Maybe he was only interested in taking care of himself and spouting his hurtful opinions to validate his own self-righteousness. Maybe he had little or no respect for other people's feelings or lives. Maybe he thought he was perfect and had to show others where they fell short of his mark; the fact that he could so easily attack her family without taking time to get to know them proved it.

She sat up and rubbed her eyes, refusing to let any more tears fall for Will. He was not worth wasting any more time or energy. There were far more important things to think about now. She tried to focus on Robyn and be happy for the new development in Robyn's life. She thought ruefully that her roommate had probably been excited and happy about Dave but was too kind to tell Liz in her misery. She refocused her mind briefly and let herself be happy. Going "public" at LDS singles functions was huge! If they were to break up now, one of them, by unwritten singles ward code, had to change wards or go to the family ward so they could erase the "damaged" brand from their respective foreheads and get back on the LDS dating trapeze.

That was why Liz was not at the dance pulling a LeAnn and trying to feel better by flirting shamelessly with any and every male character who walked by. She and Will had gone public way too soon, and she dreaded the poorly hidden glares, clucking tongues, and mock sympathetic glances in her direction. She knew all the girls would jump at the opportunity to date Will; he was probably dating again already. The girls at school wouldn't waste any time getting him back on the singles circuit. She had received several dirty looks from some and had been approached by others who wanted to know what was up with the two of them. She let them guess, of course. It was much more fun that way.

Her mind wandered back to the institute waterskiing party they had gone to a few weeks before at Echo Reservoir. She had worn a tank top over her black racer-back swimsuit, cut-off denim shorts, and a camping hat. She was surprised at how many girls had gone to such great lengths to do their hair and makeup when they were just going to get wet. Many had fancy sarongs and cover-ups and coordinating beach towels and beach bags, and Liz had felt completely out of place from the start. Robyn had been there, flirting outrageously with Dave, and Will was running around madly trying to get things organized. She had found a spot in the shade, away from the beach, and she curled up on her towel and let herself get lost in a book. She planned to go waterskiing later, but for that moment she was content to sit back and ignore the mayhem.

It hadn't been five minutes before two girls plopped down next to her. "Whatcha reading?" one with pink sunglasses asked.

"The complete works of Jane Austen," Lizzie explained, slightly baffled why these two girls would want to join her. They seemed to make the rounds pretty well with the guys, but she had never seen them speak to any other girls. "Right now I'm in the middle of *Pride and Prejudice*."

"Wow, no wonder Will likes you so much," the other one said. Her scanty tankini looked rather worn near the straps. Lizzie wondered if she realized it might fall off at any moment. "You're, like, way smart!"

Liz raised an eyebrow as Pink Sunglasses pulled a face. "Oh my gosh, when Brother Light was our home teacher he would not shut up about that book! I'm sick of hearing about it." She extended her hand and smiled brightly. "I'm Charlotte, and this is my sister Mariah."

Liz smiled to herself. If only they knew what she knew! "Nice to meet you. Liz Benson."

"So, Liz, do you and Will hang out a lot?" Mariah asked, abruptly changing the subject.

Liz had no idea how to respond. "Why do you want to know?" she blithely asked.

"Because, there are like, tons of girls who want to hook up with Will, but he's, like, the untouchable man," Charlotte explained. "I mean, we see you guys together all the time but no one knows if you're dating or friends or what. So what's the deal?"

"I'm really surprised you would ask something like that, since we don't even know each other," Liz told them frankly.

"Come on!" Mariah begged. "Doesn't it make you feel cool to know everyone is talking about you and all the girls want to *be* you? Everyone is dying to know."

She smiled coolly. "Invite me to the funeral."

Charlotte looked at her oddly, unsure of what to do next. Liz let them know the conversation was finished by returning her attention to her book, and the two got up and left. She sighed as Will came up from behind and laughed as he sat down next to her.

"That was one of the funniest things I've seen in a long time," he told her as he stretched his lean, tan legs out in front of him.

Liz wanted to die! "You saw that?"

"Yes, I did. Do you feel cool now?" he teased. She shook her head and covered her eyes. He scooted a little closer to her, and nodded toward the collection of girls in sarongs and toe rings who were now gathered around Mariah and Charlotte. "You know they're all talking about you now."

"I figured," she sighed, grateful to see Robyn had joined them. Maybe Robyn would help her by dishing out some new, outrageous gossip and deflect the attention away from her. Robyn was always good for a new, juicy tidbit.

"Well, I say we give them something to talk about!"

"Will, no!" she shrieked as he picked her up under her knees, tossed her down, and started wrestling with her in the sand. She pounded his chest with her fists, but the struggle continued while people turned to see what the commotion was all about. Robyn grinned, and others looked on.

Suddenly Brother Webb appeared almost on top of them, looking down, hands sternly placed on his hips, shaking his balding head. "Will, this is embarrassing! Do you want everyone to see that this girl can take you down?"

Will sat up in protest as Liz raised her hands in triumph. "Oh, yes!" she howled.

"That's why she's my girlfriend."

Liz looked at him in surprise while Brother Webb nodded approvingly. "I agree. You need someone to kick you in the tail every now and again." He clapped his hands together. "Is the 'first couple' ready to go out on the boat?"

Will conspicuously took Liz by the hand and walked to the boat with her. He helped her in, then got her a life jacket while others climbed in and Brother Webb revved the boat, the propeller sputtering and spitting water out the back end. And that was it. They were official. They'd gone public.

They joined the two sisters Mariah and Charlotte in the boat, along with two guys from Will's ward. Lizzie watched Mariah and Charlotte try to put on their best charms for the two guys. She had to admit, they were good-looking guys; at least the two sisters had good taste in men. When Mariah, the one in the worn tankini, got to the reservoir, she went out skiing. When she tried to ski out of the wake, she turfed it and snapped one of her straps. She was hysterical, but Liz calmly wrapped her in a towel and sat next to her while they drove back to the beach, Mariah clutching her suit tightly to her chest. Will had watched as she escorted her to where Liz kept her purse. Lizzie had a mini sewing kit in one of the side pockets, one of the many insane tricks she claimed to have picked up from her mother, and she sewed Mariah up. In less than five minutes the suit was fixed, Mariah was off flirting with some guys in the hot dog line, and Liz got back in the boat. "When was the last time I told you that you were way beyond perfect?" Will whispered in her ear as she sat down beside him. She smiled up at him, and he wrapped his arm tightly around her. *Having a boyfriend may not be half bad after all,* Lizzie thought to herself and quickly stole a little kiss from Will.

Lizzie sighed at the memory as she got up from couch and walked in her blanket cocoon towards the kitchen. She found a package of light popcorn and stuck it in the microwave. She stared numbly at the eerie green light coming from the microwave before the popping sounds jolted her back to life. Remembering where she was, she helped herself to some of Robyn's diet soda, then collapsed onto the couch and tried to stop dwelling on all the memories that refused to leave her. It was late, but she picked a pointless screwball comedy from Robyn's collection and put it into the DVD player. She needed to forget and laugh at something completely mindless. She could deal with reality tomorrow.

Maybe she would get up and try the ward activity tomorrow. She hadn't been to an activity in her own ward for two months since she had been attending Will's for the summer. When she first started going with Will, Liz could only think of how out of place she felt. She had confided to him almost right away about the awkwardness. He knew people were talking about them, and he hoped to avoid more gossip by making it clear that they had come together. As institute president, he was a very public figure in Latter-day Saint campus life, and people enjoyed talking about his dating life, for whatever odd reason. He didn't know why, and he really didn't care.

Or at least that is what I used to think. I don't know what to think now. All I know is that he doesn't want to be with me, unless I learn how to love the right way. Whatever! Lizzie thought to herself. She could feel the tears falling down her face again, soaking the pillow beneath her. She pounded her fist into the pillow. She hated letting this control her! She had to conquer it!

Lizzie sat up with renewed determination and turned the pillow over to the dry side. Laying her head back down, she promised herself that this would be the last night of Will. She would allow herself to think of him for one last time. But in the morning, she would be over him and life would go on.

* * *

THE phone suddenly rang, jolting Lizzie out of a fitful sleep. "Hello?" she mumbled as she grabbed the receiver, looking at the clock. Just past midnight. She grabbed the remote to turn the movie off so she could hear better.

"This is the operator. Will you accept a collect call from LeAnn?" a recorded voice asked.

Lizzie said yes and then heard, "Lizzie, is that you?" LeAnn's feeble voice came from the other end of the line.

"LeAnn, what's wrong? Are you okay?" Something in LeAnn's voice sent all of Lizzie's radars up. Her baby sister had never called before, and the late hour and sound of her voice frightened Lizzie as never before.

"I need your help. Please come get me." LeAnn's wavering voice faltered and she burst into tears.

"LeAnn, what happened? Where are you?" Lizzie reached for her keys and purse and began walking towards the door.

"It's not my fault, Liz. He said we were going to get married!" LeAnn said between sobs.

"*Who did?* What are you talking about? Where are you?" Lizzie demanded, panic rising with each word.

"I'm at a gas station in Mesquite," LeAnn sniffled. "Please come get me."

"Don't go anywhere. I'm on my way."

Lizzie ran out the door, forgetting to put on shoes. She didn't care that she was only wearing loose-fitting exercise shorts and a baggy T-shirt. She got all the way to her car when she remembered to turn back, grab her flip-flops, and lock the front door in one mad dash. Sprinting back to the car, she slammed the door shut, catching her purse in the door. Frantically she opened the door again, threw her purse in the seat next to her, jammed the key into the ignition, kicked the clutch into place, and . . . nothing. Lizzie's shoulders slumped over, and she slammed her hands on the wheel.

"Start, dang it! Start now!" Lizzie yelled at her inert car. "This isn't happening to me!"

"Hi, Liz."

Lizzie heard a knock at her window and jumped. She looked up and saw Will standing there with a confused look on his face. "Are you okay?"

"I'm sorry, Will, I can't talk to you right now. I'm in a hurry! I have to go!" Lizzie fought back the urge to cry. How could this be happening? How could he be here at this moment? So much to say and think and do, and no way of knowing how to begin.

"I stayed up all night last night studying and just got off a late night at work. I should be sleeping now, but I wanted to talk to you. Do you have a minute?" Will looked at her sincerely.

"I'm sorry, but I really can't talk right now, Will. This is a really bad time." Lizzie couldn't fight back the tears anymore. She tried again to get the car to start, but nothing happened. Not even a courtesy "chink-chink" noise. The convertible wasn't going anywhere.

Will's sincerity turned to concern. "What's going on, Liz?" He opened up her car door and offered a hand. She took it and stepped out of the car. "Get in my car. Wherever you need to go, I'll take you." She did as she was told and walked over to Will's car and climbed in. She sat there silently, staring straight ahead. He sat down in the driver's seat, poised to start the car while she sat and said nothing. Resting his hands on the wheel, he prompted her, "Lizzie, this would probably go better if you told me where we are going."

Lizzie sighed, not sure what she should tell him. Wasn't this the same Will who had warned her that her sister was headed for trouble? Now here he stood, at the perfect moment to say, "I told you so," and rub it in her face. She probably wouldn't blame him for it, either. But this was her Will. Despite everything that had happened, she could never lie to him. "It's LeAnn. She just called me collect and said she's stranded at a gas station in Mesquite."

The corners of his eyes conveyed weariness as he digested what she had told him. She prepared for his lecture, but was surprised when he started his car and jerked it into reverse.

"What are you doing?" she asked.

"We're going now."

"But you don't have to . . ."

He looked over at her, pausing for traffic at the end of the driveway. She saw the anguish in his own eyes as she searched them, looking for reasons why he would do this at a moment's notice. "I know that, but she needs us and we're going."

Great Irony and Revelation in the Virgin River Gorge

JUST past St. George, a beautiful expanse of majestic rock and river weaves its way through the mountainous region that separates the land of Zion from the rest of the world. Lizzie usually loved this part of the drive. She recalled many family drives where she and her father would try hard to ignore the incessant chatter from her mother and LeAnn, and would marvel at the geologic formations and at the engineering feats that managed to perch a treacherous, curvy road precariously on the steep cliffs of the Virgin River Gorge.

This time it was different. She glanced over at Will, and her heart broke just a little. He was so kind and selfless. She couldn't help but feel guilty for all the horrible things she had thought about him just a few hours ago, thoughts motivated by anger and selfishness. The light reflecting off the rearview mirror revealed his bloodshot eyes with dark circles beneath them. When he came to her house to talk, and most likely officially break up with her, hadn't he said he had been up all night studying for an exam? And then spent the entire day at work? That would mean he had gone nearly two days without sleep, and now he was going on his second sleepless night to help her rescue her sister. She shook her head and looked away, trying to hide her tears. How could he do something so generous for her when their relationship was over? *I guess this is what the gospel is all about,* she thought to herself. *Selfless service without question.* The Savior would have done as much, and as quickly. Will proved to her yet again what an amazing person he was—a person who deserved much more in a girlfriend, and a wife, than she could offer. It was better for him to find that out now.

Lizzie heard the syncopated blinks of the turn signal, and she realized that they had reached the exit LeAnn had indicated in her hysterical phone call. She bolted up in her seat and anxiously searched the parking lot of the gas station that lay just off the exit ramp.

Will pointed to a girl at a table just inside the convenience store window, visible from the road. "Is that her?" he asked.

"Yes, that's her!" Lizzie cried. She didn't even wait for the car to come to a complete stop before she pushed open the door and ran for her sister. LeAnn had seen her flying across the parking lot and ran for her too, nearly colliding with her, sobbing. All the pent-up energy and stress finally bubbled over in Liz as she burst into tears as well, wanting to hug and kiss and strangle her sister all at the same time. "What on earth were you thinking?" she yelled when she regained her composure.

Will pulled them into the store. "Why don't you two run into the bathroom and get cleaned up?" he instructed. "Wash your faces, do whatever you need to do. I'll get some caffeine so we can make the drive home." He glanced at his watch. "It's 5:00 a.m. right now, and it will be around noon when we get back to Salt Lake." He raised his eyebrows questioningly as he looked to Liz. "Unless you want me to run you up to your parents' house."

Liz shook her head as LeAnn headed into the bathroom. "No, I can't ask you to do that. You've already gone above and beyond the call." She felt herself losing her composure once again, but she struggled to stay strong. She did not want him to see her cry again. "Thank you, Will," she whispered.

He bowed his head as he cupped her chin in his hands and tilted her face up to look at him. "You know there's nothing I wouldn't do for you, Liz." Her lower lip started to quiver as he pulled her into a hug. It felt so good to be there. She wrapped her arms around him and relished being in his arms one more time. She looked up at him and saw him looking back at her. She wanted to kiss him. Oh, how she wanted to kiss him! Instead, she pulled away and searched his eyes for a moment before turning around and going into the bathroom to wash her face.

When she came back out, Will had gassed up the car and had three extra-large sodas waiting for them in the cup holders. LeAnn, face freshly scrubbed, bounced into the backseat cheerfully and buckled up, while Lizzie slid into the front and clicked in.

"Ooh, what do we have here?" LeAnn asked pertly. "Mountain Dew?"

Lizzie shot a reproving look at her while Will accelerated and sped up the entry ramp to I-15. "Root beer for you, young lady," he answered. "The drivers, however, may need to visit their bishops and discuss the Word of Wisdom after consuming their beverages."

Lizzie smiled at him, then turned back to face LeAnn, who looked out the window, watching intently despite the fact that it was pitch black and she could see nothing but the dark shadows of the mountain. "So?" Lizzie prompted her sister, ready for an explanation.

LeAnn looked back at her innocently. "What?"

Lizzie's brow furrowed. "Are you going to offer me any kind of explanation about why we had to drive several hours to save you after you were abandoned in a parking lot outside Mesquite?"

"He's such a jerk. I can't believe he left me here," LeAnn responded bitterly. Then she fell silent.

"LeAnn Valoy Benson!" Lizzie exploded. "What is wrong with you? You take off without telling anyone, wind up in nowhere Nevada, and now you're complaining about a guy? What is going on here? What are you thinking?"

Will put his hand on Lizzie's shoulder. "Calm down, Liz. She'll tell us when she's—"

"We were going to Vegas to get married," LeAnn said a little too simply.

Both Will and Liz grew silent. Will put both hands back on the wheel and steered silently while Lizzie processed what she had just heard.

Lizzie took a deep breath. "LeAnn, you are sixteen years old. You are barely old enough to date yet, let alone get married. What made you think you could just run off and get married?"

LeAnn glared back at Lizzie. "Who died and made you my mother? I don't need you to tell me what to do." LeAnn turned her head and looked out the window again.

Anger, disbelief, and total outrage built up in Lizzie. "Excuse me? LeAnn, you called *me* in the middle of the night to come rescue, and that is all you have to say? How about a 'thank you for saving my sorry butt'?"

"Right, whatever, thanks." LeAnn continued to stare out the window.

"Do Mom and Dad even know where you are?" Lizzie demanded. "And who were you going to marry?"

"It doesn't matter now, does it?" LeAnn just rolled her eyes. "And it was no one you know." It was a lie, and they both knew it.

Lizzie just about jumped into the backseat to wring her little sister's neck. She clenched the leather seat tightly to try to control her rage. "LeAnn, start talking now! Do Mom and Dad even know where you are?"

"No. They think I'm at youth conference."

Lizzie took a deep breath, closed her eyes, and recomposed herself. "You skipped out of youth conference to get married?"

She shrugged. "I didn't really skip out. I never even went. Youth conference is for goody-goodies," LeAnn said with a shake of her head, as if Lizzie were the idiot.

"You still haven't told me who the guy is." Lizzie clenched the seat so tightly that her fingernails left marks in the leather.

"Like I said, no one you would know." LeAnn turned her attention back out the dark window.

"It was Ryan, wasn't it?" Lizzie demanded reproachfully. She was blinded by her anger, but her heart softened a bit when she saw the hurt and anguish on her youngest sister's face. She tried so hard to hold in the tears that filled her eyes.

"It doesn't matter now who it was, because he's gone," she replied tersely, trying to mask her feelings. She turned away and buried her face in her hands, holding her sobs in. "We had a fight and he left."

"Lizzie, why don't you call your parents and tell them where we are and what happened?" Will interrupted calmly. Lizzie looked at him, sighed, and reached in her purse for her cell phone.

"You can't call Mom and Dad!" LeAnn yelled and snatched at Lizzie's cell phone.

"Excuse me?" Lizzie asked incredulously.

"They don't know where I am. You can't tell them!" LeAnn protested, still frantically grabbing at the cell phone.

"LeAnn, do you really think you can get away with this? You think that you can lie to Mom and Dad, run off and try to get married, and get stranded at a gas station, and that I'm *not* going to tell them?" Lizzie shook her head. "Little girl, you have lost it. Mom and Dad are probably sick with worry right now. They need to know!"

"You have no right to do that! Give me that phone!" LeAnn yelled and tried to push her way over the seat.

Will firmly but gently pushed LeAnn back down, skillfully managing to keep his eyes on the road at the same time. "LeAnn, she's calling your parents. They have every right to know where you are and what you have done. Sit down."

LeAnn looked as if she could spit on Will but instead just sat back and resumed staring out of the window. Lizzie took another deep breath and dialed her parents' number.

The phone rang once before Lizzie heard her father's voice. It was the wee morning hours, but Lizzie could tell she had not awakened her father. He sounded anxious as he said, "Hello?"

"Dad, it's Lizzie."

"Lizzie! Have you heard from LeAnn? She's missing and we're worried sick!" Her father's scared voice broke Lizzie's heart. "She didn't show up at youth conference, and she hasn't come home all night."

"LeAnn is with me, Dad. I'm sorry I didn't call you sooner. LeAnn is okay. Well . . ." Lizzie didn't know what to say next.

"What? She's okay! Why is she with you? What is going on?" Her father sounded relieved and confused at the same time.

"We're driving home right now, Dad. We're leaving Mesquite, Nevada," Lizzie replied, trying to cover the anger in her voice. Her father was clearly worried and upset, and she didn't want to make it worse.

"Mesquite? What are you doing in Mesquite? How did you get there?"

Lizzie looked at the unrepentant sixteen-year-old girl in the back-seat and decided not to tell her parents what had happened. "She's okay, Dad. I've got her and I'm bringing her home. I'll let her explain everything when we get there."

"Lizzie, is that you?" Her mother had gotten on the line. "Is she okay? We've been hysterical! What is happening?"

"Mom, it's okay. We have LeAnn with us. She's going to have a lot to tell you." Lizzie glanced back at LeAnn again before going on. She wasn't sure how much of LeAnn's story she should share, but if LeAnn didn't tell them the truth when they got home, Lizzie would fill in the gaps. "She called me tonight and asked me to come get her in Mesquite. We left immediately. She made some bad choices and realizes that now."

LeAnn snorted in the backseat. "As if . . ." she muttered under her breath. Will started to look like he may lose his temper with her as well.

"Mesquite? Why was she in Mesquite?" her dad inquired, puzzled, while her mother yelled at the same time, "Are you sure she's okay?"

"Dad, I'll let her tell you when she's ready," Lizzie restated.

"You keep saying 'we.' Who are you with?" her mother demanded.

"Will." Lizzie bit her lip.

"Will? Will Pemberley? What does he have to do with this? I thought you weren't speaking to him anymore!" her mother yelled.

Lizzie knew Will could hear everything they were saying. The crow's feet at the corners of his eyes wrinkled just a bit as he suppressed a rueful smile and shook his head, but he reached over and touched her hand supportively. They looked at each other for a moment, each knowing what the other felt. As he turned his eyes back to the road, she kept looking at him, full of gratitude, as she said to her mother, "Will drove all night to go rescue my sister, without me even asking him to. LeAnn is safe with us now, and we'll be there in a few hours, okay?"

"Tell Will thank you for me, Lizzie," her father said sincerely.

Lizzie looked at Will, who was still listening to her conversation. She raised her eyebrows and Will smiled. "Tell them to get some sleep and we'll be there in a few hours," he whispered.

"Okay, Dad. We'll be there in a few hours," Lizzie said, and then yawned. "Bye."

It was quiet once again in the car, except for the sound of the road beneath them. Soon the sound lulled LeAnn to sleep. Liz impulsively reached out to touch the curls at the back of Will's neck. She rubbed the tightness out of his upper shoulders, forgetting for a moment that they had been angry at each other, forgetting that they had fought. He relaxed visibly under her touch, but still kept his eyes on the road.

"You haven't done that for a while," he said quietly.

She smiled wryly. "I haven't seen you for a while."

He nodded. "It's been too long, I think. We do great things together, including but not limited to saving damsels in distress, whether or not they deserve it."

Liz laughed a little, glancing back at her sleeping sister. She reached around her waist to remove the sweatshirt she had tied around it, and tucked it around LeAnn. Her sister curled more tightly into a ball on the backseat and let out a little moan as she got settled. Lizzie turned back to the front and took a deep breath, letting out a long, sad sigh. "I still can't thank you enough for helping me. You are such a good person to do this, without question. You knew I needed help and you just did it. You willingly helped my sister despite the fact that she and my mother were rude to you." She wrung her hands in her lap. "I don't think I'll ever be able to repay you."

He reached over and took her hand. "I don't want you to repay me. I just want things to be like they were. One fight shouldn't change all that we have together."

Liz thought about that. So had they broken up? She wasn't sure anymore. "We had a huge fight, Will, and not about something trivial. You said I couldn't love. I know I'm not the greatest girlfriend, and I have a few things I need to learn before I am going to get any better, but what you said can't be ignored."

Will drove on silently without responding. Lizzie looked out the windshield at the long dark road ahead of them and wondered how this night would end. "I wish I could go back and take back what I said that night," he said softly.

"Don't we all?" Liz asked sarcastically. Will sighed in the darkness, accompanied by a long pause that made Liz fidget in her seat. She knew she had just said the wrong thing.

"Liz, before we go any further let's get a few things straight. I miss you. I love you. I want to apologize for what I said that night. I was wrong. I'm not perfect." He spoke slowly and in short spurts as he squelched his anxiety and expressed his thoughts.

Liz sat quietly watching the white line on the side of the road go by, unsure of what she should say next. Just a few hours ago, she had sworn to herself that she would never let herself think of him again. Now he was sitting here next to her, declaring his love. She wasn't sure she could form a cohesive thought and respond appropriately.

Fortunately, she didn't have to; he pressed on after her considered silence. "I have been miserable these past few weeks. And then I realized that I couldn't lose you." Will stopped speaking and glanced quickly at her to gauge her response.

Liz felt herself wavering between tears and anger. She bit her lip and found herself shaking her head. "Will . . ." she began, but the words jammed together in her throat. He reached over and took her hand. She didn't pull back.

"Will, I don't know what to say. Earlier tonight I thought I'd never see you or speak to you again. Now you want to take it all back and act like this never happened?" Lizzie felt a tear trickle down her cheek. She wiped at it with her free hand.

He shook his head. "No, I don't want to act like it never happened. That isn't possible. It happened and it won't be ignored, but I think we can be better for it in the future," Will said thoughtfully.

"How so?" she inquired.

He took a deep breath and let it out slowly, but still did not speak. "Are you cold?" he procrastinated. "Is the air conditioner too cold? You can change it if you want." Will nodded towards the control panel.

Liz shook her head in frustration. "I'm fine."

Sensing her annoyance, Will continued. "I know I told you that you couldn't love, but I was wrong." He paused not for effect, but because he felt her hand tense in his. "You do know how to love. You just don't know how to show that you love."

Liz released his hand and sat up straight in her seat. She took in a sharp breath and looked blankly through the windshield.

Will hung his head and shook it back and forth. "Wait, Liz that still isn't right. Let me try again."

Lizzie almost imperceptibly nodded her head and allowed a tear to roll off her chin.

"You show your love; I just didn't know how to read the way you show love. And you get scared easily in this relationship and try to hide your feelings sometimes—I think to protect yourself. Every date is a struggle with you. I feel like I have to chip through your tough exterior and get to the soft, mushy inside every time I see you. If I didn't know that soft, mushy inside was in there, I would have given up ages ago. But I fell in love with the mushy inside."

Liz didn't move, trying to digest his words but getting stuck on the word *mushy*. The white line continued to fly by as the road whizzed under the wheels.

"You have your own unique way of showing love. You are a discriminating personality, and I mean that in a good way. I think most couples probably have a problem with miscommunication at some point in their relationships. Not just misunderstanding each other, but sometimes not appreciating the way each shows their love." He glanced over at her again, wishing he could say this to her while looking in her eyes so she could see that his words weren't just words. "You carefully select who you will let into your own private world. That is the first way you show love: you let them in. I was thinking tonight, before I came over, of all the ways you show your feelings. You send cards and write love notes, and you e-mail your sister in England twice a day. I'm a doer. I do things to show my feelings. It's not that you don't know how to love. I was wrong when I said that. You do know how to love; I just didn't know how to see it yet." Will paused and squeezed her hand. "And maybe I wasn't ready to accept how in love we were yet."

Lizzie turned and looked at Will. This was not what she expected to hear.

"I thought I was ready for a new relationship," he continued briskly. "When I met your family and saw how serious they were about marrying you off as fast as possible, I got scared. I realized that maybe I wasn't ready yet. When I didn't see you, though, I realized that ready or not, I want to be with you." Will spoke confidently. Lizzie had never felt so scared and certain at the same time.

The silence in the car was deafening. Will began to wonder if his words mattered to her at all, if the damage was too great to be repaired.

"Mushy insides, huh?" Liz smiled at Will with one raised eyebrow.

"Would you prefer 'gooey'?" Will teased back, relieved she was smiling.

"I like to think I have a creamy, chocolate, cashmere inner core," she said slyly. "So I'm crunchy on the outside, chewy on the inside?" They both laughed.

She sighed as their laughter faded away. "You are right, Will. You didn't say anything I didn't already know. You're the first man I have ever loved, and I don't know how to handle that. Before you, I never showed my feelings to anyone, but I never realized that until now. I think we have a long road ahead of us." Her chest tightened as she realized the gravity of her words and the commitment she was about to make. "But it's a road I'm ready to travel with you. I love you, Will." She realized as she said it that she had never said those three little words to him.

Will picked her hand up and kissed it. "I love you too."

Lizzie felt the relief of a thousand-pound yoke lifted from her shoulders. She turned on the radio to keep them awake, but just knowing that things would be okay—with her sister and with Will—drained all the energy from her. The worst was over. She put her head on against the window and was asleep before she had a chance to say good night.

A Young Woman Faces Her Fate

"WOW," LeAnn commented as they pulled into her parents' driveway. "I never knew I was so popular. Welcome to the Benson used car lot."

Will pulled into the Benson driveway and turned off the car. He gently woke up Liz, who had been asleep for several hours. She lifted her head and looked around, feeling guilty for falling asleep and surprised to see how many people were there. She saw her mother's minivan parked halfway in the garage. Her father's small pickup was parked behind that; he must have called in to work, because usually he was gone at this time of day. Merry's car was on the grass, Collin's Euro van was parked neatly at the curb, and Bishop Young's car was behind it. Liz smiled ruefully at her sister. She knew LeAnn and her parents had a long, rough path to tread.

They had not gotten the car doors halfway open when the front door of the Benson home flew open and their mother came running to them, faster than they had ever seen her move. LeAnn's tough demeanor seemed to crumble when she saw her mother's tear-streaked face, and she ran to her. Soon her dad joined them, and Liz's eyes welled up once again when she saw the relief and anguish on his face as he crushed LeAnn to his chest, rubbing her hair, holding his wife and youngest daughter close.

Will turned to Lizzie. "If it's okay with you, I'm going to head back to Salt Lake now. Do you think you can get a ride back home?"

Lizzie looked at him questioningly and slowly nodded her head. "Yes, I think Collin can take me. Or someone else. Are you sure you don't want to stay? You need to get some rest!"

"This is a family affair. I'll just be in the way. And I'm ready for a nap," he admitted, "in my own bed. Call me when you get back to Salt Lake. We'll make sure we get your car fixed." With that, Will gently kissed Lizzie and got back in the car.

Merry and Collin stood in the shade of the front porch, waiting for everyone to come back in. Much to Lizzie's surprise, Austen appeared at the front door and came out to join her. He wasn't exactly a welcome sight, Lizzie thought, angry at him for hurting Jana.

"Hey, Liz." Austen attempted to greet her with a hug. "What's up with my second-favorite Benson babe?"

Lizzie hesitated a moment. "Austen, I've had three hours of sleep and a really bad night, so I'm just going to get down to it. Why haven't you called Jana?"

There comes a time in a man's life when he realizes that whatever it is he just did, he did it wrong. Austen Young took one look at the clearly aggravated Lizzie and realized that he was in the doghouse. Liz's voice was biting and angry, and he was not so sure he liked having that anger directed at him.

"I wrote her two letters, but they both came back to me," he stammered. "I lost her e-mail address, and I had the wrong phone number. I got some bookstore in England instead of her room." Austen looked at her very feebly, hoping that whatever it is he did wrong, he had just made it right.

Lizzie nodded broodingly. She believed him about the bookstore, since she had called the same bookstore by mistake herself. That still wasn't enough, though; he couldn't possibly think he was off the hook.

Austen figured he needed to keep explaining since Lizzie looked like she could bite. "So after I kept getting the wrong number," he rambled, "and couldn't e-mail, I just figured I would wait for her to get back. I mean, she'll be gone such a short time. I know she's coming back soon. I kind of wanted to surprise her at the airport."

Lizzie fumed. "It never occurred to you to get her info from me or any other member of my family, or even your sisters for that matter? Jana will be back in two weeks, Austen, but I'm not sure you should go get her at the airport. She thinks you are intentionally not writing or calling. What kind of an idiot are you?" Lizzie's exhaustion and exasperation clearly showed.

Austen looked even more guilty. Maybe there was some truth to what Lizzie said. "I didn't think it was such a big deal," he said meekly. "I went for lots of weeks without writing Jana on my mission."

Lizzie rubbed her eyes and let out a long sigh. *Silly, clueless boy.* Could she smack him and get away with it? "Austen, that was different. She understood that you were in the jungle back then. She never missed a week writing you, though. Now you have a computer and a telephone, not to mention ample time to write!"

Austen suddenly looked worried. "She really thinks I didn't write her on purpose?"

Lizzie shook her head in disbelief. With the little reserve energy she had left she confirmed, "Yes, Austen. She thinks you don't love her anymore."

Austen's panic set in. Finally! "Lizzie, you have to help me. I have to fix this!" he said desperately.

"Austen, again, I'm tired, so maybe I'm just a little confused. You go nearly two months with no contact, and you expect her not to think that something's wrong? And your sisters have made it pretty clear that you want to date other people, and . . ."

Austen started to laugh. "Is that what this is all about? My sisters trying to hook me up with Julie? Please, Liz, give me some credit for having a little taste. Julie just wants to get married, and I'm an easy mark. She'll take the next guy as easily as me. Let's just say she tried real hard at Yellowstone to . . . hmm, how can I say this tactfully?" He thought a minute. "I can't say it nicely. She tried real hard, but I made it clear that there is only one girl I want, now or ever. Does that make you feel better?"

"Yes!" Liz had never felt so relieved. "But you need to make it clear to Jana, not me! She hasn't heard one thing from you since she left, and she's really hurt. You promised to keep in touch and you didn't. That's not okay!"

"Liz, you know how I feel about Jana," he said quietly. "What can I do to make things right with her?"

"My advice?" She thought a moment. "Get your tail end on the next plane to England. And have a couple dozen roses, some balloons, a giant teddy bear, and lots of chocolate for her."

He laughed. "One of those big heart-shaped boxes of chocolates?"

"Definitely," Liz agreed. "The bigger the better. You know how cheap we Benson girls are. One good box of chocolates is enough to buy us off."

"You really think I need to fly to England? I just can't call her?" Austen asked anxiously.

"Do you want to lose her forever? Or do you want to prove you love her?" Lizzie said.

"I love her," Austen said with a little worry still in his voice.

"Then take a diamond ring too." Lizzie smiled at him. Austen looked at her and then smiled too.

"You think that will do the trick?" He laughed. "Okay, but what if a plane ticket is out of the question? I don't exactly have money or a job yet!"

"Well, then you better think of something quick. I'll even help you by giving you her phone number and e-mail address!" Lizzie teased as she smiled at Austen and then spontaneously reached up and hugged him.

"So was that Will in the car with you?" Austen said teasingly.

"Yes," Liz said shyly, unable to contain her smile.

"And? How are things going? I thought y'all broke up," Austen prodded.

"Looks like we're back together. Stay tuned!" Lizzie laughed and hugged Austen again, then suddenly remembered how tired she was. Things would work out for Jana and Austen. Things were working out with LeAnn, a little bit at a time. Merry and Collin would be an ongoing project, but she knew that at the very least she would always have odd anecdotes to tell about them. She smiled to herself. *My work here is done.*

* * *

"So even though you're just a little bit *too* domestic, girl—no offense or anything—you do make a mean glass of lemonade," LeAnn was saying to Merry as Liz woke up on the couch.

Merry beamed. "Thank you, LeAnn! I do try, and Collin loves it. Maybe I could teach you sometime."

Lizzie laughed as LeAnn's face fell. "Yeah . . . uh . . . right."

"What did Austen want to talk to you about?" Merry inquired when she saw Lizzie was awake.

"Austen," she mumbled sleepily and tried to recollect her thoughts. "He wants to marry Jana . . . !" She accepted the offered glass of lemonade from Merry and guzzled it down.

Merry's face showed confusion. "I thought they hadn't spoken since she went to Oxford."

"Really? That's so, like, bitter. Where have I been?" LeAnn asked.

"Mesquite," Liz quickly replied, eyeing her sharply.

"Ouch. That's harsh, Liz," LeAnn replied, showing little remorse.

"Austen now sees the error of his ways, with a little help from me, and he wants to make up for it," Liz explained, changing the subject. "I think it really was nothing more than a careless mistake. He's going to be working his tail off to show Jana how sorry he is. Trust me; I made sure of that!"

LeAnn grinned. "You tell it, girl! He better be good to Jana or we'll take him down, make him sorry he ever lived." Shaking her head, Merry pursed her lips in disapproval.

The girls looked up as their parents walked into the room. Their father sat down on the couch with a grim expression on his face. Their mother looked at LeAnn apologetically as she sat next to him.

"Your mother and I have been talking about what just happened, LeAnn, and we have decided to have a family council to decide your punishment."

"What?" she cried angrily. "I'm fine, no one got hurt, and the only wrong thing I did was tell a little lie."

"But that one lie could have had eternal consequences," Merry pointed out. "Too often we fail to see how what we do today has an impact on tomorrow, but it does."

"Whatever, Merry," LeAnn spat. "You don't know anything about real life. It's more than Personal Progress and enrichment night. You're totally clueless." Her eyes narrowed and she folded her arms as she sat back, refusing to make eye contact with anyone. "It's no big deal."

"Yes it is!" Brother Benson declared firmly. The strength, anger, and fear in his voice caught them all off guard. Never before had he raised his voice to them. Even Sister Benson was taken aback. "You are very lucky your sister cared enough to drive all night to rescue you, and I think you owe her and Will a huge apology and thank-you."

He stood up and paced for a moment, looking very distressed. "I blame myself for this."

Sister Benson put her hand reassuringly on his hand as he passed. "Elray, don't blame yourself!" she exclaimed. "LeAnn made a mistake. But she's old enough to learn from her mistakes. I'm sure it will never happen again, right, LeAnn?" Her expression pleaded with her youngest daughter, whose face brightened when she realized she just might worm her way out of trouble.

She nodded pertly. "I promise, Daddy."

He stopped his pacing and looked at her squarely in the eye, staring her down. LeAnn stopped nodding and leaned back into the couch cushions, then rubbed her lips together nervously. She had never seen her father so upset. And her mother had never scolded her like that before.

"It's just not that plain and simple anymore, LeAnn. My job as the father in this family is to make sure I teach you right from wrong, and then enforce it. It's clear to me that I have not been doing my job as well as I should. I'll tell you right now, LeAnn Valoy Benson, what happened last night will *never* happen again."

Her eyes widened in shock as he placed his hands behind his back and leaned toward her. "But, Daddy, I know, I—"

"I have decided that the new system around this house will revolve around trust and responsibility," he informed them while Lizzie and Merry nodded in agreement. "Since you made such a wild, reckless decision and then lied to cover your tail, I think an appropriate consequence is to lose your driver's license indefinitely."

LeAnn gasped and started to cry. Sister Benson immediately went to her, cradling her daughter's head in her shoulder.

"Lizzie, Merry, what are your thoughts?" Brother Benson turned to them.

Merry looked helplessly at Lizzie, who nodded again.

"I think it's a good idea."

"Liz! You're such a traitor!" LeAnn yelled angrily as the tears disappeared. "Come on! This is so unfair," she pleaded, then turned to her sister, pointing. "Lizzie did tons of things when she was a teenager, and you never took away her driving privileges!"

"Don't even try and play that card, LeAnn. I lost my driving privileges a dozen times, spent most of high school without an allowance, and had to keep my curfew if I wanted to keep the keys to my car," Lizzie stated firmly. She tried to put a comforting arm around LeAnn, who violently shrugged it off. "You probably think we're just being mean, but you did something monumentally stupid and dangerous. *You* have the choice here. Prove to Dad that you have earned the right to get your license back, earned the right to his trust, and you'll get it back." She turned to her father. "I believe that is how the system works, right, Dad?"

He nodded, sitting back down and putting his arms around LeAnn as well. "You might not realize how sick with worry we were when we realized you were gone. And how upset and angry we became when we realized you had lied and run away. You know how to do what's right. At least we've taught you that. Now you have to prove to us that you can choose to do it. Show us you've earned our trust, and we'll give your license back." He reached onto the floor and picked up her purse, setting it on her lap. "Your license, please."

"But Dad, I just barely got it! Please! I'll do the dishes for a year and keep my room straight and go to Young Woman's every week. I promise!" LeAnn begged. "Please!"

He smiled at her tenderly but firmly. "License. *Now.*"

LeAnn angrily reached into her purse and pulled out her newly minted license. She looked pleadingly at her mother, clutching her license tightly. "Mom, do I really have to?"

Sister Benson looked again to her husband, then gently took the license from LeAnn's hand. "You will get it back when you have proved you are responsible."

Again LeAnn grew angry. "Now how am I supposed to get to Angie's party tomorrow night?"

"I think you better sit that one out, LeAnn," her mother whispered when she saw the shocked, angry expression on her husband's face. Clearly, LeAnn's turnaround would take a while.

Merry rolled her eyes at her sister's audacity, but Lizzie just smiled ruefully. Maybe a few hours was a little too soon for LeAnn to grow up and face the consequences of her actions. Lizzie thought it unfortunate that LeAnn would have to recognize and learn her lessons the hard way, that going against what the Lord has asked can bring nothing but sorrow.

16

Getting It Right

JANALYN BENSON looked exhausted. She had been awake for nearly twenty-four hours, and her mother was talking so much, it didn't look like she would be able to sleep anytime soon. Sister Benson was rapidly peeling potatoes while excitedly rattling off every detail of Merry's wedding dress. The Benson house was turning into a living, breathing wedding reception beast that had spawned in the living room and was slowly creeping its way up the stairs. Their father was busy mowing the lawn. Why that was necessary when the reception was at the chapel was beyond Lizzie's comprehension, unless he just wanted to escape the confusion of the mad weddingfest inside. LeAnn had been sentenced to vacuum duty, Merry and Collin were off getting a marriage license, and Lizzie and Jana were tying tiny bows on little bottles of bubbles. So many things needed to be done for the wedding the next day, but Lizzie could see the bags under her sister's eyes and realized a little intervention would be necessary if all the plans for tonight were going to go well.

"Mom, I think we need to let Jana get some rest. She's had a long flight," Lizzie said, hoping there was no sound of conspiracy in her voice. "Jana, why don't you go take a nap on the couch?"

Jana looked at Lizzie with gratitude. "Mom, would you mind telling me about the dress later? I really could use a nap."

Their mother took one look at Jana and saw the dark circles compounding under her eyes. "Oh, dear, you do look tired. There is an eye mask in the freezer for those bags under your eyes. Why don't you take that with you? Oh, and hanging in your closet is your dress. Try it on before you go to sleep."

Lizzie suddenly hopped up from her seat and blocked Jana's exit from the kitchen. "Actually, Mom, you forgot Jana's bed is covered with Collin's stuff now! Jana, why don't you sleep on the sofa?"

Jana looked at her sister in disbelief. "The couch is covered in tulle and gauze for the reception. Can't I just sleep in your bed?"

"No! My bed is covered in Merry's boxes. Sorry! Just sleep on the couch." Lizzie practically pushed her sister into the living room, ran over to the couch, and shoved all the wedding paraphernalia onto the floor. Then she quickly ran across the room and grabbed a quilt off her father's recliner. "Here you go! A nap on the couch will be perfect!"

Jana looked at her sister and wondered what on earth had gotten into her, but she was so tired that she lacked the energy to point out Lizzie's apparent bout of temporary insanity. She accepted the quilt gratefully and crashed on the couch, asleep before her head hit the cushion.

Lizzie quietly slipped from the room, ran to her bedroom, and pulled out her cell phone. "Austen, she's asleep! Let's go!"

* * *

JANA stirred on the couch and fitfully turned over onto her side.

Lizzie knelt down at the end of the couch, where her sister couldn't see her, and slowly reached over the arm and tickled her sister's foot.

Jana kicked her foot in protest, but continued to sleep like a baby.

Lizzie looked at the doorway, where her entire family was crouched just out of sight. They waved at her to do it again. Lizzie deftly reached over the edge of the couch and tickled Jana's foot more persistently.

Jana kicked once more and blinked her eyes. In front of her sat a dozen yellow roses, her favorite. "They must be for the wedding . . ." Jana muttered, half-asleep. And then she rolled over to face the back of the couch.

Lizzie nearly let out an audible groan. She paused for a second, reached up, and yanked Jana's big toe as hard as she could.

Jana sat straight up on the couch. "What the . . ." She looked around. "What the . . . ?"

Tied to her wrist was a long, yellow ribbon, trailing all around the living room, around the roses, and out the door. What was going on? Jana rubbed her eyes and slowly stood up. A small envelope propped up on the roses said *OPEN ME* in Austen's familiar block handwriting. She slowly walked over to the card, subconsciously allowing a soft smile to spread across her face. Picking up the card, she leaned over to smell the roses. Could these really be from Austen?

CLUE #1—FOLLOW THE YELLOW RIBBON ROAD.

Jana looked suspiciously around the room, certain she was being watched. Where had her entire family gone? she wondered, while Lizzie flattened herself across the floor under the dining room table, filming with the video camera from a cat's viewpoint. Jana slowly untied the ribbon from around her wrist and began to follow the satin trail out the door.

The ribbon went out the front door and looped around the columns on the porch. Dangling in the center of the columns was another note. She opened it.

CLUE #2—BUY TWINKIES AT MAVERIK.

Jana laughed out loud and looked around the yard. "Austen? I know you are behind this! Where are you?" Lizzie ducked behind the front door, still trying to film through the screen, as Jana turned around to see if Austen was there.

Jana slipped under the ribbons winding all around the front porch and skipped down the sidewalk. Suddenly, Lizzie called out, "Jana! Take my car! You'll get there a lot faster!" Lizzie smiled at her sister and ran down the sidewalk after her. Handing her sister the car keys, she gave her a quick peck on the cheek. "And Mom wants me to tell you to run inside and change your shirt so you don't look like you slept in your clothes."

Jana looked at her blouse and then at the keys in her hand. After she quickly shook her head no, she practically ran to the convertible. Lizzie watched her sister drive south toward the gas station, and then she ran for her dad's truck.

She hopped in and headed for the Circle K on Twelfth Street. When she arrived she pulled out her cell phone and called Will. "She should at Maverik any minute now. I'll call you when she leaves the Circle K."

"Subject in sight, video camera recording," he deadpanned quietly, trying to remain hidden around the corner of the Maverik store while still getting a good shot of her. Jana rushed to the empty Maverik, unaware that she was being taped.

Jana had practically hopped out of the convertible to run inside, presumably to buy Twinkies. She scanned the aisles up and down, but couldn't seem to find them. She ran back down the obvious aisles, horrified at the lack of Hostess products.

She approached the counter, trying her hardest not to appear a nervous wreck. "Excuse me, do you have any Twinkies?" she asked as politely as possible, hoping she did not sound totally desperate and anxious. The cashier looked out the window at Will, who waved and nodded.

"I am sorry, I only have one package left. I was saving it for my lunch break," the cashier said.

"I'll give you five dollars for it!" Jana surprised herself with the degree of force that came from her own mouth. *This cashier cannot possibly understand the importance of Twinkies at this exact moment,* she thought.

"Um, no thanks." The cashier looked at her as if she were crazy. Then he winked at the window and Jana knew something was up.

"What *do* you want for the Twinkies?" Jana demanded, ready to barter her sister's car in exchange for them.

The cashier raised his eyebrow, leaned across the counter and said, "Name five types of cheese."

"*What?* What does that have to do with anything?" Jana blurted out and giggled uncontrollably. Whatever Austen was up to, it was typical Austen.

"You heard me: name five types of cheese." The cashier still kept a poker face.

"American, cheddar, gouda, Swiss, and provolone," Jana rattled off surprisingly quickly.

"Hmm . . . Nope, none of those fit my crossword. Try five more." The cashier lifted his newspaper slowly, provoking Jana to near exasperation.

"What? You have got to be kidding me!" Jana exclaimed.

"Do you want the Twinkies?" he asked dryly. Jana nodded anxiously. "Then solve my crossword for me!"

"Oh my gosh! Um, Monterey Jack, Limburger, Velveeta, string, American!"

"You already said American."

"Oh, good grief! Mozzarella!" Jana practically yelled.

"Voila! We have a winner!" The cashier brandished a pencil from above his ear and filled in the little blocks with painstaking exactness.

"My Twinkies, please!" Jana demanded.

"Oh yeah, right. I'm supposed to give you this too." The cashier reached into his breast pocket and pulled out a little white card, just like the two she had received before this. In her excitement Jana nearly jumped over the counter to grab it from him.

CLUE #3—GO TO THE CIRCLE K AT 12TH AND WALL
AND BRING BACK SOME ROOT BEER
IF YOU KNOW WHAT'S GOOD FOR YOU.

"Whoo-hoo!" Jana cheered and ran for the door.

"Hey! Don't forget your Twinkies!" The cashier held up a box of the wholesome goodness. Jana grabbed the box and ran for the car. She started the engine and peeled the tires as she raced away.

Lizzie was ready in her black fatigues, crouched behind an orange garbage can at the next stop. She was laughing so hard, she had to struggle to hold the camera still while the cashier at the Circle K made Jana perform some clogging moves for the crowded store. They applauded her appropriately, and shy Jana even took a sweeping bow as she blushed and took her root beer and ripped open the next card.

CLUE #4—YOU KNOW WHERE TO GO. AND BRING THE GOODS!

She hollered, "Wahoo!" again as she leapfrogged over the door of the convertible and sped away.

Lizzie doubled over in laughter from her perch behind the trash can. Picking up her cell phone, she called Austen. "Austen? She's on her way."

☆ ☆ ☆

AUSTEN sat on a rock overlooking the valley and checked his watch every five seconds. How long did it take to drive ten miles anyway? And then hike up a mile? The suspense was killing him. Suddenly he heard a rustling in the woods. "Jana?"

She slowly walked up the last few steps of the patch. "Hi, Austen," she said softly. She placed the six-pack of root beer and the box of Twinkies down on the rock, but didn't move closer. Suddenly a rush of confused emotions flooded her mind. Why hadn't he called her for two months? Was this his way of apologizing? This game was exciting, but there were still questions to answer.

"Hey, Jana," he said awkwardly. He stood up and walked closer to her. When he got closer and saw her tender, confused expression, he melted. He spoke softly, "I've missed you so much. You look beautiful. I never forget how beautiful you are."

A tear trickled down Jana's cheek, and she shook her head softly. "Austen, this isn't that easy. Where have you been?"

"Jana, I am sorry. I was stupid. I didn't realize how dumb I was. I should have tried harder . . ." Austen choked up. Looking at Jana and seeing her in pain made him realize how careless he had been. "I don't know what I was thinking. I didn't think it . . ."

"Austen, Lizzie already told me. It's okay," Jana said in her most caring voice. She couldn't take watching Austen's discomfort and distress. "I just needed to hear you say it."

Austen hung his head and shook it. "Jana, I have always loved you, and I always will. I am sorry. I just didn't realize not writing would be a big deal. I thought you'd understand." He looked at her with his eyes pleading for forgiveness and understanding.

"I love you too, Austen, and I do understand what happened," Jana reassured him. "Just don't ever let it happen again."

"I promise!" Austen said eagerly, wrapping his arms around her for a long hug. The sun had set over the valley below, leaving the sky above them a deep violet, painted bright with stars so close they could almost touch them.

A few feet away in the woods, Lizzie, dressed all in black, quietly crept through the dark.

"Caw-caw! Caw-caw!" a mannish, very unbirdly voice called through the dark.

Lizzie suppressed a giggle and moved towards the voice. "Will, where are you?"

A hand suddenly emerged and waved at her from the trees. Will was wearing all camouflage and hiding near a fallen log. He smiled, his white teeth making him more visible in the darkness.

"Hi!" Lizzie whispered. "What's going on? Is she there yet?"

Will signaled for Lizzie to be quiet and pointed to the video camera. She looked up the hill to where Austen and Jana were sitting on a rock, looking very much in love. She smiled to herself and then turned to look at Will. He looked absolutely adorable dressed all in army camouflage, sprawled out on what appeared to be an army blanket. So very unlike the usual proper Will. He turned just in time to catch her checking him out and winked at her.

"Come on!" he whispered, crawling Marine-style down the hill. Obviously he was having just a little too much fun with this! Lizzie watched him slink across the ground and attempted to follow suit. She moved about five feet when her shirt snagged on a twig. She tried pulling herself loose, but she was stuck. She started to laugh at her current situation.

"Shh!" Will hissed at her. "They are going to hear you!"

Lizzie covered her mouth, rolled over, and kept laughing.

"You're hopeless!" Will whispered. Suddenly, Will smiled, stood up, grabbed Lizzie, threw her over his shoulder, and began to run down the mountain.

* * *

SOMETHING rustled in the woods and distracted Jana. "What was that? Is someone out there?" She grabbed the flashlight and shone it into the woods.

Austen quickly reached over and pushed her hand down. He didn't want her to catch Will setting up the video camera on the tripod. "It's nothing, probably just some squirrels bunking down for the night."

He moved to stand in front of her and suddenly couldn't find the words he had rehearsed a hundred times. He caught his breath and just stared at how beautiful she was in the light of the rising moon.

"Jana . . ." he began, but tears came to his eyes, his throat caught, and the words wouldn't come out. She stepped closer to him and held his hands. Looking up into his blue eyes, Jana felt tears forming in her own eyes.

"I—" Austen paused and swallowed. "I love you."

"I know. I love you too," Jana said with a single tear rolling down her face.

Austen took a long breath and paused to look at Jana before taking a step back. Grasping her hands tightly, he knelt down on one knee before her. Jana began to tremble.

"Janalyn Benson, I have been in love with you for as long as I can remember. And for as long as I can remember, I have wanted to marry you. I am so happy when I think of spending all eternity holding your hand and standing by your side. I cannot wait to have a family with you. Or to have you as part of my family. Or just to wake up in the morning and see you next to me. You bring the sunshine into my world. You are the only woman I have ever wanted." Austen paused and let out a deep breath.

"I love you, Austen," Jana whispered, still trembling.

"Janalyn Benson, will you marry me?"

Jana paused, almost unable to move or respond. The pause was brief, but to Austen it felt like an eternity. Suddenly, Jana smiled, tipped back her head, and yelled, "Yes!"

"Woo-hoo!" Austen jumped up and grabbed Jana around the waist and kissed her. Giddy with excitement and relief, he laughed and kissed her again and again.

Jana kissed Austen back and laughed and smiled and kissed him again. She pulled back, looked him in the eye, and barely whispered again, "Yes, Austen Young, I will marry you!"

She put her left hand up on his cheek to kiss him again and suddenly saw the glint of a diamond on her own hand. "What?" she stammered.

Austen laughed and pulled her hand down. "What, you thought I wasn't going to give you a ring? I may just be a poor returned missionary, but I can still afford to get you a ring!"

"But when did you . . . ? How did . . . ? Austen, I'm confused!" Jana looked at the ring on her own finger, wondering how it got there.

"It's been there all night!" Austen smiled.

"What?"

"I put it on your hand when you were asleep on the couch. I can't believe you didn't notice! You almost woke up when I put it on you!"

Jana laughed and shook her head as she stared at the ring, then examined it a little more closely. She looked at him with unmasked love and affection, then leaned over and kissed him again. This was one time when words were not nearly as useful as a warm kiss.

In This Happy Way

LOUISA BENSON always had a readable expression on her face. When she was happy, her whole face glowed with a radiant light that beamed from within. Lizzie had seen that expression on her face earlier that morning when she had emerged from the Salt Lake Temple, holding her daughter's hand as Merry made her first appearance as Mrs. Collin Light. The same joyous expression covered her father's face and those of Collin's parents as well. The glow seemed enough to outshine Sister Light's hot-pink lipstick—a small miracle in itself.

At this moment, however, the fear and panic on Sister Benson's face was almost more than Lizzie could take. And for once, she worried with her mother instead of rolling her eyes at her. It was ten minutes before Merry's wedding reception was supposed to start at the stake center, and everything that could have possibly gone wrong had. First, they had been locked out of the building. The scheduler thought they were coming the night before to decorate, so he had waited patiently for an hour the previous night before heading home. The family had arrived en masse to decorate after the wedding luncheon and had wasted precious time milling around in the parking lot until someone produced a key.

Then the decorating frenzy began in earnest. The lattice backdrop had been set up against the north wall, and Mrs. Benson chatted away happily until someone pointed out that the basketball hoop still rested in its lowered position. A key was found, and the mechanical hoop-raiser hummed, buzzed, clanked, and then stopped with the hoop halfway up. Austen and Will took turns jumping up to try and pull the hoop back down, while Collin frantically tried to push it all the way up with the head of a dust mop, ignoring the flecks of dust that settled on the shoulders of his white tuxedo like flakes of gray snow.

The two-layered cake, with marzipan frosting, beaded edible pearl accents, and fresh flowers, arrived in three pieces, which meant immediate surgery in the kitchen. Several young women from the Bensons' home ward arrived to help assemble the refreshment plates; they discovered that the monogrammed napkins said *Merry Christmas, Together Forever* under the image of the temple instead of *Merry and Collin, Together Forever.*

Lizzie could see her mother across the room, talking to the photographer, gesturing with one hand while the other played with the jeweled brooch that secured her pink silk scarf to the shoulder of her cream mother-of-the-bride suit. But despite the mayhem, she knew that the frantic scenes were not the cause of her mother's panicked expression. The reception was moments away from starting and the bride had yet to show.

Even normally placid, serene Jana began to worry. She sidled up to Lizzie, who had been putting the finishing touches on the table displays of Collin and Merry's childhood pictures, and whispered, "You don't think Merry's changed her mind, do you?"

Lizzie muffled a laugh, though she had to admit to herself that the thought had crossed her mind many times while they waited. "Well, the time for that would have been before going to the temple, Jana. I can't imagine Merry ever being late for anything, let alone her own wedding reception, but I guess there's a first for . . ."

Her voice trailed off as the distant sound of police sirens drew near the stake center. In a moment, they seemed close enough to be in the parking lot. Lizzie's head cocked to one side thoughtfully as she followed the sound and the others outside to discover the source of the commotion.

Three police cars, lights and sirens blaring, pulled up to the front of the building, escorting one silver Euro van, with a bride at the wheel. *This is not a good sign,* thought Lizzie.

"Gracious, child, don't you know how you've worried your poor husband?" Sister Benson's voice rung like a bell above the din of the nervous chatter, her face illuminated by the flashing red and blue police lights that continued to blare. They had parked in front of the main entrance to the stake center, where the entire street could see them. A flushed Merry, veil flying, skirt gathered in her hand, emerged from the van looking rather embarrassed at being spotted by the crowd gathered around. Guests had started to pull into the parking lot, and half the ward spilled out from the kitchen and cultural hall. She looked around sheepishly as Collin burst through the assemblage.

"Merry, my snoogums, are you all right?" he asked anxiously, grasping her hands dramatically and clutching them tightly to his chest. "We were worried sick about you."

"Worried she changed her mind, eh, boy?" Brother Light guffawed loudly, jabbing his son in the ribs. A few people laughed out loud while LeAnn nodded in agreement and Sister Benson buried her face in her hands, humiliated. A police officer had joined them in the center of what was rapidly becoming a huge crowd. Across the street, people were even starting to step out of their houses to investigate.

"I guess I know how to make a memorable entrance," Merry offered feebly as the officer approached with a grim expression on his face. Lizzie smiled. *Poor Merry!*

"Who is responsible for this young lady here?" he asked, looking around.

"I am," Collin and Brother Benson said in unison.

The officer looked each of them over carefully as he cleared his throat, and Merry lowered her head, snuggling into Collin as he wrapped his arms protectively around her. "I guess I better speak with both of you then. I pulled this young lady over, going eighty-seven miles per hour in a twenty-five-mile-per-hour zone. She claimed she was on her way to her wedding reception, but I had no way to verify this—"

"Are you *kidding*?" Liz burst out incredulously, motioning to the bride, the gown, the groom in the white tux, and the assembled wedding party. Did he think they were dressed like this just for kicks?

One very stern look in her direction silenced her, however, and he continued, "She was speeding in a residential area, driving recklessly, and failed to provide proper identification and proof of insurance on the vehicle she was driving, which is registered to someone other than her. All of these are excellent reasons for me to take her in and book her right now." The cop rested his hand menacingly on the shiny handcuffs hanging from his belt.

An audible gasp escaped from the crowd. Arrest the bride? Lizzie could see the thoughts that were racing through her mother's head right now, images of her daughter behind bars, her mug shot complete with wedding veil gracing the front page of tomorrow's newspaper.

"But I put an emergency call in to my chief," the officer continued, pausing for effect—or torture. "He said I have special permission to let her go, just this once, as long as we can take some cake back to the station." And then he cracked the biggest smile Lizzie had ever seen as members of the ward laughed with relief and burst into applause. Merry, trembling with joy and relief, almost collapsed into Collin's arms as her mother and father sighed with gratitude. Lizzie was sure the ticket they were preparing for would have cost almost as much as the wedding.

The photographer quickly began snapping shots of Merry and the police officer. Sister Benson placed her hand to her head as if to verify that her hair wasn't standing on end. Then she patted the side of her head while she took a deep breath to recover. "Well, my goodness, why are we all standing around?" she called. She clapped her hands together, ushering everyone back inside. "We have a wedding reception, people! Move it, move it!"

Liz's cheeks puffed out as she let out a sigh of relief. Her mother caught her by the elbow and whispered, "Will you and Jana find a way to fix the basketball hoop? I don't know what I'll do if Merry has that ridiculous net hanging down in her face during the pictures."

Liz grinned with a gleam in her eyes, marveling that the woman could be so composed on the outside while so frazzled on the inside. "Of course, Mother. I would be happy to."

"And would you please hurry and put your dress back on?" she called as Lizzie skipped off. "Our guests have already arrived and there you are, running around the gym in your jeans. I might as well have had twelve sons, with all the jeans I've seen today. And don't forget to put a girdle on under your dress. It does wonders for your figure!"

Lizzie stopped, quelling the urge to roll her eyes at her mother, and went back to kiss her on the cheek. "I know, Mom. I know. You're still completely insane, but I can only hope you'll be this composed when I run off to Vegas with my hairy biker boyfriend and we come back with matching tattoos."

"I should be so lucky, Lizzie!" she exclaimed in reply. "Then I wouldn't have to plan your reception." She winked at her daughter, and then pointed her in the general direction of the rest room. "Now go! And make sure you put on some of that lipstick I got to go with your dress. I know you don't care for pink, but it will look marvelous with your summer tan. And, here, let me fix that stray hair for you." She licked her fingers and reached up to tuck a flyaway hair from Lizzie's face.

"Mom, *ick!* That's why hairspray was invented!" Lizzie cried in disgust.

"Well, fine, do as you please. Just get dressed! We should have been doing pictures a half hour ago." Straightening her skirt, Sister Benson licked her fingers once again and smoothed her own hair, threw on her best portrait smile, and went to join the bride and groom.

Jana, Liz, and LeAnn were soon set to join the rest of the family in the receiving line. The girls wore matching pink dresses with satin bodices and full-length tulle skirts—with girdles and corsets underneath draining Lizzie's will to live—and held daisy bouquets bound with pink satin ribbon. As the girls approached from the rest room, their mother gestured as subtly as she could toward the half-up, half-down basketball hoop and gave Lizzie a look of desperation.

After a moment of whispering among themselves, LeAnn went to the nearest table, grabbed a couple of folding chairs, and dragged them over to her parents, setting them just under the hoop. The guests in the line had to move around them as they worked, but Jana and Liz climbed onto the chairs, holding their tulle skirts up, and quickly wove some fresh daisies from the centerpieces into the hoop's netting so it matched the decor. Making the best of an insane situation, Collin and Merry laughed and joked as they began receiving their guests, saying they would greet them under the basketball hoop in true Mormon fashion. Jana and Liz hopped down and stood back to admire their work.

"We are amazing," Jana said with mock smugness.

Lizzie nodded in agreement. "'Nuff said." She looked around ruefully at the mayhem that surrounded them as they took their places after Merry in the receiving line. "Remind me never to get married," she told Jana.

Her most beloved sister shook her head. "Sorry, I can't do that. There's a young man over in the corner who would never forgive me if I made that promise. Besides, wasn't it William Shakespeare who said, 'Methinks you protesteth too much'?"

"Protesteth, huh?" Lizzie shook her head. "A summer in Oxford, and that is the best you can come up with?"

Jana laughed and bopped her sister over the head with her bouquet.

As the reception wound down, they finally found a few moments to break free from the drudgery of their wedding duties. LeAnn wandered off to join some of the young women in the kitchen, Jana and Liz went to look for their boys, and Merry and Collin went to cut the cake and pose for another round of pictures. Jana and Liz found Austen and Will deep in conversation near the refreshment table. Jana smiled indulgently at Austen as she came up from behind him, placed her hands on his shoulders to massage them, and teased, "I see you're making sure no one else gets any of the food," as she pointed at several dirty plates scattered on the table.

Austen looked up and pulled her onto his lap, wrapping his arms tightly around her so she could not escape. "We decided the catering at this reception needed quality control," he told her.

Will nodded in agreement. "It's really a service to Merry and Collin. It's our job to ensure that all the guests receive high-quality food attractively arranged on the plate."

Liz laughed. "Please! That's the lamest excuse for overeating that I have ever heard."

"If you think I'm bad," Austen said, pointing to the punch table, "check out my dad."

Liz and Jana turned to see Bishop Young at the decorative silver punch fountain, continually filling a cup, guzzling it down, and filling it again. They laughed. "Oh yeah, we should have considered the bishop and his weakness for spiked tropical punch when choosing the beverage." Liz nodded with a shrug. "At least we know there won't be leftovers!"

Will raised an eyebrow. "Spiked? Austen, what kind of operation does your dad run here?"

Liz laughed. "Come on, Will. Mormons get loopy on Nyquil. We're talking 7-Up here. And there will be plenty of that left since we used a lot less than Mom thought we would."

Jana nodded in agreement. "I think we're going to have a twenty-year supply of nut cups left over too."

"Nah," Austen told her, holding her a little closer. "We'll just save them for our reception." Jana's eyes glowed, and she reached up to gently touch his cheek while she gave him a soft kiss. The ambient light reflected off the diamond in her engagement ring, revealing the pink glint in her princess-cut solitaire.

Liz absentmindedly pulled fresh flowers from the floral centerpiece on the table, weaving a daisy chain as her mother shrilly called for all the single girls to come vie for the bouquet Merry was about to throw. Jana hopped up, calling behind her, "Come on, Lizzie! Let's see who the next victim is!" She reached down and tried to pull her sister up.

"Not even!" she replied, digging her feet in. "I'm not going to take part in some ridiculous tradition that only serves to reinforce the stigma of the single girl with no prospects." She placed her daisy chain around her neck, sitting stubbornly still while all the other girls in the room stampeded for a prime position near Merry.

Jana stopped and stared. "What have they been teaching you at the U?" She ran back and pulled persistently at Lizzie.

"No!" she protested again, as all the other girls crowded closer around the bride. "I don't think I can handle that sort of commitment yet!"

Jana looked at the boys. "Will you guys give me a hand here?" she implored. "Poor misguided Lizzie needs a little persuading." Without another word, Will gladly hopped up, walked over to Lizzie, and picked her up caveman style, tossing her over his shoulder while she pounded his back in protest. He pushed his way to the front of the giggling gaggle of girls and placed Lizzie down right in front.

"Merry! Right over here, if you don't mind!" Will hollered and stepped back as the whole room laughed.

The glowing, ecstatic bride turned so her back faced the throng of anxious girls. Collin beamed at her as she counted off, "Three! Two! One!" and tossed her bouquet wildly behind her. Time seemed to stop as Liz realized she was penned with nowhere to run. Shrieks and laughter filled her ears. She closed her eyes and stuck her arms up over her face to protect herself from the hopping mass of madly flailing arms and fingernails as the girls crushed in around her. Somehow, some way, the bouquet dropped into her hands. She stared in complete disbelief as the horde of girls melted away, shoulders slumped with disappointment.

Several girls moaned as Liz shrieked, "No way!" They reached for the bouquet once more as she threw the flowers at Jana. Everyone around them laughed as the girls dispersed, but as she returned to their table, Austen and Will seemed to be laughing harder than the rest.

"So now Will knows how you really feel about marriage, Liz," Austen grinned, giving Will a good-natured jab in the ribs.

Jana handed the flowers back to her sister. "These really are yours, Lizzie. I don't need them."

"She's going to be a tough sell, Will," Austen informed him.

Will nodded grimly. "Yeah, but I'm breaking her in a little at a time."

"Excuse me? You're breaking me in? Like some stubborn barnyard mule?" She glared, pretending to be offended, but her smile gave her away.

He nodded, holding his hands up. "Your words, not mine." She laughed as he pulled her into a hug.

"I don't think so!" She reached up to give him a good-natured, loving whack upside the head. "Come on, Merry and Collin are about ready to go. I want to blow bubbles as they leave." She pulled her hidden stash of wedding bubbles from her bag under the table and passed them out.

Jana looked at them slyly and motioned for them to come closer. "I have something better." Reaching into a backpack she had kept under Austen's chair, she showed them a bag filled with shaving cream, sandwich cookies, soap, and silly string. They looked at her in surprise.

"Why, Miss Janalyn Benson," Lizzie said in faux shock. "I am quite surprised at you. And more than a little disappointed that I didn't think of it myself!"

Jana giggled, eyes bright. "LeAnn decorated the Euro van, but I have it on good authority that the happy couple will be leaving in Dad's truck tonight. I thought the four of us ought to make sure they have a proper send-off in an appropriately decorated vehicle." She giggled again, highly pleased with herself.

"Oh, how I do love this girl of mine," Austen said, beaming with pride. The foursome hurried out the door where Collin's Euro van was parked, soda cans tied to the bumper, the back window covered with soap writing that declared, "Just Married."

Austen and Will spotted the truck and began a friendly competition, seeing who could spray the most silly string on it while Jana and Liz doodled hearts and swirls all over the windows and stuck the creamy side of the half-opened Oreos cookies on the side windows before finishing the job by writing LOVE LIGHTS in large bold letters on the back window. "Let's just hope our friendly police officer doesn't pull them over for driving with an obstructed view or something," Jana said, standing back to admire their work.

"Maybe we should leave a bag of Oreos in here for them to bribe the cops with!"

Jana laughed.

"All right! Neon colors!" Austen and Will were hooked on the silly string. Jana just shook her head.

"Don't you dare shoot that at the bride!" Lizzie cried out as the boys debated whether or not they should shoot it at Merry and Collin when they came out instead of blowing the wedding bubbles.

Jana pulled Lizzie aside, watching the boys with a gleam in her eye. "Those two really are partners in crime, aren't they?"

Lizzie nodded with a smile, the joy and love in her eyes unmasked. "Yup. I think you and I will have our hands full." The doors opened, and they turned to the emerging couple and started blowing bubbles while Austen aimed the can and let loose a barrage of day-glow-green silly string.

"Hey!"

"Oh, sorry, Natalie," Austen apologized, stopping when he realized it was his sister. "At least this stuff doesn't stain." He paused. "Does it?" Lizzie knew he was envisioning the green silly string permanently staining the bride's white gown and the groom's tux.

"It better not stain, Austen!" Natalie scolded. "This is a silk dress." She grabbed the hand of her date, and they continued to a car parked at the far end of the parking lot.

Lizzie could not contain her delighted grin. "Was that James Smith with Natalie?"

Jana nodded. "Apparently they have been dating for months, but they didn't tell anyone because she knew how Erin felt about him and she didn't want to hurt her sister's feelings. When Julie and Erin started dating twin brothers at BYU, she and James decided to go public."

Lizzie mulled this over as the doors burst open again and a flood of people ran out holding their tiny bottles of wedding bubbles. Merry and Collin weren't far behind. They ran through the doors and out to Brother Benson's truck, flanked by their tearful mothers and the rest of their families, friends, and well-wishers. Collin's mother and Sister Benson exchanged a sobbing hug as the couple drove off, and Brother Light clapped Brother Benson heartily on the back before picking him up in a monstrous bear hug.

"Yup, we're family now, old boy. Hopefully we'll be sharing grandbabies before too long!"

Lizzie stifled a laugh as her father's weary eyes grew wide at the thought. He already had a pre-headache look on his face. She made a mental note to give him a cold-pack and a double dose of aspirin when they got back to the house. Yes, the thought of those little Lightlings made Lizzie feel a migraine coming on as well, but she knew she would just have to work through it. Baby steps, just like Robyn said.

As the crowd thinned out and the parking lot emptied, Lizzie's thoughts returned to Erin and Julie. "Twins, huh?" she asked Jana.

"Identical. And they are both in law school right now. Julie is in heaven," she replied, laughing a bit. "I hear she's even starting to be nice to people."

"She is? Well, I'm very happy for them," Liz said graciously. At least she would try to be happy for Julie.

Jana sighed, radiating sheer joy. "Oh, Lizzie, who knew things would end up like this? Did you know everything would end in this happy way?"

Liz did not hesitate. "I did. I never doubted for a moment that you and Austen would end up living happily ever after. I even think Merry and Collin will too."

"I thought you were the ultimate pessimist."

"I still have an inner pessimist, but I'm learning to control her," she answered lightly but seriously. She wanted to make a concerted effort to look at life from a different perspective, hopefully a better one. She had decided recently to try to believe the best of people, to let herself care about them and be cared for in return, and she had not been let down yet. She knew she would eventually be let down some of the time, but her new outlook was a much more pleasant way to view the world.

"And what about you, Lizzie?" Jana asked softly, glancing at Will, who was gleefully shooting the last of a can of silly string into the air with Austen, judging height and distance. She smiled at the boys. "When do I get to see you so happy?"

Lizzie thought a moment and grew serious. "I can never be as happy as you, Jana. I'll never be as good or as faithful as you, so I can never be as happy. But I'm figuring things out. I'm a work in progress."

"Yes, you are," Will interrupted, joining her with an empty can in his hands. He wrapped his arms around her waist and pulled her close. "Good thing you have me around."

She playfully slapped his chest. "Good thing you have me," she corrected. "It's actually very frightening to consider how boring your life would be without me." Then she let herself sink into him, resting her head against his chest.

"Good thing we have each other," he finished softly. Liz knew that there, with Will, in his arms, was the most perfect place for her.

"Good thing," she echoed quietly.

About the Authors

ERIN ANN McBRIDE is a native of the Washington, D.C., area. She is an events and tradeshow manager, currently putting her talents to work as a gun-show planner. She also runs her own business, Events by Erin, on the side. When she is not busy planning dates, parties, and weddings for her friends, she can be found volunteering at the local fire department, where she is a certified firefighter and EMT. Erin Ann graduated from George Mason University and holds a bachelor's degree in political communication and broadcast journalism. She loves to travel. She also enjoys romantic dinners, moonlit walks on the beach, chick flicks, roller coasters, and professional sporting events. Erin Ann is a member of the Langley Young Single Adult Ward, McLean Virginia Stake, and a veteran of many other singles wards. She would like to point out that Juli really was given a "lights and sirens" police escort to her wedding reception.

JULI HIATT CALDWELL was born in Anaheim, California, the fourth of seven kids. She went to school in Utah, then spent some time working as a nanny in the Washington, D.C., area, where she met Erin Ann for the first time. She met her husband, Bryan, on a trip to Utah to visit her family, and they became engaged three weeks later. They have been married for six years and are the proud parents of the two craziest, most adorable little girls on the planet. She and Erin Ann coauthor "A Single Thought," a weekly column for *Meridian* magazine. Juli enjoys music, reading, going to the beach, riding bikes, yoga classes, and working out at a local gym. She spends most of her time with her girls, playing with them, chauffeuring them to piano and dance lessons, and cleaning up their messes. She lives on Florida's beautiful Space Coast and is currently at work on a second novel with Erin Ann.